Haunted Creek

By the same author

Moorland Lass
Bitter Inheritance
Yorkshire Rose
Lavender Girl
Summer by the Sea
Shadows on the Moor

Haunted Creek

Ann Cliff

ROBERT HALE · LONDON

First published in Great Britain 2011

ISBN 978-0-7090-9275-9

Robert Hale Limited
Clerkenwell House
Clerkenwell Green
London EC1R 0HT

www.halebooks.com

2 4 6 8 10 9 7 5 3 1

Typeset in 11/15.3pt Janson
Printed in the UK by the MPG Books Group,
Bodmin and King's Lynn

For Neville,
with thanks for the
Australian adventure.

ONE

Gippsland, Victoria, Australia: January 1875

'YOU'RE A BRAVE one, to come all across the world by yourself!' The bullock cart lurched into a pot hole and the woman steadied herself with a hand on a bag of corn. 'What did you think to Melbourne, then? Not as fine as London, I'll be bound.' She sounded envious of the traveller. 'I was born near Melbourne. This is as far as I've been.'

'I've never seen London, Mrs Carr,' the passenger admitted and the older woman leaned forward to hear her. 'I come from a village in Yorkshire. This is ... it's all so different.' *A neat little stone-built village with pretty cottage gardens ... not like this.*

It was nearly journey's end after endless weeks of sailing from England to Melbourne, with plenty of time to get used to the idea of leaving home. Rose had arrived at the other side of the world and then the journey through Victoria had begun. There was no railway east into Gippsland and the roads were rutted tracks through dense forests with no signs of civilization; no villages, no church steeples and no people. Only the wild, dark green woods.

Rose had been lucky to get a ride but the bullock cart seemed very slow after the mail coach. Cobb & Co. had stopped to change horses many times; fresh horses to keep up the cracking pace. They'd left Bourke Street in Melbourne at one o'clock yesterday afternoon and rattled east, reaching the Bunyip River just as darkness fell. (What *was* a bunyip?) The night stage was frightening and hardly any of the passengers slept. The track was very rough, the horses floundering through deep mud at a place called the Gluepot before toiling up the steepest of hills.

Before daybreak, Rose had stepped down from the coach at the little town of Moe, aching and weary. There she'd had hours of uncertainty until she found a way of getting into the hills. The Carr family said they had room for her on their cart, so she stayed in a small boarding house and joined them early the next morning. Thank goodness, this was the last leg of the journey. It was also the slowest, in a lumbering cart drawn by eight bullocks with long horns. By evening, not long now, she would be on their Australian farm with Luke. Dear Luke! A real farm of their own and a new house to live in!

Rose had married Luke Teesdale a year ago just before he came out to Australia, promising to follow him as soon as he had somewhere for them to live. Leaving home was nothing, she'd told herself. Not compared to the promise of the future: a farm of their own in a new country and, above all, the chance of happiness.

On either side of the road were huge trees. As they came out of the valley and slowly crawled into the hills, the trees had seemed to get bigger, crowding in across the road and mercifully shading them a little from the pitiless afternoon sun. A familiar smell came wafting into the cart at intervals and after a while Rose realized it reminded her of Grandmother's washing day: these giants must be eucalyptus trees.

There were woods everywhere here – the Australians called them 'the bush' – and huge bogs like the one round Moe that they called swamps. The birds she had seen were big and brightly coloured. It was a new world, different from anything she had seen before, and frightening in its silent emptiness. Rose had thought there would be more villages, more people.

'Now, I always say a country girl fares best in Australia.' Mrs Carr poked her husband in the back. 'Get a move on there, Bert. There's folks coming up behind us and they'll get there first …'

Her voice was drowned in an uproar as the cart keeled over sideways in a rut that was deeper than usual. The hens swinging in a coop under the cart started to cackle, the bullocks bellowed and a rather thin cow that was tied to the back of the cart moaned plaintively. A saddle horse beside the cow plodded on as though nothing had happened. This was a whole farm on the move, ready to claim some land and settle down. But now it seemed that a race was on.

'Have some sense, Martha. You can't hurry cattle and you know it.' Mr Carr clamped his teeth more firmly round his pipe. 'Get up there, lads, get up.'

When order was restored Mrs Carr started again, fanning herself energetically. 'You'll be feeling the heat, dear, straight from England ... My Bert has ambitions, otherwise we'd not be here. We had a little place near Melbourne, growing vegetables, but Bert wanted to get bigger and then he heard about this land for selection. So here we are, but they told us in Moe that there's only one good block of land left near the creek and another lot has their eyes on it.' Her faded blue eyes looked at Rose curiously. 'So your man has a block already? He'd have got one of the better ones, then. When I first saw you in Moe, I said to myself there's a handy young woman, she'll make a settler.' Mrs Carr was scrawny and brown, her work-worn hands folded over a faded print dress.

'I hope so.' Rose wiped the perspiration from her face. It was hot under the canvas and the bullock cart was stuffed to bursting with the Carrs' possessions, including two small boys, Charlie and Peter, now mercifully asleep. They were bound for a place called Haunted Creek, where Luke said in his letters that he had bought a farm and built a house.

It would be wonderful to have a home of their own. Rose had lived with family all her life and longed for a little kitchen with a good cooking range and a cat on the hearth rug. She imagined the house neat and orderly, the way you could keep things if you got up early in the morning.

The road was getting steeper and the bullocks slowed down even more. Rose could have walked faster. 'So what can you do, my dear? Can you milk a cow and bake a loaf?' Mrs Carr smiled. 'You'll soon learn, any road. Now if you're able to teach children, or nurse folks that's sick, you'll be right welcome up here. From what I've heard, there's not enough good women to do those kind of jobs.' They had passed a tea house where the road divided and the track had come close to the Latrobe River again an hour ago. A few sheds were dotted about and Rose saw some fences, signs of farming and a relief after the endless bush, but no people. Although she was a country girl, Rose had never been far from the neighbours in Yorkshire.

'I'm a farmer's daughter, Mrs Carr. Used to milking and all that ... I like to grow vegetables and herbs, but I suppose it will be different here.' There were many packets of seeds in the big brass-bound trunk that Rose had sent off to Australia months ago; there was lavender oil, dried sage and plenty of pepper.

Other women on the ship had told her that they'd packed bone china and silk dresses for their new life. 'You can't get good china in the colony for love nor money, they say.' But Rose had packed seeds and cooking pots and pans, wrapping them in material to make tablecloths and curtains. The ladies in silk had been bound for Melbourne, not the Haunted Creek. They had looked at her with pity when she told them where she was going.

'You're off to where? In the wilds of Gippsland, miles away from civilization? I wonder what you've let yourself in for, dear. I only hope you've got a good husband,' one woman had sniffed. 'You'll likely be stuck alone with him for months at a time.'

Another had said, 'You must have married a well-off-chap with a big grazing property. There's fortunes being made from sheep, they tell me, and some of the farms out there are as big as an English county. Stations, they call them.'

Rose said nothing. Her man had bought fifty acres and at the place Luke had settled in, the land was being divided up into small units, more on an English scale, thank goodness. That had led her to think that there would be a village or two ... but where were they?

The cloud of dust behind them whirled up and enveloped the cart as two horsemen overtook them on the track, not slowing down and not even looking at the bullock dray. 'Now that's vexing, that is.' Mrs Carr frowned. 'They'll be the ones, they'll get the block near the creek. And we'll get the hill ... just our luck.' Bert hunched his shoulders but said nothing.

'Those men might not be going our way,' Rose suggested, smoothing down her dark hair. 'They didn't look like settlers – they had no baggage, did they? How could you settle without your belongings?'

But Mrs Carr was convinced that they were selectors. 'If they were neighbours, they'd have waved, or stopped for a chat. And they wouldn't have covered us in dust – that wasn't friendly, like.' She wiped her grimy face.

Shadows across the road grew longer as the afternoon wore on. The strange thing was that the sun, though heading for a sunset in the west, was travelling through the north instead of the south. You could tell because the mountains were to the north of the valley; the bullock team was labouring up the hills out of the flat land. There was a lot to learn about Australia.

The road levelled out along a ridge and Rose could see a few scattered houses where a track led off towards a river. 'Used to be hundreds of men down there,' Mr Carr said as they peered into the deep river valley. Rose could see huts and some sort of machinery. The Tangil gold rush was almost over, Bert said, but men kept coming, still hoping for a big find.

The cart rumbled on through the hot day, lurching from side to side. In spite of her excitement, Rose was dozing when Mrs Carr put a hand on her arm. 'Now, we're coming to the place – the creek we're looking for. You won't mind if we try to find our block first?' She looked at Rose, almost pleading. 'I know you'll want to meet your man, but we've got a race against time …' She consulted a rough map showing the outlines of vacant lots. 'Hey, Bert, turn down here. This must be it.' A mark was blazed on a tree where a narrow track turned down into a little valley.

The road was steep and Bert hauled the bullocks to a halt. 'I'll go down myself and see. Might not be able to turn cattle round down there,' he muttered.

'May I come with you?' Rose jumped down and nearly fell, clutching the wheel of the cart for support. She was aching and stiff from sitting for hours; it would be good to walk for a little. Martha joined her and after tying up the lead bullock, they all walked down the track.

Between trees the water gleamed invitingly and the land levelled out as they went along. Bert kicked at the earth at the side of the track. 'Good red soil,' he said. 'This'll do me nicely.'

They heard a shout and Rose looked up to see two young men watching them. 'Sorry, folks, this is taken!' The man who spoke was laughing. 'We got here hours ago. I've staked my claim and put a hut up – see?' A few young trees had been felled and heaped together. 'There's good places over the hill.'

Bert's face dropped when he saw the men. 'This is the block I want,' he said obstinately. 'I'm a veggie grower, I've got a wife and two children—'

'Hard luck, mate,' the second man said with rough sympathy. 'But t'other land's not bad, just a bit steeper, going down to Haunted Creek.' He came closer and stared hard when he saw Rose. 'My – it isn't young Rose – is it? Nay, I never expected you for another month or two, lass! Oh, Lord!' He turned away.

It was hard at first to see in this thin, bearded stranger the good-looking Luke Teesdale she had married. He wasn't even pleased to see her! Perhaps he felt shy; it was strange to meet again after so long, and in front of strangers. Rose had imagined such a warm welcome … not this. To come all this way, through these dark and frightening forests, for this.

The others watched as Luke walked over and gave her an awkward peck on the cheek. 'Well, I suppose you'll have to make the best of it. You'd have been better to come next year.'

Rose was lost for words. Her husband couldn't look her in the eye. He didn't ask how she was, but stood with his arms folded, looking grim. Bright hopes faded as she looked at him.

The other man, a curly-haired lad with a lopsided smile, came across and shook her hand. 'Pleased to meet you, Mrs Teesdale. Luke has been looking forward to seeing you here. I'm Jim Carlyle, we'll be neighbours.' He at least had a few manners.

'I knew it – they're the ones that passed us on the road!' Martha glared at the two young men. 'They beat us, after all.'

'I've had it booked for a while, you know,' said the lad called Jim. 'Just had to get here myself and stake it out ... Luke's been helping me.' He turned to the Carrs, dusty and disappointed by the track, shoulders drooping. The little boys had run after them and now they began to cry. 'There's plenty of room for us all. I'll show you if you like.'

Bert Carr roused himself. 'We'll camp for the night by the track and look for a selection tomorrow,' he said shortly. 'Right, Martha, let's feed these boys.'

Back at the cart, Rose wished them luck and tried to hide her own disappointment. 'Thanks for the lift. We'll be seeing you again, I'm sure,' she said as brightly as she could.

Luke picked up Rose's bag and led her away. The horses were left with Jim. Her husband seemed ill at ease and she supposed the sight of her had been a shock. 'But you knew I was coming?' she asked him.

'Oh aye, I got your letter, but I worked out it would take longer.' He looked quickly at her, and then away. 'And then it was too late to tell you to wait a bit ... but hell, it was always going to be a bit of a shock for you at first. It's not like Kirkby, you know.' His smile was bitter.

This was not encouraging, but Rose tried to pull herself

together. 'Well, I knew it would be different. What have you been doing, Luke?'

'I've promised to help young Jim there to build a house. He helped me with mine. But he only got here this arvo to stake his claim – he's been working for a man in Moe. And ... well, I was going to do a bit of tidying up at our place.'

That didn't sound promising, but Rose was too tired to care. 'All I want is a cup of tea and a bed to sleep on,' she said quietly, just like an old woman.

'There's the creek,' Luke said suddenly as the track turned sharply. 'Our place is up there on the little ridge. It's a grand spot, it's not far now. I suppose you must be tired.'

Tired was not the word for it. Rose had travelled across the world, only to find that her husband was not expecting her. But at least she was here at the Haunted Creek at last. The water looked cool and clear. Luke was right, it was a beautiful place, dotted with tall, graceful trees with trunks like pale ivory. Their site was a clearing among the trees and looked down on the water. Across the creek she could see distant mountains, blue and mysterious, soaring above ridge after ridge of dark green forest. Lonely and frightening in its size, it was still a beautiful scene.

Rose turned from the view to look eagerly for the house.

There was no farmhouse waiting for her, no civilized place in which to rest her weary bones. The only building was a small hut. Dismayed, she walked up to it. The walls and roof were made of big slabs of rough tree bark. The door creaked as she went in to stand on the earth floor. There was no fireplace; cooking must be done outside. Benches, a table and a bed were made from rough hewn planks. The one room was dark and stuffy and full of the buzz of flies. Outside was bare earth, with no sign of a garden.

'It's got a glass window,' Luke said defensively. 'Not many folks have glass at first, you know.'

So this was home. How could she live here? Was this how all the settlers lived? Surely most women and plenty of men would want something more civilized than this.

A big white bird flew off with the harshest cry Rose had ever heard, a desolate sound echoing through the trees. 'Cockatoo,' Luke said. 'You'll like the birds here.'

'What sort of farming are you doing, Luke?' Rose asked faintly. They would need some money quickly, to build a decent house.

Luke looked away. 'Well … I've got a few beef cattle, young ones, they'll be a while growing before I can sell them. I've a few chooks. We can have eggs for tea …' He broke off and looked past her. Rose turned round but she was too late. A flying charge knocked her off her feet.

Luke laughed so much he could hardly finish his sentence. '… and a goat. This is Gertrude, Rose. She maybe thought we were going to feed her.' Rose struggled to her feet and the goat wandered off.

There was a sort of twilight here, more than in the tropics she had travelled through; there, night fell quickly like a curtain dropping on the day. 'Are you going to wash before supper?' She looked at the sweaty, dusty young man.

'I'll take a dip in the creek – are you coming?' Luke's white teeth flashed in a grin that lit his dirty face.

'No, thank you. I'll take a wash in a basin, if you have one.' Rose longed for cool water, but she couldn't bathe in the creek until she had worked out whether they might have neighbours that walked this way. She had never done more than paddle in a Yorkshire beck.

Luke laughed again. 'There's no crocodiles round here, you know! You'll have to rough it a bit if you're going to be a settler.'

'So I see.' Rose bit her lip and went back to the hut, while Luke went off with a towel to the water. Perhaps one day she'd be able to laugh like Luke did. But he must have had a hard time. She knew that he had saved fifty pounds and had been able to buy land for a pound an acre, but instead of the neat fields she had imagined, all around them the huge trees crowded in. Was this the land he owned, or was it somewhere else?

There was a rough veranda on the side of the hut and Rose sat down there in the last of the daylight. It had been a long day and the days ahead would be difficult. But they would settle down; she and Luke would be established in time. Anything was better than staying in Yorkshire.

A huge spider scuttled across the dirty floor, its body as big as a saucer. Rose shuddered. Was it poisonous? A lot of women wouldn't stay here. They'd take one look and go home.

Rose would have to stay in Australia because her father had married again. Of course, folks said it was a good idea, but why he'd picked that Pearl Harley, Rose would never know. He went and married a shrew, that was the only word for it. She found fault with everybody, nagged her husband and seemed to hate her step-daughter.

Rose had been expected to earn her keep by working on the farm and this she would have enjoyed, but for the new wife. What else could she do? At school they'd said she would make a good teacher, but she never got the chance to train for it.

Looking round rather desperately for escape, Rose was interested when Luke came to their farm one day. He had been hired by her father to hoe turnips and he was full of plans for going to Australia. Lounging on the cowshed door while she milked, he told her about the wonderful prospect ahead. 'You can buy land for a pound an acre. I've been saving since I left school,' he said. 'I'm off in a month or two. Want to come?' He grinned.

Looking up from her milking stool, Rose considered him. They had been at school together but she hadn't thought about him much. Luke was well made and strong, cheeky and always cheerful, and he seemed determined to succeed. 'You can write to me when you get there,' she told him. 'Tell me what it's like.'

For the next few weeks Luke visited every day and talked about Australia, where the sky was blue and the days were mostly sunny.

He had chosen a place in Victoria, where there was good rainfall and a climate like Italy. You could grow grapes and lemons, he said. Imagine picking a lemon or an orange from your own tree! It was too good to be true … and a nice long way from Yorkshire and the dreadful Pearl.

Luke had beguiled her with his stories of a warm sunny land and in the end he had proposed marriage. He told her she was a bonny lass and just right for the colony, and the week before he sailed they had been married.

Rose thought that her stepmother Pearl might have encouraged him, to push Rose off to Australia out of her way. It was exciting, but theirs was not exactly a romance, although she hoped for love. Rose had wanted to get away and Luke had decided he needed a wife. After a few months of silence he had written to her.

There was a sound and Luke was there, grinning through his beard. 'Is supper ready?'

'I don't know where anything is,' Rose said quietly. 'It's too dark to find my way around.' It was hard to think of housekeeping in this rough place.

Luke shrugged and lit a lamp, then brought out a loaf of bread and a few eggs from a cupboard. He lit a fire in the clearing outside and boiled a tin can of water, putting the eggs in the can and making tea when it boiled. He looked better for a wash and smelled of soap. Coming to sit beside her, he put an arm round her. 'Got a kiss for your old man?' His beard was rough and Rose flinched. 'Suppose I might have to shave now there's a lady in the house.'

As they ate, Luke was quiet. 'Your mother sends her love,' Rose said into the silence. He asked her then for news of the village, but he seemed to have something on his mind. 'What are your plans for the farm, Luke? Where's your fields?'

Luke stood up and looked into the darkness. 'I'm sorry, but this is it, lass,' he said sombrely. 'Good land, it grows the biggest trees in the world, and that means something. But you've got to chop 'em down first.' He stopped and then went on. 'To tell you the truth, Rose, it's killing me. The gum trees are hardwood, blunt a saw in no time. I've got my fifty acres but this bit is all I've managed to clear.'

The little farm was only a dream; it might be years away. 'So what are you living on, Luke?'

'Not much … odd jobs here and there, and for meat what I can shoot, mostly. Kangaroo's not bad and the ducks are good to eat. But I've got a plan to get rich and then, you'll see, we'll build a fine house.' There was a gleam in his eye. 'I'm looking for gold. Anybody can go along the creek and pan for gold. It washes out from the banks into the water and you don't need machinery. All you need is a shallow pan and a bag to put the gold in!'

'You're going to be a gold miner? But Mr Carr said it was all over. Most of the gold has been taken out by now.'

Luke laughed. 'I'm going to be a gold prospector, Rose. Not really a miner – you don't dig for alluvial gold. We've had no luck yet, but you'll see. One day we'll strike it rich.'

TWO

ALTHOUGH HE SAID little, Luke's arms were warm and comforting and for a short time some of Rose's doubts faded. She had longed for love, for this reunion, ever since Luke had left England. As long as they could learn to love each other, this was where she belonged. Life would be hard, but they would face it together.

Long after Luke was asleep, Rose stared into the darkness; the doubts loomed again. If only they had got to know each other in England, had established their partnership before taking on this new venture.

The 'farmhouse' was a huge shock. How could anyone keep it tidy or even keep their clothes and food clean in a place like this? You wouldn't be able to invite anyone in, even for a cup of tea; you could take no pride in your work. Rose was too tired to make any plans for improvement but she doubted whether anything could be done. What would her father say if he could see her now? She imagined a huge spider, crawling over the wall towards the bed, and drew the sheet tightly round her although the night was warm.

The darkness was full of shrieks, wails and hoarse cries, frightening even behind a barred door. At first Rose started at each new sound, while Luke slept on. What unknown creatures lurked in this wild place? Instead of the sleepy twitter of birds in an English wood, there were howls, long drawn-out sounds of misery floating up from the creek below them. They must be dingoes. There were weird moans from among the trees. No wonder it was called the Haunted Creek.

The bed was fairly comfortable after the hard and narrow bunks on the ship, but Rose could not sleep. For the first time, she was worrying about money and how they would make a home and earn a living. Money had not seemed very important in her life up to now, on a well-established farm where in most years there was a profit.

But Luke was a dreamer, it was clear. He was spending time running about with Jim – what had they been doing in Moe that day? Their next plan was to start searching for gold instead of getting on with the work of carving a farm out of the bush. It looked as though Rose would be the one to make a garden and with luck she might be able to sell herbs and vegetables to the local folks. But how many people lived here? She was in the dark in more ways than one.

A harsh scream pierced the night and after a while Rose decided it must be a bird. But what sort of bird? Beside her, Luke continued his regular breathing. It was a blessing that he seemed to be at home here. Perhaps she would get used to it, in time.

Just before dawn she dropped into a light doze and soon afterwards Luke got up. He ate the last piece of bread and put on his boots. 'I'm off to help Jim,' he said. 'We've got to get a fence up so he can get his block registered and all that.'

Rose sat up in bed. 'Jim's got to do this urgently?' Luke nodded. She bit her lip, realizing she would need to tread carefully and not seem to be taking charge. 'But Luke … wouldn't it be better if you spent some time here, improving our place? I can help you, there's two of us now …' She stopped as she saw his obstinate expression.

Not looking at Rose, Luke stood up. 'As a matter of fact, I have to help Jim. I owe him.' Going to the door he added, 'Don't worry, lass, I'll be back about noon – it'll be too hot to work by then.'

'Owe him? What do you mean?'

'Well, he lent me some money when I was short, see? I'm paying him back in labour.' He banged the door and was gone. Luke was going to work, but the earnings were already spent. It looked as though they'd be eating a lot of kangaroo.

Rose peered round slowly, avoiding the eye of That Spider who now sat on a chair, watching her in a far too intelligent way. She was on her own in the forest, in a rough cabin with no water and no food. *Babes in the Wood* came to mind and Rose laughed at the thought. Things had to get better; they would get better than this.

There was no privy, of course. Luke had waved a vague hand in the direction of the forest when she'd asked. 'Anywhere you like,' he'd laughed. Surely he could have built a little shelter for an earth closet? Luke had not tried very hard to make a home, but to be fair he hadn't known exactly when to expect her.

Outside the hut in the fresh morning, the world seemed less hostile. Rose decided to wash at the creek and then bring some water back for making tea.

The morning light fell softly through the trees, their pale trunks glimmering in the first rays of the sun. Here there was green grass, even in the summer heat. A light mist moved up from the water and there was the rustle of birds in the high canopy of branches. These trees were taller than any she had seen before; Rose had to tip her head back to see the tops of them. The shade was lighter than the heavy gloom of summer under English trees, the sunlight glancing off the shining gum leaves as they moved in a soft breeze.

The peace was shattered as a peal of heartless laughter made her start. How could anyone be so cruel as to laugh at her predicament? She looked round but saw no one. It would be easy here for people to hide behind the trees ... The laughter came again and then died away in an evil chuckle, a horrible sound. Rose shuddered and remembered some tale of a laughing bird. It was hard to believe that a bird could sound so evil.

The creek wound through the bottom of a little valley, the clear water flowing in and out of the shade of trees and bushes on the bank. Rose went down to the water and bathed her face and hands, then filled the can. There was a crock of flour in the hut and she could make a bread cake, once she had lit the fire.

Floating through the trees she heard children's voices and realized that the Carrs' bullock dray was camped quite close. There was a splash and a lot of shouting. Little Peter Carr came running towards her. 'Mrs Teesdale!' he said breathlessly. 'Charlie's fell in the water!' The little boy was about six and very frightened. Rose took his hand and they ran along the bank to where Charlie was thrashing about in a deep pool made by a bend in the creek. He seemed to be entangled in some branches that had fallen into the water.

On the opposite bank, a small figure could be seen hurrying towards them. Martha Carr, the children's mother, was not frightened. She was annoyed. 'Charlie! Stop that at once and come out of there!'

Charlie surfaced, gulped air and cried out, 'Save me!' The poor child was drowning – or was he playing the fool? She couldn't afford to wait and see. Rose took off her long skirt and jumped into the water. She gasped with cold as she went down, her petticoat floating up round her legs. The water was deeper than she expected, but she managed to grasp the child firmly under his arms.

'Keep still, Charlie!' Rose tried to hold him up, but then she realized that the boy was swimming strongly, quite at home in the water. 'You bad boy, you made me jump in for nothing!' He made for the bank and hauled himself up, and Rose followed, water streaming from her long hair.

Charlie lay on the bank panting and laughing; he had been trying to frighten his brother and she had fallen for it. He looked up at Rose with hangdog eyes. 'Me ma'll kill me,' he muttered, still giggling. 'She's done it before.'

Rose laughed, slightly hysterically. 'You probably deserve it, you horrible boy!' It had been a frightening two minutes.

Martha stamped along the bank, uttering threats, and Rose stood protectively in her wet petticoat in front of the lad. 'I think he's learned a lesson – he won't play about in water again, will you, Charlie? Next time, you might really need help and I wouldn't believe it!' She had been told that Australians had a strange sense of humour and this seemed to prove it.

The sun was gaining height and its warmth would soon dry her light cotton underclothes. It was embarrassing to walk about without her skirt, but the most practical thing to do. Rose picked up her skirt and turned to go. 'I'd better go and make myself some breakfast.'

'That bloke of yours gone off and left you already? Some men don't know how lucky they are. Well, girl, you'd better come and have breakfast with us, then. And after that we're off to look at this here block of land.' Martha led the way along the creek to where their cattle were grazing not far from the cart. Blue smoke curled lazily into the air and Rose could smell coffee and frying bacon. Their camp seemed to be a much more civilized place than her new home. Rose put on her skirt as they neared the fire, where Bert was frying the breakfast in a huge iron pan.

'Your man – Luke, you call him? He'll be able to tell us who lives round here and where – even draw us a map. We must find out where everybody is,' Martha said firmly as she took over the cooking.

'Well, it's nice to be sociable …' But what was the hurry? They could meet the neighbours when they'd established a homestead and Rose herself didn't want any callers while she was living in a hut like that.

Bert shook his head at her. 'It's nothing to do with being sociable. If we're going to select land it has to be good for growing onions and greens. Locals can tell us that. And there has to be somebody here to buy them off us.' He took a deep slurp of his coffee. 'Does anybody live up here, barring a few crackpot gold miners?' Bert was short and solid and never seemed to waste words. 'The gold fever and maybe the whisky gets a lot of 'em and they go right off of their heads … that's what you hear.'

Rose hid a shudder, but she was feeling braver already, with breakfast inside her and her clothes drying out. 'Of course you'll know better than me, but I was brought up on a farm,' she told them. 'I think this soil is good, but we're high up in the hills. I noticed the air cool down as we came up from the valley yesterday. If it's too cold, crops won't grow.'

'Aye, well, we are in the hills, it's true,' Bert agreed. 'But beggars can't be choosers, Rose. Valley land is all taken and folks are spreading out all over these hills. River land's best, but that's gone now. I'm looking to find a block further along the creek.'

Rose knew she should have been trying to clean up the hut, but it would be interesting to go along with the Carrs to visit the block. Martha was friendly and it would be good if they were to be neighbours. The bullocks were left to their grazing with young Peter to guard them.

A rabbit ran across the track and the Carrs all yelled at once. 'Rabbit pie!' Martha said, her eyes shining. 'They'll be right handy.'

'If we can keep them off the crops,' her husband reminded her. 'I thought it would be over cold for them up here. They led us a merry dance at Melbourne, I can tell you.'

There had been rabbits at Kirkby, but Rose hadn't thought of them as a nuisance. 'They're not an Australian animal, are they?'

'Nobs brought 'em in for the hunting,' Bert said briefly. 'Rabbits to feed the foxes, so they could chase foxes on horseback, like what they do in England.' He laughed. 'But rabbits, they got out of hand and it's folks like us that suffer when there's too many.'

'But you do like your rabbit pie, Bert,' his wife reminded him.

The available block of land on the Haunted Creek was not far from Luke's land and covered with the same big trees, apart from a clearing by the water. 'A miner lived here in the sixties, they say,' Bert told them, but there was no sign of a house. It might not be true. Then he found a broken clay pipe in a heap of stones and the place took on a new meaning: it had been somebody's home.

'Them stones were probably the fireplace,' Martha said. The rest of the hut, if there was one, had dissolved back into the earth. Roses were blooming among the wattles down by the creek, perhaps the remains of a forgotten garden.

'When folks walk off the land, the bush soon takes over,' Bert said as he turned the soil with a stick.

'Was all this land used at one time?' Rose wondered. She had thought that this was wilderness and the settlers were the first on the land, but Bert nodded.

'The miners spread out a bit, of course, and then all this land was leased as a cattle run, the Wattle Tree run, thousands of acres without fences. They turned cattle loose and collected them months or years later. Up the road here there's a little place called Wattle Tree; there's a few houses and maybe a store. At least I hope so.'

The land turned out to be a useful piece of dirt, as Bert said. It sloped up fairly gently to a level plateau and this, Martha decided, was where they would build a house if they settled here. Bert was handy with a hammer, and they would get sawn timber and do the job properly – none of your slabs of bark for the Carrs. 'Luke needs to get sawn timber, too,' Rose said quietly, looking at the roses peeping through the wattles. 'Maybe you could get a load together, save in some way.'

When she got back to the hut, Luke was sweeping the floor and doing his best to clean the place up. 'Thought you'd gone back to England,' he said with a grin. He had a brace of rabbits hanging up outside and some onions in a bag. 'We'll have a grand tea, better than last night. Jim made me come home early – said you need company.'

Luke was happy to draw a rough map of the area for the Carrs while the rabbit meat was stewing in a big cast-iron pot. 'It'll be good if they stay, somebody for you to talk to when I go prospecting,' he said happily. 'I'll likely be gone for a few weeks at a time.'

Rose turned to him in shock. 'Weeks? But I thought we'd be farming! It's a gamble, isn't it, looking for gold?' How could she stay here alone?

Changing the subject abruptly, Luke pointed to the map. 'There's a few folks round here. I think the Carrs would be able to sell vegetables. Down here towards the Tangil River there's a pub called the All Seasons: it was busy in the gold rush days and there's a few miners left. Landlady's a bit of a character. Maeve they call her. Irish, I suppose. There's not many women up here, though. And then—' He pointed to a track leading out of the Haunted Creek '—this goes up the ridge to Wattle Tree. There's a store there, a few houses and a little school, that's used sometimes as a church. Mrs Jensen is the schoolmistress and her son Erik farms a couple of blocks. I reckon he's a big bore … but very straight, you understand.'

Rose nodded, trying to take it all in.

'Then there's a farmer, Ben Sawley, a bit further along who's cleared his land, has a few cows and breeds donkeys. He grows whatever he thinks will sell.… Last year he grew a lot of onions – I got these from him.' Luke looked at Rose and added, 'I've met him once or twice at the All Seasons … don't know if he has a wife. There's a few more … the store's here, they have a load of bairns … and some folks have built a grand house on this hill.'

Against all the signs, Rose persisted with her dream. 'When your land is cleared, Luke, could we keep milking cows?' A dairy herd would be a little oasis of civilization in this wilderness. 'I could sell butter to all these people.'

'No, Rose.' The rather hard voice was firm. 'I milked enough cows at home – don't want to be tied to a cow's tail ever again. You can milk Gertrude the goat when she comes into milk. There maybe will be dairy herds here in time, if more folks come. Somebody might build a butter factory like I hear they're doing in some places, for the farmers to deliver their cream to. But that's all in the future. Haunted Creek is pretty quiet at the moment. Gold's the thing, I tell you.'

As they ate the meal, Rose said, 'Do you remember old Mr Alsop at Kirkby, Luke? Well, he died and his lads are fighting over the will....'

Luke listened in silence for a while and then stood up with an impatient gesture. 'I hope you're not going to be talking about Kirkby all the time, Rose. You're here now and we have to make the best of it, not be looking back all the time.'

Rose felt tears rising and turned away from him. She would not show any weakness; she would be strong. That Spider was sitting at her feet now, mocking her, and she tried to laugh. 'You're right, lad. Let's make the best of it and start farming. That's what we're here for.'

The Carrs decided to buy and were pleased with their selection. 'It's a good thing,' Bert said to Martha a few days after they had settled in, 'our block has a little creek running down to the big one. Plenty of water.'

They were sitting at the top of the ridge, looking over their land. 'Yes, Bert. And I'll tell you something else – if you leave that line of thick trees on the ridge we'll be sheltered from the worst of the storms.'

Martha and Bert had strolled through the neighbourhood, looking at the lie of the land and the progress of the local folk. They had visited Rose and walked up the hill to Wattle Tree and now Martha said, 'Jim Carlyle beat us to the level block, but he'll have no water on his land as far as I can see. He'll need to dig out some dams to catch the winter rains. We've got the best deal, I'm thankful to say, in spite of the race to get here first.'

'It was no race – you can't hurry cattle,' Bert reminded her. 'They'll not be pushed.'

Martha continued. 'But what worries me is that poor English lass, the mess she's come to. I was shocked to see their place. That Luke should be horsewhipped for bringing her out, telling her the farm was ready. Everybody knows it's hard enough for young women in the back blocks, even if they're used to our climate. Most men make a bit of an effort, build a house that keeps out wind and rain and rats ... I wouldn't live like that for very long and I doubt she will.'

'But if you go back, folks say you've failed. And they're married, so she'll have to stay. A woman's place is with her husband,' Bert said heavily.

Martha sighed. 'Maybe she'll straighten him up, if she's got the character. Poor Rose! I've only known her for a week or two but I feel right sorry for her. I suppose we owe her for pulling Charlie out of the creek, although I know he was shamming. That was quick of her, that was, and she thought he was drowning.'

'There'll be plenty of chances to help her, you mark my words.' Bert got stiffly to his feet. 'It's time you put those young monkeys to bed.'

THREE

THERE WERE FLEAS in the dust of the floor and rats scuttled about in the roof of the hut at night, to say nothing of spiders. Rose was used to the realities of farm life, but nothing like this. They lived for most of the time outside in the bleak back yard. How long would it be before they had a decent home?

For a few weeks Luke tried to please Rose in practical ways, doing things like putting up shelves in the hut, although she seemed to get no closer to him emotionally. The loving relationship was not developing; it seemed as though a part of her husband was private, shut away. She hoped it was just the effects of isolation and that he would change in time.

One day as she was washing clothes in the creek, Rose looked up to see a figure towering over her. Then the enormous grey kangaroo turned and bounded into the bush. Were they dangerous? Luke had not warned her of any dangers at all, but Martha Carr had mentioned snakes, so she kept a watch for them. If a snake bites you you're as good as dead, Mrs Carr said, but they usually avoid people if they can. Perhaps Luke didn't want to frighten her.

'What about men like Ned Kelly?' Rose asked one evening. She'd read about bushrangers before she came to Australia; gangs of outlaws could be anywhere. People on the ship had warned her about them. 'There's no police anywhere near Haunted Creek. I suppose our cattle are worth money, it would be easy to gallop off with them.'

'Don't be daft, woman,' Luke said shortly. He was drinking beer from a bottle that had been submerged in the creek all day to cool it. 'The Kelly gang's hundreds of miles from here, up north. Remember, it's a big country! And, anyway, they mostly steal from rich folks, not poor cockies like us.'

'Cockies?'

'The folks on the grazing runs call the selectors cockatoos – they arrive in flocks and get in the way. Don't worry so much, lass.'

One or two trees were chopped down and Rose helped to clear away the branches, but it was a slow job and by the end of a month she could tell that he was getting restless.

Luke was unwilling to work long hours. 'Tradesmen in Melbourne have worked an eight-hour day for years. Why should I kill myself out here?' he demanded.

'I've never heard of an eight-hour day. We worked at least twelve on the farm at home.' Rose stopped; she had noticed that her voice was getting harder. She must try not to be bitter, try to be loving.

One Sunday night, Luke started to pack a bag. 'I'm off down the creek with Jim to look for gold tomorrow. You'll be all right, won't you?'

Rose swallowed. He was so casual! But she was not going to plead with him to stay at home. She was a settler's wife; she must not seem to be afraid. She would refuse to think about snakes, outlaws, howls and shrieks and she would stare down spiders with big goggling eyes.

One night they had climbed the hill behind the hut so that Luke could show her the unfamiliar southern stars. 'The Southern Cross,' he said, gazing at the bright cluster low in the sky. 'Shining down on the best place on earth. This is our country now, lass.' She had heard the growls, the grunts, the rustling all around them that night, but Luke had only mentioned the croaking of bullfrogs. 'It's not like Kirkby, Rose, you mustn't expect it.'

'So I've noticed,' Rose murmured, peering into the rustling darkness. Heaven knew what was out there, a few yards from their hut. Now, she would have to face her fears alone. 'Just one thing, Luke,' she said, more calmly than she felt. 'Why is it called the Haunted Creek?'

There was a slight pause before Luke answered. 'Surely you don't believe in ghosts?' He put a casual arm round her. 'It's just a name, that's all, from the gold mining days. Most of the haunting was done at the All Nations hotel. They say some of the miners couldn't get enough of the place in the old days, stayed there for weeks at a time.'

There had to be a better explanation. The roses down at the bottom of the Carrs' place ... perhaps there was a grave there. She'd realized that people were not buried tidily in churchyards here, because there were few churches and not many cemeteries as yet.

Jim Carlyle arrived with a backpack about seven the next morning. 'Good day, Mrs Teesdale, I've come to take your husband off your hands for a few days. I'm sure you'll enjoy a bit of peace for a change.' He was a likeable lad but there was something of the rogue about his crooked smile and Rose wondered whether Luke would be better off without his influence. She gave him a mug of tea while Luke tied a pan to his bundle.

'Where are your horses? Won't you be riding?' she asked Jim. Surely it would be easier to travel with horses, the ones that had overtaken the bullock cart on her way to Haunted Creek.

'Well, you see, they're borrowed from a neighbour when we go to town. We haven't got ourselves nags as yet,' Jim said airily as though he could pick up a horse any time he wanted one.

The men went off and Rose was left alone in the little clearing, listening to the hum of bees in flowering trees high above her head.

There was very little housework in a bark hut. Perhaps she should try to make some proper bread? That would be challenging without the comfort of a kitchen and a coal oven. Mrs Carr – Martha, as she liked to be called – had given Rose some yeast with instructions for making a loaf in the cast-iron pot. 'You bury it in the embers of a fire and then it's an oven, a camp oven,' she had explained. 'It bakes the bread very well, if you get the heat just right.'

It would be a good idea to try the method while Luke was away, in case the first batch was not eatable and it had to be given to the hens. The embers would need to be hot enough to cook but not burn the bread. First she'd lock up Gertrude, in case she interfered with the process.

The goat watched with interest from her pen as Rose kneaded the dough, working on a board set on a convenient tree stump near the hut. It was a very hot day and the bread rose quickly. In Yorkshire, it had nearly always been slow to rise. Over there, they would be struggling through winter snow. It was hard to imagine that she was in the same world ... but she must stop thinking about Yorkshire.

By noon, the birds had fallen silent and the gum trees seemed to shimmer in the heat. The bread went into the pot and Rose pulled the embers of the dying fire over the camp oven. As she did so, a sudden breeze blew through the trees and sparks flew up from the ashes. They landed on a pile of dry gum leaves and a blaze sprang up immediately. The hens cackled in alarm and Gertrude bleated.

Rose looked round wildly. With all her worries, she'd never thought to be afraid of fire. She now had a fire on her hands and if it spread to the bush, those oily gum leaves would go up like a torch. Where was the water? She rushed over to the buckets, but they were empty. Fetching water from the creek had been planned as her next job.

Fanned by the breeze, the fire ran along towards a tree with long ribbons of dry bark hanging down from it. If the flames got into them, the whole tree would burn and the hut would be gone in a few minutes.

Rose bit her lip and fought down panic. Luke had left a shovel leaning by the door and she snatched it up and began to dig a shallow trench in the dry earth between the fire and the trees, to try to contain it. It was the only thing she could do. Dirt wouldn't burn, surely? Everything in this place seemed likely to burn. The summer sun had sucked all the moisture out of the earth, the hut, even the people, everything except the grass down by the creek.

Digging feverishly, she hardly noticed when the wind changed until the blue aromatic smoke came back towards her, making her cough. She could now see little, but the dreadful laughter began again. 'Don't sit there laughing, come and help me!' Rose called to the bird. The fire was gaining ground and she was not going to be able to stop it now.

Just as the wind seemed to gain strength and the fire rose higher, a figure appeared in the smoke, carrying a basket. 'Please help me, there's a rake by the fence,' Rose called and went on digging.

The woman nodded and took up the rake. For some minutes the fire seemed to be beating them and Rose despaired of the hut; they would lose what little they had.

'Keep going!' the woman encouraged her. Gradually they gained ground and, working together, they were able to contain the fire, pushing it back to the open hearth, and then beat out the flames. A few wisps of smoke still rose up from the ash, but the fire was ringed with bare earth. It was safe.

Gasping, Rose sat down suddenly on the bench beside the door as her legs gave way. 'Thank you. I was in real trouble until you came.'

The woman smiled. She wore a plain cotton dress and bonnet and was browned by the sun. 'I am so glad I was here at the right time. I've been picking blackberries … You must be Luke's new wife. I'm Freda Jensen. I teach at the Wattle Tree school up on the ridge yonder. It was built last year.'

'Yes, I'm Rose Teesdale.' The name was still unfamiliar. Rose mopped her brow; the heat was intense. They sat quiet for a while and a bird flew down onto a stump, evidently looking for insects in the newly turned earth. It looked like a kingfisher. Then Rose moved slightly and the bird flew up into a tree, making the unearthly laughing sound she had come to hate.

'That was the bird, Mrs Jensen!' Rose laughed herself. Those dreadful sounds came from this bird.

'The kookaburra – it's called the laughing jackass. He always seems to turn up when you make a mistake.' The older woman went over to the fire site and hooked off the cooking pot with a forked stick. 'I'm afraid your cooking is ruined, Rose. What was it?' There was a blackened lump in the pot.

The relief was enormous. Rose realized that if the fire had got away it could have burned miles of bush, right up to the Wattle Tree settlement. She would clear a wider space round the site of the cooking fire and she would be much more careful in future.

The women looked at each other, both covered in grime from the fire. 'I'll go down to get some water …' Rose began, but Mrs Jensen stopped her.

'No, come home with me and we'll have a cup of tea with Erik. It's not far to walk. You can wash your face at our house. And please call me Freda. There's not so much call for formality in the bush.' The teacher certainly had a determined way with her. She picked up her basket.

Rose was still shaky and in no condition to argue and so, with a backward look at the smoking embers, she walked with Freda up the steep track to Wattle Tree. Her right hand was painful and, looking at it, she realized that it had been burned at some time while she was fighting the fire.

The sound of hammering grew louder as they approached a new wooden house at the side of the track. Freda led the way round the house, which was built of rough sawn timber. 'Erik is building a veranda … it's almost finished.' She waved to the workman but went on inside and showed Rose to a small bathroom with a wash-stand, basin and ewer, soap and towels – how civilized! 'There's water in the jug. Wash while I put the kettle on.'

The bathroom mirror was much better than the cracked one at home and Rose saw that her face was browned by the sun and her dark eyes had a haunted look. She smoothed down her hair, which was singed at the front.

Feeling cleaner but still shaky, Rose joined her hostess in the big kitchen. Freda had also washed and put on a clean apron. As she poured the tea, a large figure appeared. 'Erik, come and meet Mrs Teesdale – Rose. This is my son, Erik with a "K", named after his father.'

Erik Jensen. So this was Luke's 'big bore', this blond, suntanned giant with blue eyes that made her knees turn to jelly. *It must be the effects of the fire, I'll recover soon.* Whatever had come over her? This was like no feeling she had ever experienced, this sudden strong attraction; terrifying, in fact. She leaned against the table for support.

The big man reached out a huge hand. 'Welcome, Mrs Teesdale.' He looked at her intently. Erik took her hand and then he felt her wince so he held it, turning it over very gently in his. 'A burn, eh? We'd better do something about that. What do you normally use to treat burns?'

Her hand was certainly burning in his. It was his touch that affected her; the pain of the hand was nothing. *Concentrate, lass, stay practical.* 'We always used lavender oil ...' Rose stopped, almost blinded by the look of concern in his eyes.

'Why didn't you tell me?' Freda put down the teapot and looked at the burn. 'Tea leaves, I think. Sit down, my dear.' She put a spoonful of cold wet tea leaves on a piece of cloth and tied it round Rose's hand. 'Now, hot sweet tea. You've had a difficult morning.'

That was putting it mildly. Rose had nearly burned the parish down and now she was nearly swooning like a heroine in a romantic novel, just because of a neighbouring farmer's blue eyes. Ridiculous, she told herself.

It was past the middle of the day, time to eat, but Rose did not feel hungry.

Freda cut slices of new bread, buttered it and added hunks of cheese, talking as she worked, telling Erik about the fire. Rose quietly drank her tea, waiting for the churning feeling to subside. Erik had fair hair bleached almost white by the sun, blue eyes and a very determined chin with a dimple in it. He looked like a sunburned Viking. 'You did well not to panic, Mrs Teesdale,' he said quietly, and his mother nodded.

'Rose did very well.'

'How's Luke getting on with the clearing?' Erik wanted to know. 'I'm doing the same thing myself, but of course I've been here longer than he has. It's hard, slow work, making a farm out of the forest.'

Rose nodded. 'Yes, I'm hoping he will get some more land cleared soon, and cut some wood for a proper house. He's not at home at the moment.' Both the Jensens looked at her with serious faces. 'Luke has gone looking for gold, to get some money together, you see.'

There was a short silence and then Freda said quietly, 'Perhaps he should have stayed with you just a little longer.' So he should, but what could she do? Freda must be worried about her.

Erik cut in quickly. 'I'm sure Rose can look after herself very well!' His eyes were bright; his smile lit up the room. 'You'll soon get acclimatized. There's so much to enjoy – you're a country girl, yes? If you love being outdoors, this is the place for you.' The cheerful words made her feel less afraid.

'I do. I like growing things,' Rose told him, striving for calm. 'Looking after animals, too. I'm used to sheep and cattle.' She paused and changed the subject. 'Do you farm with your father, Erik?'

'No, I'm afraid he died before I was born. He was a sea captain, not a farmer – he came from Sweden.' Freda's eyes went to a framed photograph of a bearded man in naval uniform. She was a widow, and she had survived.

After the meal, Rose was taken on a tour of their little farm and she managed to keep her distance from Erik, walking beside Freda. The disturbed feeling slowly subsided but a sort of glow remained.

The first thing she saw was a neat vegetable garden, with rows of beans, tomatoes and potatoes. Here too were all the herbs that Rose and her grandmother had grown and others as well. Carefully,

Freda pulled sprigs from some of the plants and gave them to Rose. 'Take these cuttings; they should put down roots if you keep them watered in soft earth.' The strong scents of rosemary, lavender and mint brought back memories of her old home. 'You'll find that they grow all the year round here.'

The Jensens' land was divided by wood and wire fences into fields that had been sown with grass and clover. There was a substantial stack of hay and a few farm buildings made from slabs of bark, rather neater than the hut Rose lived in. One enclosure held pigs and Erik explained that once the big trees were cleared, the pigs rooted out the bushes, turned over the land and manured it.

There was a flower garden round the house and Rose wondered how she could ever develop a garden from the dusty, parched earth round her hut. It seemed so easy here, where everything was neat and orderly. 'It's all wonderful, but what I like best is your house,' she admitted. The roof was of corrugated iron and it had gutters connected to a rainwater tank. These folks had no need to go down to the creek for water; the tank would collect it from the roof every time it rained.

'Luke can do the same thing, it's not too difficult. But now, of course, I'm saving for more land. We need more stock to make a proper living.' When Erik spoke he gave her all his attention.

'Of course, Luke is a countryman too,' Freda put in. 'Town folks have a harder time of it. How long have you been married, Rose? I gather you were married in England, you must have known Luke for a long time.' They were both watching her reaction. 'So you'll know how to handle him, of course.'

It was hard to tell what that meant. 'Well, we went to the same school, but I didn't see much of him until … until he decided to come here and asked me to join him. We were only married for a week or two before he left.' Rose glanced at Freda. 'He should be successful, don't you think?'

Freda nodded, but doubtfully. 'As long as he sticks to a plan, and you may have to help him to do that. Now, Rose, if you pick some blackberries where I did, you'll be able to make some jam.'

'That's a pleasant young woman,' Freda said to her son as Rose went off down the track. 'But I wish her luck with that husband of hers. I wonder if she knows what he's really like?'

Erik picked up his hammer and some nails. 'He might settle down, now that she's arrived. I hope so. We'd better keep an eye on her, just in case of trouble. She's got character; she'll make a settler before too long.' He laughed in his carefree way. 'Pity there aren't a few more nice girls in these parts. Now, how high do you want this top rail? I know there's a plan, but I'm making it up as I go along.'

Freda looked at the rail, measuring it with her eye. 'That's about right, where it is now … I think young Luke should grow up a little. We all know what's been going on in Moe, although Rose won't have heard of it.'

Erik hammered in a nail violently. 'That bloke's had plenty of time to clear some of his land but he hasn't been there often enough. It's not fair to his wife.'

That night Rose sat beside the fire, listening to the bush waking up as the creatures of the night started their activities. The usual twittering and rustling, the croaking of frogs and the whine of a mosquito was becoming the familiar background as the sun set. She would manage quite well without Luke. She had even found out from Freda how to remove That Spider and his friends from the hut. You clamped a basin over the thing, slid a piece of paper under him and then he was trapped and you could take him outside. This was priceless knowledge.

Gradually Rose became aware of a new sound: a low moaning, coming from among the trees at the back of the hut. The sound rose and fell like a lament and died away on a sobbing wail. Rose felt herself go cold as she listened. When it started up again after a few minutes, she gave herself a mental shake. What would her grandmother have said?

'Right, Grandmother, I will face it,' Rose muttered and walked firmly to the trees. In the last of the light she looked up at the branches, dark against the sky, just where the sound was coming from. Was it a bird? As her eyes got used to the darkness she was able to see that two branches were rubbing together, moving with the variable wind. As the branches moved, the sound rose and fell.

No doubt, Rose thought as she went to bed, all the strange noises in the bush had an explanation and one day she would understand them all. The real danger was not the howls, shrieks and moans, but fire. She had never seen anything burn so quickly as gum leaves and she would make sure that the fire was out every time she left the hut.

If Luke could build a house like Erik had done … At the thought of Erik, she blushed in the darkness. Erik was a potential danger just like fire; his intensity could consume you.

About midnight, Rose woke to the sound of voices. Men were tramping past the hut, talking as they went. Who were they, out at this time of night? She cowered in the bed, afraid they would knock at the door. They seemed to stop and she heard one say, 'That's Teesdale's place but he's never there. He's done nothing with it.' He was relieving himself on the path – she could hear him. 'I'll give him some fertilizer.'

There was a coarse laugh and another voice said, 'Well, we all know where he spends his days and nights, don't we?' The men moved off down the track.

FOUR

'PISS OFF!'

Rose jumped in alarm as the hoarse voice cut into her thoughts. She was wandering by the creek in the cool of the evening, picking up stones and putting them into a bag lying on the bank. 'What you want the bloody stones for, anyway?'

On a rock by the side of the creek was a big, wide-brimmed hat, underneath which was a bushy black beard. There must be a bad-tempered man under there somewhere, thought Rose, but he was not visible. A younger man lounged nearby. Were they bushrangers? They looked like outlaws, rough and dirty.

'I thought everybody was friendly round here,' Rose said to the hat, her heart beating quickly. She had nothing worth stealing, so why should they bother with her?

'We're on a selection just up there. Teesdale's it's called. I'm picking up stones to make a fireplace. That's all.'

It was the day after her fright and Rose had decided to make a safer place for the fire before she tried to cook again. 'My name is Rose Teesdale,' she offered.

The man spread large hands in a gesture of disgust, twisted and gnarled by age, crusted with dirt. 'Waste of time. Go back to where you belong – this country is no good for the likes of you. You'll be eaten by dogs or bit by snakes down here.' He sniggered. 'And that's if the blokes don't get to you first. We're short of women in the bush – it makes us ready for anything.'

'I'm ready for anything,' the younger man said with a leer. 'How about it, missus?' He had a face like a rat.

'Now look …' Rose began, ignoring the leer. 'We're hoping to start a little farm. There are other families here, doing the same thing. Maybe you have a farm yourself, but surely there's room for all of us.' It was better not to think about the outlaws.

'I'm no bloody farmer. I belong to the bush,' the hat growled. 'But I'm warning you for yer own good, Haunted Creek is no place for a woman. There's things down here as you didn't ought to meddle with, see. And there's ghosts as well, that come crowding in on dark nights … down the Haunted Creek.' He paused, evidently for effect, and went on in a hoarse whisper, 'Have you heard dingoes howling in the dark of the night? Well, one night they'll be howling at your door!' His voice rose on the last words.

In spite of herself, a shiver ran through Rose. 'I suppose you say that to all the women you meet. Maybe you should be on the stage!' She turned for home but continued at the water's edge, choosing flat stones for her bag as she went. The sun had gone down behind the ridge, leaving the little valley in shadow. Leaves rippled in the breeze and the creek gurgled quietly on down to the Tangil River.

Now the dusk was falling quickly, as it did here. When Rose straightened up, four men were blocking her way, all with ferocious-looking knives in their hands. She was about half a mile from home and much further from any help.

Holding up her head, Rose walked steadily forward. Surely they wouldn't attack her? This was supposed to be a Christian country and Queen Victoria ruled the Empire – it was not the jungle, after all.

The rat-faced man dropped his knife suddenly and grabbed Rose in a powerful grip. 'I'm taking her into the bushes, teach her a bit of respect. Haven't seen a woman for months.' His laughter was pitiless. However Rose twisted and fought, she was caught fast. His arms were round her and he held her close to his body, clamping her between powerful legs while he tied her wrists. He reeked of beer and stale sweat. Dragging her away from the others with both huge hands round her breasts, he taunted her. 'Come on, you know you like it. Women like a bit of rough play and they never get enough of it.'

'Won't you help me?" Rose screamed to the man in the hat, but he too laughed. 'My turn next, when she's calmed down a bit.' She was going to be raped by the outlaw and there was nothing she could do.

Another man called, 'Leave this one for me, Joe, if you don't mind.' He came up to her, taller than the rest and moving smoothly, like a cat. His face was scarred, perhaps with a knife like the one he held. 'Benny, give her to me. I want her. You owe me, y'know. I helped you out last week.'

The cultured voice was even more sinister than the rough voices of the other men. He was as unkempt as the others and his right hand twirled the big knife dangerously.

'You want the bitch? She's probably no good for fun anyway. Too respectable.' The man holding Rose gradually let go and the tall man took her arm and marched her down the track.

The villain was looking down at Rose with a strange expression. If she could keep him talking, she thought desperately, maybe she could appeal to his better nature. 'Who are you?'

'We're bush workahs, that's who we are.' It was not the voice of a worker. But he was obviously a rapist; the upper classes sometimes took it as a right.

The hat man shouted, 'Make sure you teach her a lesson, Lordy,' as she was pulled into the shadow of the trees.

'Please untie me and let me go home.' Rose looked up at the man who held her with one powerful hand, the other holding a knife close to her throat. He was still edging her away from the other men.

The man they called Lordy looked to be the most dangerous of the four, lean and very agile. As soon as trees hid them from view, he cut the ropes on her wrists, but still held her.

Rose was almost fainting from fright. 'Please … let me go,' she gasped. But the man smiled evilly and kept on walking for several minutes. Then he stopped and backed her up against a big tree. This was it … Rose closed her eyes. It might be over more quickly if she didn't fight.

'Just get your breath back,' Lordy said. He stepped away and looked at her as she opened her eyes. 'I want to apologize for frightening you,' he said quietly. 'Please allow me to escort you home, Mrs Teesdale.'

Rose had no alternative but to walk beside him back to her hut. What now? Was he going to rape her later? There was no point in running away – he would easily catch her. 'What is all this about? Why threaten me?' Surely there was nothing to lose by asking questions.

'They don't like strangers, as you may have gathered.' There was a laugh in the deep voice. 'I'm not quite so prejudiced, but it seemed best to appear to go along with the chaps. They can be quite difficult, y'know, when they really try.'

Was it possible that Lordy had actually saved her from the others? 'Are you … bushrangers, like Ned Kelly?'

The tall man beside her shook his head sadly. 'My … associates are former jail birds, I'm afraid. Incarceration sours the temper, they tell me, especially when the convict is originally innocent of crime.' They walked on in silence until they reached the hut. It was nearly dark.

Looming above her in the starlight, Lordy looked down at Rose and she quailed again. He had seen that the hut was deserted. Slowly, deliberately, his arm came up and he raised his hat. 'Jasper Barrington, at your service – I should have introduced myself. My advice to you is to go to see Maeve at the All Nations hotel. Maeve is a very sensible woman and if you intend to stay here, you will need her help. Good night, Mrs Teesdale.' He vanished into the trees, leaving Rose shaking with relief.

As she locked up the hens and fed the goat, Rose thought about her situation. Why had Luke left her alone here? She had obviously been in real trouble, those few minutes by the creek. Did the men want to discourage settlers for some purpose of their own, or were they just looking for an excuse to assault her? And why did they all carry big knives? She would keep well away from anyone she met down there in the future … but life must go on. Perhaps she should carry a knife herself.

Once she got her courage back, Rose thought she would go to see this woman Maeve. She might even meet Luke on his way home – he had gone that way.

For a few days, Rose concentrated on her work. She built a ring of stones to enclose the cooking fire. She had plenty of sugar and so she picked blackberries and boiled them up to make jam, thinking that Luke would be pleased with a variation in their diet. Some of the yeast that Martha had given her was still alive and so she made good bread with the camp oven method, watching it carefully. Part of the dough was saved, to make the next batch of bread.

One day rain fell and she collected as much as she could in pots and buckets, pouring it into the rainwater barrel. She hammered nails into the posts that framed the hut, to hang up kitchen utensils, and the kookaburras chuckled as they watched her. They were almost like friends by now.

At the end of the week, Rose realized that it must be Sunday. How different from Sundays at Kirkby, with church bells ringing and people in their best clothes. She bathed hurriedly in the creek and put on a clean dress.

Freda and Erik came to see her during the afternoon, bringing fresh vegetables. Rose felt uncomfortable and remembered to be on guard, but the big man was open and friendly and she soon relaxed a little. 'I know how hard it is at first,' Freda said, waving her thanks aside. 'People tend to live on dry food, flour and sugar, and that's not healthy.'

'Luke not home yet? I want to see him.' Erik looked round and although she had done her best to tidy up the site, their home looked very shabby to Rose as she saw it through the visitors' eyes. 'Onions are fetching a good price down in the valley. Luke should dig some ground and get some seed in as soon as he can. I could take yours in with ours in the cart, once you have a crop.'

Rose sighed. 'But there's a lot to do first. We have to get rid of all these trees ...' She waved her hand at the surrounding bush and then drew the kettle on to the fire. 'Let's have a cup of tea,' she said, hoping to change the subject.

Freda sat down thankfully but Erik paced restlessly about, looking at the land and the patch that had been dug. 'Good land,' he said when he came back. 'You could grow crops between the trees at first, you know. Get some income, while you clear the rest.'

Rose produced some scones she had made on a plate over the fire, peppered with a few currants, and the visitors seemed impressed. 'You sell your vegetables in Moe?' she asked. Moe was where she had left the coach road and joined the Carrs in their bullock dray.

'Mostly, although the All Nations and the miners' camp take quite a lot. There's a few miners left, of course. But I really want to start a dairy herd and then we could make butter and cheese.' So this was why Luke found the big man boring. 'And you could perhaps advise me, Rose.' Erik smiled devastatingly at her and she felt like telling him he was wasted in the bush. Those blue eyes should have been charming the young ladies of Melbourne.

When the visitors got up to go, Rose wished they would stay longer. 'Come to see us as soon as Luke gets back,' Erik said firmly. He had a touch of his mother's schoolteacher ways, Rose thought. It had been a relief to talk to them after being reduced to conversations with the hens and the goat, although Gertrude the goat seemed very understanding. Watching the Jensens disappear out of sight, Rose decided to take Gertrude for a walk.

'Come on, Gertrude, we'll go and find some fresh greens for you.' Rose unhitched the animal from her tether but kept the rope in her hand. She did not want to lose a valuable goat, even though milk was just a hope for the future.

Gertrude bleated happily and led the way to a patch of fresh grass in a little clearing. Here they were still on Luke's land, but Rose was not sure where it ended. The area had been surveyed and there were pegs at intervals, but it was not all fenced as yet. 'Goats don't like gum trees, I know that,' Rose said as Gertrude sniffed disdainfully at a trailing bunch of eucalypt leaves.

Gertrude was enjoying the walk so much that Rose let her set the pace and lead her further away from the hut, although she kept looking back to work out where she was and see the reassuring wisp of smoke from her cooking fire. It would be easy to get lost here. Suddenly Gertrude jerked the rope out of her hand and trotted off on an errand of her own, her udder swinging jauntily. They should never have come so far from home! They must have walked a couple of miles and one stretch of bush looked so much like another....

Rose told herself severely not to panic. She had been here before with Luke and she knew roughly where she was. But where was Gertrude?

Calling at intervals, Rose tried to walk in a straight line. There was no goat to be seen and the only thing to be heard was a magpie's liquid warble, that changed suddenly to the crack of a whip and then to the grating of a saw. Nothing here was what it seemed. Surely there were no people about? Then Rose remembered she'd been told about the lyre bird that imitated all the sounds it heard in the bush. Maybe next week it would be chirping 'Gertrude!'

The eucalypt forest shimmered in the heat and the scent was heady and penetrating; it seemed to be growing stronger. Surely the goat would come back to her? She was tense with worry when she eventually saw Gertrude's black and white head among the trees. The goat was towing someone else on the other end of the rope. It was Lordy, the sinister gentleman worker.

'Mrs Teesdale, your goat, I presume?' Lordy handed over his end of the rope and raised his hat. Was his face really evil, or was it just the scar? He had been kind … and his old-fashioned, precise way of speaking was somehow reassuring.

'Thank you, Mr Barrington.' Rose had run towards the goat when she first saw her and now they were in a clearing she remembered, but it was changed. The eucalypt smell was overpowering and soon she could see why. Her heart sank; the rapists were here in the bush.

The trees had been stripped of leaves. A man with a cart was tipping piles of gum leaves into a metal tank, from which steam leaked out in several places. A big fire roared under the tank. Whiskery Joe was leading an empty horse and cart away, recognizable by his big hat and beard. Several other men were stoking the fire or adding more greenery and all around them were leaves and branches of eucalypt. All the small trees had been cut down and branches lopped off the large ones.

'Please allow me to set you on the road home,' Lordy said smoothly, guiding her away from the scene of action. 'It really will not do for the other men to see you. Consequences might follow, y'know.' Rose shivered. After they had walked for a while, Rose turned to the man beside her. 'Please tell me … what are those men doing? Working on a Sunday, too?' She passed a hand over her hot face.

Lordy looked at her, then sat down on a log and drew Rose down beside him. 'Let us have a short rest. Don't be afraid, Mrs Teesdale, I won't harm you. Quite the reverse. I was trained to protect females and I quite like goats.' This was just as well, because Gertrude had sidled up to him and was nearly sitting on his knee. 'These men with whom I have the misfortune to work are distillers of eucalyptus oil for the British market. They are called eucy men and they roam the forest with big knives and a portable still, as you could see.' He looked earnestly at Rose.

'And evil intentions,' Rose reminded him. 'Why are they like that?' Heaven help any woman who met them in the bush.

'Here today and gone tomorrow: they move about to get the best leaves. The work is hard and – well, you could say the workers are a little uncouth. They see no polite society, y'know.' Lordy shook his head sadly.

Rose couldn't help smiling at the lack of polite society; the men she'd met the other day obviously didn't want any. 'Distilling, that's a harmless thing to do. But why do they hate me?'

Lordy sighed. 'The selectors are cutting down the trees. Do you not see? There is a great tide of selectors flowing into Gippsland, taking the land for farming. Soon the forests will vanish and the woodsmen fear that eventually there will be only farm land, or at worst, desert. There will be no room for the men with big knives. On their system, most of the trees will grow again … but not with yours. Do you see the difficulty?' He smiled and looked more sinister than ever. 'That is the extreme view, of course. It's probably shared by the kangaroos and wallabies, I am bound to say. I'm afraid that the threat of rape was real. They think it's the best way to discourage settlers, y'know.'

Rose swallowed. 'Well, they could have had the leaves from all our trees until we clear the land if they'd been civil. But surely if people are going to live here, we need farmers?' There should be room for everyone here. And if people were going to keep on coming – Rose knew that ship after ship was bringing folks in from England – they would need food.

Lordy leaned towards her and Rose flinched. 'Do allow me, Mrs Teesdale, to remove this spider from your hair.' It was a huntsman spider, nearly as big as a saucer, with eight thick legs, just like the ones she was battling at home. It must have dropped on her from above as she walked through the bush.

Rose shuddered but managed not to scream. 'Thank you again, Mr Barrington.'

They watched it scurry away and Lordy said, 'How very composed you are for a young woman. The bite of the huntsman spider is only mildly toxic, of course.' He paused. 'I don't wish to alarm you, but the redback spider bite is potentially fatal, especially to children or old people. If you see a spider with a red spot on its back, avoid it at all costs. And the white tail spider can cause you pain – watch out for them in the house.'

Rose stood up. 'It's time I went home, Mr Barrington. Are there any other dangers in the bush that I need to know about?'

Lordy got up from the log, appearing to think deeply. 'I am trying to remember my first impressions ... but I came here from a war in Africa, so the Tangil valley was a haven of peace to me.' He looked at Rose and added, 'They say the Australian bush is the safest jungle in the world. Remember that, if ever you feel afraid.'

FIVE

'PLEASE, ARE YOU Mrs … Maeve?' Rose looked up at the tall, stately woman behind the bar before glancing round nervously. Her nerves had suffered after the encounters with the wild men and she longed for Luke to come back, to give her some peace of mind. But Luke was still away from home.

The big room was dark and the smoke-blackened beams and battered chairs and tables looked as though they had been there for centuries. It was the first time Rose had been into a public house and it was hard to know what to expect, what would lurk in those shadowy corners. A morning visit had seemed the safest, when most people should be sober and she hoped the eucalyptus oil men would be working.

The owner of the grandly named All Nations hotel nodded and smiled, revealing two gold teeth. 'Myself it is. You'll be new round here, then. What can we be doing for you?' She was handsome in an Irish way, with dark hair and blue eyes.

'Well …' Rose breathed in the fumes of stale beer and tobacco, overlaid with the smell of cooking. What did she want? Lordy had told her she would get good advice, but about what? Rose stood looking down at her dusty dress and boots. She was hot and tired from the long walk down the side of Haunted Creek and far from her usual more confident self. 'Do you happen to have seen Luke Teesdale? A young man with curly brown hair?'

Maeve's expression altered and the soft voice seemed to harden a little. 'You'll be Luke's woman then, and just arrived in the colony.

Tell me, are you married properly, church and all – or just living together?' She put her head on one side.

This was impertinence and Rose stood up straight with indignation. "Of course we are married! I'm not a loose woman! We were married before Luke came out. And what is it to do with you, anyway?' She was about to sweep out, but stopped herself. Three dusty figures were eating plates of bacon and eggs at one of the tables and they looked up at this, so Rose dropped her voice. 'Why do you ask?'

Maeve shrugged big shoulders clothed in flimsy green silk. 'Then it's too late, there's nothing to be done at all. If you were living in sin with the lad, and many a good girl is too, you could give him up and find a better prospect. There's plenty of good men out here that's looking for wives, you must know that. But—' She spread her hands '—if you're legally wed, you'll have to make the best of it. That's all. I'm thinking of you.' She looked Rose up and down.

'I'm not complaining,' Rose said frostily. 'I just asked whether you know where he is.'

Maeve ignored the frost and went on, 'You're stuck, that is unless you go back home and say you couldn't stand the climate. Some women do that. The truth is they find the men too rough and the life too hard in a bark shelter or a tent.' Then she added, 'Come and have some breakfast, girl dear, you look as though you could do with a feed.'

Rose felt sick, but she would not back down in front of this cynical woman. 'No, thank you, I have no money with me.' Why did she think so little of Luke?

'I'm not asking you to pay, don't be silly,' Maeve interrupted. 'Here, come through,' and she led Rose through a door in the back of the bar. 'This is my room – customers don't come in here. Now you can cry, if you're that way inclined. I didn't mean to upset you, but what I said is the honest truth. Men are disappointing, most of them.'

Rose sank down into a comfortable cane chair and looked at the room, trying to calm herself. In contrast to the gloomy bar this room was light and pleasant, with curtains framing a window that looked out on to a garden. A bowl of roses stood on the table and there were books on a shelf. What luxury! Would she ever be able to coax roses to grow, or have a nice room to put them in? It seemed impossible.

Maeve went off for a few minutes and came back with a tray on which there was a china teapot and cups. 'The cook's making you breakfast. Now, drink this tea before you do anything else.' There was kindness in her eyes as she looked at Rose. 'Sure and I was too honest with you … but I thought you'd have known by now and be weighing up the choices.' She poured two cups of tea. 'How well do you know your husband? Maybe you're not long married, still have stars in your eyes?'

Rose sipped her tea from the delicate china cup. This was why women wanted to bring china and silk to Australia, to give a feeling of civilization in a most uncivilized place. Would it make any difference, in the end? She looked over at her hostess, dressed like a lady in this bush shack of a public house. Maybe it was important to keep to your own standards, no matter what your surroundings were. 'I knew Luke at school, we come from the same village, Mrs—'

'Maeve Malone I am, but Maeve'll do,' the woman said. 'And you must be Rose, English Rose.' She laughed. 'You seem so much more English than Luke.'

She knows my name, Rose thought. Luke must have told her. 'We got married and then he came out straightaway afterwards. I probably don't know him very well, really.'

'You got married because you fell in love, I suppose, as folks do. He's a nice enough young fella. Or maybe he needed a wife and you wanted a change of scene and a man of your own. That happens, too. Well, it's your business, not mine at all.' Maeve went to the door and took another tray from a large man in a cook's apron. 'Get this down you, it'll do you good.'

Rose ate the scrambled egg on toast and she could feel her spirits rising a little. When she had finished she said, 'So you do know Luke? Have you any idea where he may be?'

The woman gave her a pitying look. 'Come with me.' They went along a dark corridor lined with walls of pressed tin, decorated with scrolls and flowers. 'Imported from the old country, every sheet,' the landlady said proudly, running her hand over the embossed patterns. 'If ever I leave, I'll take them with me. Now brace yourself, girl, he'll not be a pretty sight.'

Maeve opened a door at the end of the corridor and Rose peered into the room fearfully. It held a marble wash stand and a huge brass bed. Luke was on the bed, lying on his back with his eyes closed. He was deathly pale, his breathing hoarse and ragged. His shirt was dark with perspiration. Light filtered dimly through blinds so that she couldn't see him clearly; there was a sour smell in the room.

Rose's heart beat wildly as she looked at him. 'Is he ill? What happened? Did a snake bite him?' She walked towards the bed but Luke did not stir. He was either asleep or unconscious. 'Oh Luke, what have you done?'

'He's dead drunk, girl. Did you never see a man drunk before?' Maeve shook her head. 'And never be after blaming me. I keep good order in this house and I never encourage the men to drink too much. It's bad for them and bad for trade. But Luke had grog with him on the diggings, he was brought in on a barrow. It was none of my doing.' She turned and led Rose out of the room. 'If you can wait a few hours, you can take him home. He'll be sober enough to walk by then.'

Rose swallowed and thought for a minute. 'Yes, I'll wait. But where's Jim Carlyle? He went looking for gold with Jim.' She felt anger rising, a cold anger. How could Luke be so thoughtless when there was so much work to be done?

'Jim Carlyle brought him here and then went off again. He's a waster, that one.' Maeve's mouth shut in a straight line. 'You might like to stay here for a bit. I've work to do, but you're welcome to put your feet up on the sofa in my room. And think what you'll say to your husband, I reckon.'

What would she say? That she was disgusted, she was bitterly disappointed and wished she'd stayed at home. Gradually the anger gave way to sadness and Rose slept a little. When she woke, Maeve gave her soap and a towel and directed her to the wash house. Feeling more normal, she went back to the sitting room clean and cool to find Maeve there, adding up accounts. 'You're looking better, Rose.'

'I feel better, thank you. You've been very kind. So tell me, Maeve, what do you know about Luke – that I might not? He went off to look for gold over a week ago, that's all I know.'

Maeve put down her pen. 'Luke said his wife was coming out, but he thought not until the autumn. He talked about starting to build a proper house, but I gather he didn't get round to it.' She sighed. 'He's quite pleasant, isn't he? Not a bad young bloke. But he's weak, Rose ... he's easily led and he has bouts of the drink. Doesn't drink all the time, but when he does ... it's bad. I used to tell him to go home and chop down some trees, make a bit of progress. He's all talk, that one.'

'I didn't know,' Rose said in a small voice.

'There, I didn't mean to upset you, but we gotta face facts. You have a choice, Rose, in spite of what I said. There's always a choice. Several, in fact. Unless you're in the family way. A child would alter things a bit.' Maeve moved round in her chair to face Rose.

This was impertinence again. Should she talk to Maeve, or keep her own counsel? Rose was tempted to go out, away from the pub and wait for Luke somewhere else. But Maeve obviously had years of experience and she might give good advice in her softly spoken, brutally forthright way. After a pause she said quietly, 'I'm not pregnant.'

'Stay that way, girl, if you can. It would only complicate things. Now, about your choices. You can let him stay in charge, tell you what to do, and make progress in his own time. I don't hold out much hope, although if he does find gold he might buy some more land.'

'But what else can I do?'

There was a flash of gold as Maeve smiled. 'You could go home to dear old Mother England, to live with the fact that you've failed to make a go of it. Or you could do what I did, and take charge yourself. Mind, you've got to be strong. This is a hard country. Can you be strong enough?'

'I can try. You mean I ought to decide what we should do and tell Luke?'

'Persuade him, more like, lead him – you can't drive a man except to drink. You'll have to have a plan and the guts to carry it out, take him along with you, as you might say.' Maeve laughed. 'The only thing you can really take charge of is yourself.'

There was silence as Rose digested this.

'My man was restless, always off on a new venture, and in the end he went to America and didn't come back. They sent to tell me he'd died, not long ago. Left me with a little baby, too.' Maeve laughed. 'But we beat them all in the end. My boy Paddy Malone is a doctor in Melbourne, Doctor Malone. And I've a good business here. So it can be done.'

Maeve made it sound almost easy, but Rose frowned. Luke wasn't likely to go to America, so she would have to work round him. 'I need a plan, you say. But I've just arrived here, I don't know where to start. And I can't chop down trees, or make fences. That's what we need.' Going home to Yorkshire was not an option, so she would be strong.

'You need cash, lass. Anything can be done if you have the money. Did you bring any with you? Then hang on to it, don't give it to Luke.' Maeve nodded. 'Look around and see what you could make or grow that folks will buy. You're off a farm? Good. You might have to be the farmer, you know.'

The huge cook came in and Maeve gave him instructions, while

Rose thought hard about what she could do. It was taking her mind off the problem of Luke's drinking in a very positive way. Vegetables could be grown eventually, but it would be months before they could be ready for sale. The hens she had were laying well, but only enough for their own needs … what if she bought more hens and sold eggs? Hens didn't cost as much as a pig or a cow. She had enough money to buy a few hens.

When the cook had gone Rose tentatively spoke her thoughts. 'If I forget about the horrible hut for a while and think about making money, we could keep more poultry – they don't need fences. Is there a sale for eggs here?' She thought that most families would keep hens; settlers would be self-sufficient.

'Now you're talking!' Maeve looked pleased. 'I could take several dozen eggs a week and so could the store at Wattle Tree, and that's just a start. There's still a lot of miners about, that need to eat, and folks working in the bush that buy all their tucker, tree fellers and the eucy men that make the eucalyptus oil. You'd be surprised how many men there are skulking about in those trees, right up into the mountains, with not many settlements up from here.'

'And eggs are handy food for men on their own – don't take much cooking.' Rose nodded; she remembered the 'eucy men' only too well but she couldn't imagine them buying from her. 'And most of these workers will be your customers?'

Maeve laughed. 'Of course! What would single men do at all but come to the pub at night, whenever they come out of the bush? And buy their tucker from me when they go back to work. Now I think about it, there's nobody keeping poultry seriously here. I have to buy eggs where I can, and none too fresh they are at times.' Maeve sat down and then went on. 'You could sell dressed chickens too. Fresh meat's often scarce unless the butcher kills a bullock and nobody's keen on kangaroo.'

Rose's mind was active now. She could use the feathers to stuff pillows and cushions … and the manure from the hens would go into the soil to feed the vegetables. All they needed was a bigger hut for the hens to perch at night and more nest boxes for them to lay in. Luke would have to help, but if she worked out the likely returns from selling eggs, he might be persuaded.

By mid afternoon, Luke emerged blearily from the bedroom and stood under the pump outside in the yard. He was pale but sober and by the time he had eaten some bread and cheese with Rose, he said he was ready for the road. 'Thank you, Maeve,' Rose whispered as they left.

Lordy had been right. Maeve had given her some very useful advice and one consequence was that she and Luke would not quarrel. She had decided not to fall out with him. The plan was too important. The hard words she had ready were put aside for if all else failed.

'Be strong!' were Maeve's parting words. 'Come back and see me with some eggs.'

They walked along the track in silence for a while, following the creek back along the way that Rose had come. Many of the scattered wooden houses of Haunted Creek were falling down, crumbling back into the bush as if they had never been, as the gold field was gradually abandoned. Apparently it didn't take long for bark huts to rot away in this climate, with its hot summers and high rainfall. In some places Rose could see a stone or brick chimney standing forlorn among the undergrowth where a hut had once been, or a straggly neglected garden. Would theirs be like this in a year or two? A sad reminder of failed hopes? It was a depressing thought.

Other huts were still in use, one or two with paling fences round them and rows of vegetables near the house. There were even a few new houses. This must have been a sizeable village in the 1860s, a good market for produce, Rose thought regretfully. We should have been here earlier, before the decline. In those days, Haunted Creek was part of Wattle Tree, a big cattle run. She turned to say this to Luke, but he was trailing sheepishly behind.

The main track out of Haunted Creek was not the one that led past Luke's land, which was why she had not realized there were so many people down here. It went in the other direction down to the Tangil River.

After some time Luke said sulkily, 'I suppose you're going to tell me all my faults and what a bad husband I am. Well, you'll have to get used to it. Do you know, you're a very irritating woman – always think you're in the right.' He clenched his fists. 'You've seen nothing yet.'

Rose straightened her back a little, brushed the flies from her face and held on to the plan. Luke was waiting for a quarrel, trying to bring it on. She would not make it so easy for him. 'Well, Luke, I expect you'll have a dreadful headache. Did you find any gold?'

'A little bit – we washed some out down in the river,' her husband mumbled. 'But Jim went off with it and bought a bottle of whisky from a cart that came round the diggings, selling food and that ...' He tailed off.

'Bad luck. Maybe Jim isn't a very good friend to you.' She glanced at Luke but he avoided her eye. She had been told that hard liquor was banned on the diggings, but the rules may have been forgotten by now.

Luke was quiet again, probably with surprise that Rose was so calm. 'I'm sorry, lass,' he blurted out after a minute or two. 'I'll make it up to you, work real hard.'

'I'm sure you will, and it will make you feel better. Would you like to build a bigger hen house? I've been thinking, Luke, that I could sell a lot of eggs and that would give us a start....' Rose decided to leave it at that. Luke was in no shape for a proper discussion, but the seed had been planted. A poultry house built with saplings and slabs of bark would be a small job compared with the task of clearing fifty acres of trees.

The next morning, Luke got up at dawn. 'I reckon we need a bigger hen house, lass. You could sell the eggs to the hotel. I'll cut some slabs straight after breakfast.'

SIX

'LUKE! WAKE UP! The roof's leaking!' Cold water dripped onto Rose's face and her pillow was wet. Incessant, heavy rain had soaked the bark slabs of the roof and was finding its way inside. Luke grunted, turned over and went back to sleep.

With a sigh, Rose fetched a bucket to catch the drips and curled up at the bottom of the bed to wait for daylight. Maeve had been right; Luke was pleasant but not willing to put himself out. But then, he could hardly patch the roof in the middle of the night, and fetching a bucket was a wife's job.

The rain had changed everything, just a week or so ago. The hot weather had built up, more humid every day, until it pressed on you like a heavy weight. Huge biting flies that Luke called March flies were everywhere and they were both covered by angry red bites before the weather broke with thunderstorms.

They had watched lightning dancing along the tops of the mountains, more dazzling than anything Rose had seen. Thunder rolled ominously through the bush and far away on tree-covered slopes they saw points of fire. 'Lightning strikes,' Luke said. 'But the rain will put them out, I hope.' It was strange to see forests climbing to the mountain tops, after the bare, sheep-nibbled grass of Yorkshire uplands.

The dust outside the hut turned to mud, but the water barrels were full. A haze of green appeared where Luke had dug the earth and some of the trees started to flower. Rain made everything harder, but it was a blessing and at last Rose could start her garden.

'This is the Victorian autumn,' Luke told Rose. 'The best time of year.' It seemed all wrong to have Easter in the autumn, but everything was upside-down here. On Easter Sunday the Teesdales joined other settlers in the Wattle Tree school for a service conducted by an Anglican vicar from Moe.

The rain had stopped for a while and the trees were brilliant with new green leaves. Apart from the strange and beautiful tree ferns in the sheltered gullies, Rose thought it looked more like an English spring than autumn.

It was good to see so many people crowded into the little schoolroom, more than you'd expect when you looked at the empty bush. Some selectors were tucked into pockets of good land, surrounded by trees and hidden from the main tracks. You only knew they were there when they came out of their hiding places.

Bert and Martha Carr were there with Charlie and Peter, the boys' hair smoothed down with water and parted in the middle. Lordy, the gentleman worker, looked distinguished and altogether different, in clean clothes and wearing a tie. His back was straight and he had the high-beaked nose of authority, but the scar gave him a sinister look. The other eucy men were not there, thank goodness; Rose didn't want to meet Joe of the hat again.

Lordy nodded to Rose. 'Good morning, Mrs Teesdale. A Happy Easter to you.' Mrs Teesdale felt almost like dropping a curtsy. The moors at home were full of gentry like Lordy in the grouse season and she'd helped to cater for them once or twice.

Luke turned to Rose and whispered furiously, 'How do you know him? He's a villain.' Rose smiled; he probably was, but his manners were good.

Freda Jensen played the piano for the hymns, accompanied for some of them by Erik on a mouth organ. 'We should have a dance here one night, if the music's this good,' Luke whispered.

It was odd to hear the familiar Easter hymns so far from home ... but this was home now, wasn't it? Rose enjoyed singing, but it was so long since she had used her voice that it was husky at first.

The Reverend Horace Jennings was on a mission that day. Speaking without notes and with rather less churchiness than Rose expected, he said that he realized the effort they had made to come to the service. Anyone who was even vaguely Christian had come from Haunted Creek, from Fumina and from the farms on the Latrobe River. It was the first time that so many had met at Wattle Tree, he said, a good sign of things to come.

'You will know that a state school is not supposed to be used for religious purposes,' the reverend went on. 'The Victorian government in their wisdom has kept religious instruction out of the school curriculum. And so I would like to suggest that you, as a new community of souls, might make a further effort. You might work together to build your own little church, to bring civilization and religion to Wattle Tree and to keep the forces of darkness at bay.'

Rose looked round uneasily. On such a bright morning the forces of darkness were not worrying her but she knew what he meant. She had sensed that the eucy men carried a darkness with them. What dreadful past had made them what they were? The bush was very dark at night. Would a church make a difference? Human effort seemed so small and powerless in this huge landscape, so maybe religion would be a comfort. Perhaps anything that brought people together would make them feel safer.

The vicar was developing his theme. 'Then you might have marriages and christenings in your church, to bring your children into the light. There will be builders and carpenters among you, who can direct the work.' The men looked at each other and Rose could almost hear them thinking about all the work they had to do on their own blocks. 'Of course, some generous landowner will need to donate the land.' Some of the possible generous landowners shuffled their feet.

Judging by the number of small children at the service, Freda would have a full class of infants next year. 'Yes,' she said quietly when Rose remarked on it afterwards. 'The settlers all seem to have plenty of children to help with the work.'

Freda invited Rose and Luke to share their meal after the service. 'I want to hear what progress you've been making,' Freda said in her schoolmistress voice and Luke grinned.

'Yes, ma'am,' he said, with a mock bow. 'I'm doing my best, you know. I'm very proud of our chicken house – sheer luxury for chooks.'

While they ate cold beef and potatoes, Rose was asked to tell the Jensens what she had been doing. 'I bought some pullets from a farmer down towards Tangil,' she explained. 'We've also got some young chicks hatched out by our old hens. A bag of grain lasts them quite a while – they scratch about in the bush for insects.' She was quietly proud of the healthy little poultry flock.

'How do you sell them?' Erik turned to her with intense blue eyes and Rose had to look away quickly, pulling against a powerful magnet, or so it felt. She had to fight the melting feeling whenever he looked at her. This was very wrong in a married woman.

Rose told them she'd bought two wicker baskets and packed the eggs with dried fern to keep them from cracking. She had orders from the All Nations and the Wattle Tree store and was building up a list of customers. Erik smiled his approval with a beautiful warmth and Rose caught Luke frowning at him.

Luke chatted easily to the Jensens apart from this and it was clear how much he liked company; he was not cut out for a solitary life in the bush. Erik said little, smiled at Luke's jokes and listened attentively to everything that was said.

After lunch they all went on a tour of the farm, but by then Luke seemed less than happy. He leaned on a gate with his hands in his pockets and it was left to Rose to ask the right questions.

'Look, these trees are ring barked,' Erik told them. 'We take off a section of bark all round the tree and it dies.' He seemed pleased by her interest. 'Once the trees are dead, there's more moisture in the ground for crops and more light.' The skeleton trees looked ugly, but the crops were growing well.

'We could do this, Luke!' Rose said eagerly. 'We could grow

crops or grass and then the trees could be cut down later, when you have the time.' Luke nodded, but said nothing. Wasn't he interested? Rose touched his arm but he ignored her.

There were sheep in one paddock, black-faced Suffolk ewes. Erik said he preferred them because it was often too wet for the heavy-woolled Merino that was so popular in other parts of the country. The butcher at Haunted Creek would take all the mutton he could produce.

Rose looked longingly at the sheep. 'I hope that we can keep sheep … but fencing them in will be a problem. If they escape into the bush they might never come back.' She sighed; it all came back to fencing, to keep farm stock in and wildlife out. 'Do wallabies eat onions?'

Erik laughed. 'I've never given them the chance … probably not, I should think. But they eat our good grass, I know that much.'

Luke muttered to Rose, 'That bit about fencing was meant for me, I know it.'

Maybe it would shame him into doing some more work, although Rose hadn't meant any criticism. The fact remained that fencing was the most urgent job for them and Rose could not do it.

'We're learning, all the time,' Erik said before they left. 'I wish I knew more … it's new for all of us – this country hasn't been farmed before. It needs careful handling, we're finding that out. I've got a long way to go to be a good farmer.' How could such a large, handsome man not be confident? With such a tidy farm, he must be a perfectionist.

As they walked home Luke said, 'That Erik was looking at you a bit too friendly for my liking. I wonder why he doesn't go and start a farm of his own instead of hanging round his mother.' He'd taken a dislike to the Viking, which was a pity. Erik could have taught Luke a lot: perseverance, for one thing. Sticking at a job until it was finished.

'This is his farm,' Rose pointed out, refusing to quarrel. 'He came up here on his own at the start and then his mother joined him when the school was opened. They were looking for a good teacher …' But Luke had lost interest.

'Oh, they're so pleased with themselves! Nobody else can farm like they can.' Luke was irritated by the Jensens and Rose decided to say no more about them. 'Let's go for a walk, Rose, on a new track, let's explore a bit.'

They were wearing their best clothes but if they stayed on the tracks they could keep dry. The ground dried out so quickly here after rain. Rose trotted after Luke as he strode out on his long legs, hoping that a walk would put him in a better humour. Luke could be moody at times, and very possessive. She hadn't expected that.

Luke turned off the main Haunted Creek track and headed down a narrower one. 'I think someone lives down here, but I'm not sure.' They heard the insistent plopping of frogs and soon came to a watering hole, full with the recent rains. Several black ducks swam on the water and Luke's eyes shone. 'Good dinners there – you'd like roast duck. Wish I had my gun.'

Rose was thinking about the work she would do in the week ahead and hardly noticed the enormous dead tree standing in a little clearing at the side of the track. It took her a while to realize that it was a house and people lived in it. The top of the tree had been cut off and a slab roof sheltered the hollow trunk. A man and woman sat on stumps beside the tree and a child played on the grass at their feet.

'This is the place!' Luke was suddenly animated. 'Good day!' He must have taken this direction on purpose, to find these people. Why?

The woman nodded shyly and the man, who was probably in his forties, took the pipe out of his mouth and moved his wide-brimmed hat to the back of his head. 'You'll be yon couple from Teesdale's, I reckon.' Already their bit of land had acquired their name. 'Dressed up too! Must a bin to church.'

'And you'll be Tom Appleyard, that does the tree felling,' Luke responded. 'How's business?'

Mrs Appleyard stood up and rearranged her shawl, then gave the fire a kick and pulled a kettle over it; they were going to be given tea. Her husband grunted and pointed to a rough bench. 'Sit yourselves down. Business is good, you might say. Plenty of work felling trees for me and my mates – we work crosscut between us and we're always in work.' He paused. 'But in another way, it's bad. Bad for the land, all this clearing. We'll be sorry one day.'

Here it was again, another point of view. How could making farms from the bush to produce food be a bad thing? Why would a man question his own way of making a living? The settlers Rose had met thought that the only good tree was a dead one. Luke hated the trees that loomed over his block, shutting out the sun. Perhaps the man was a little bit strange? She sat quiet and listened while they drank sweet black tea in tin mugs, handed out by the woman.

'But it's got to be done if we're going to settle here,' Luke reminded him. 'We'll improve the land, once the trees go.'

Mrs Appleyard had evidently heard all the arguments before. 'And we've got to have a living!' she whispered to Rose. 'Tom sees that, of course.'

Tom Appleyard was clever to make a home in a hollow tree, to save building. It even had little windows cut in the bark here and there and seemed to have two storeys. 'I suppose you'll keep cattle or sheep,' Tom said to Luke, who nodded. 'Plough the land, grow cabbages and spuds, just the same as in England. That's what they all do and I must admit we eat the stuff the farmers grow – we couldn't live off the bush. But,' and his face was grim, 'you have to remember the soil's very soft, it cuts up with the hooves of animals. It dries out when we plough it. Take trees away and the dirt's nothing but powder in a few years, blows in the wind.'

They sat quiet for a while and Rose wondered why the soil here was different from English soil. Tom hadn't finished. 'Especially,' he added, 'we shouldn't farm the steep slopes, they shouldn't be cleared. They'll wash away in winter. River flat's a different matter, but even there we should be more careful. And we shouldn't drain the swamps; it'll change the river systems if we do. Swamps soak up the flood water, see.'

Maybe this was what Erik had meant about the land needing careful handling. Rose decided she would watch their soil carefully to see what happened when the trees were felled.

'Oh Lord! Maybe we should go back to England right away,' Luke scoffed. 'I believe that when you pay good money for land, it's yours. You can do what you jolly well like with it.'

'Well, it's too late. Settlers are here now and they think like you do.' Tom relit his pipe and took a few puffs. 'But kangaroos and wallabies with their soft feet, they don't cut up the land. I reckon we should be farming them, myself. Kangaroos, anyway, for meat and hides. And maybe growing trees to sell for timber, export it even. But that will have to wait until railways come up here to move it....'

Tom Appleyard was evidently well into his favourite theme, but his wife came to take Rose's mug and whispered, 'Would you like to see the house?'

'Yes, please!' Here in the bush, it was even more fascinating to see how people had their living arrangements. The Jensens' house was neat and spotlessly clean but some of the small cabins down by the creek had a tumbledown look. And now, a tree house ... Rose was amazed at how much room there could be inside a tree.

The forest giant must have been hundreds of years old; it would have been here before Captain Cook landed in Australia. The inside was hollow, but the outside seemed quite sound. 'Is it dry?' Rose had been battling with leaks for some time now.

There were two rooms, a kitchen and a tiny bedroom on the ground floor and a rickety ladder led to the floor above. 'That's for storage, and where the bairn sleeps.' In the centre of the kitchen was a large table made from the trunk of a tree, smooth and polished with use. The rest of the furniture was similar to Rose's own, sparse and homemade. And yet instead of being ashamed of her home, Mrs Appleyard was proud of it. 'Yes, dry, and right comfortable,' the woman said happily. 'I cook outside, of course. Before this, we lived in a tent. But Tom always promised me a tree house, and now we've got one.' She looked at Rose with shy grey eyes in a rosy face, wanting to be friendly.

'I like it,' Rose said gently, realizing that her own kitchen was quite good enough for the present.

As they walked home, mist began to rise from the creek and the trees were ghosts glimmering in a sea of silver. Luke shivered and lit the cooking fire, saying he felt cold, but Rose watched the moon rise, reflecting on the day. Was it true that farming would destroy the land? That was what the eucy men thought, too. The night was so beautiful that she could imagine the regret – men like Tom loved the bush, but they were destroying it. Erik realized the danger; he loved the land, too.

There would be fields and fences all around here, very soon. Quietly she wandered down the well-worn little path to the creek, watching the mist twist and swirl. Her everyday world was transformed by mist and moonlight. Rose gave a start as she thought she saw darker shapes among the shadows under the trees. Several dark shapes, moving soundlessly … and then they were gone. Rose did not see them go but they were not there any more. Had she been dreaming?

Luke wanted fried bacon for supper, so Rose set to work, still wondering what she had seen. 'Are there any … natives about here?" she asked as the bacon sizzled in the pan.

'Blackfellas? No, it's too cold, they say. They stay down in the valley and by the ocean where there's plenty of fish. No Aborigines here.'

So what had she seen? A few dark shapes that could have been kangaroos, perhaps. Better forget about it. She wondered what the original people here thought about the white settlers. No doubt they felt the same as the eucy men – their world was disappearing as the land was cleared. They were bound to hate the settlers.

Rose had almost forgotten about the shapes in the mist when they came back, one evening when Luke was away fishing with Jim Carlyle. She was at the creek in the twilight, enjoying the peace, when two dark figures came round the bend and stopped suddenly when they saw her. This time she was sure: they were real people. On impulse, she walked a few steps towards them with her hand outstretched.

SEVEN

AS ROSE MOVED forward slowly, the shapes retreated further into the misty woodland. They were slightly built females in cotton dresses and bare feet. The older one seemed to be wearing some kind of fur round her shoulders and they both carried bags. 'Who are you?' Rose asked, but the women shook their heads with a half smile and said a word she didn't understand. The younger one carried a small baby bound up in her shawl. The other woman stooped and picked something up from the ground … then they were gone. They were so silent, so rapid, that it was hard to believe they'd been there at all.

Was this where the name came from – Haunted Creek? Had the first gold miners seen dark shadows flitting by the water and thought they were ghosts? It was possible: most people she'd spoken to had told Rose that there were no native people here. It was empty country, waiting to be claimed, they said.

Slowly, Rose walked over to where the women had been standing. She had noticed since the rains a fungus that was growing in the open forest where the trees gave a light shade, a whitish, flat fungus very unlike the mushrooms she was used to. 'Probably poison,' Luke had said, but now she could see that several of them had gone; the women had collected them.

The dark mysterious figures had looked at her not as an enemy, but with a shy friendliness. Rose wondered whether they would get used to her presence so that she could talk to them. They must know so much about the plants that grew here, knowledge that was difficult to come by.

The settlers seemed to take some interest in the animals and birds, but most of them saw the bush as hostile, something to be fought. The native growth was weeds, to be got rid of as quickly as possible to make room for useful plants. And yet in Yorkshire, Rose had gathered many 'weeds' with her grandmother, and used berries, flowers, leaves and roots for food and medicine.

Rose had seen small red berries growing on low bushes near the hut and wondered whether they were good to eat, but nobody knew. 'Don't try them, they might kill you,' Luke had warned her. 'You've got to be careful in the bush, haven't I told you? Don't take risks where there's no doctors. I don't want to have to bury you in the orchard.'

Sitting alone outside the hut, Rose stirred the fire and looked up at the stars above the trees. Perhaps they should get a dog; it was lonely once the goat had gone to bed. At home she had never sat outside at night; never thought of it because decent folk were indoors after dark. She sighed and put the billy on to boil, wondering when Luke would be home. Sometimes he stayed out all night when he was with Jim, but he usually brought back fish for the next meal. She was not afraid of sleeping alone, although if native women were close there was probably a whole group, including the men.

That night Rose heard howling noises by the creek and her skin prickled, but she eventually fell asleep. Morning came quite soon and she made toast on the fire for breakfast; still no Luke. The next delivery of eggs was due at the All Nations and so she carefully arranged them in the basket. She fed and watered the animals and tried to move the cattle to another paddock, but the gate, which had no hinges and was lifted open and shut, was too heavy for her. Luke should have fitted it. She gathered some grass and threw it over the fence at them and the heifers ate it greedily. They should have been moved earlier; they were hungry and likely to cause trouble. She waited a while, expecting to hear his voice, but Luke had still not come home by the time she left.

Maeve was pleased to see the eggs. 'Come in, now, you must be ready for a cup of tea. How's things on the farm? No, don't tell me, I know. Men are such—' Maeve broke off and laughed. 'I nearly said a rude word. You're on your own again? I saw himself going down the creek with Jim and I bet he didn't come back last night at all. They took some tucker from here with them.' So Luke had called at the pub yesterday.

'I saw some Aborigines by the creek,' Rose told her, to change the subject. The memory of those slim dark figures haunted her. They were creatures from another world, but she could not imagine what their world would be like. They were closer to the earth than the settlers, that was certain.

'What?' Maeve's eyes opened wide. 'Blackfellas came round when you were on your own? They're hardly ever seen hereabouts. But they can be dangerous, you know. Can you fire a gun?'

Who would want to point a gun at such shy creatures? Rose shook her head. 'Just two women … picking some kind of mushrooms, I think. They disappeared when they saw me.'

'Just as well.' Maeve talked as she poured the tea; they sat in the bar in case customers appeared. She explained that most of the neighbours were very wary of the native people, although they weren't often seen this far inland. 'Mostly they're quiet, but you hear bad stories. And the drink – well, they can't take it. Thank goodness they don't come in here. Mind you, it could be said of some of our blokes!' Another belly laugh; Maeve was in a jovial mood today. 'A lot of miners would be better off without any liquor at all and healthier, although I say it myself that sells it to them.' Sniffing the stale beer aroma of the bar, Rose agreed. This was yet another way of earning a living that could prick the conscience. 'But you want to be careful.'

The dark people lived mostly near the rivers and swamps, Maeve said, in the valleys where there was plenty of food. Generally they were called the Ganai nation, though there were different names for five separate groups. According to some, they could murder people in their beds when they got upset – which was why she was afraid for Rose.

There was a mission further east, to convert the Aboriginal people to Christianity and persuade them into European ways. Maeve thought that this was a good thing. 'Our food and medicine must be better than theirs, stands to reason,' she said comfortably. 'They'll be better off, once they do as we do and settle down, stop wandering about.'

Rose felt a little tug of sympathy now that she had seen the people for herself. For how many centuries had they lived as they did? They must know how to survive in what could be a very harsh world in the bush. Would they really prefer dry salt beef to fungus from the forest? You could hardly blame them for being unfriendly; they were here first.

'That's one of their possum skins, over on the wall yonder.' Maeve pointed and Rose went over to the dark corner where the skin was tacked to a board. It felt very soft and warm. She realized that this was what the older native woman had been wearing. Next to the skin on the wall was a bag, woven from reeds or rushes by the look of it, rather like ones the gypsies made in England.

The door opened with a bang and Luke strode in, carrying an enormous fish. 'Hello, darling!' he shouted to Maeve. 'My special woman! Look what I've brought you this time! Give us a kiss, won't you?' He rushed round the bar at her.

'Save the fish for your wife.' Maeve twisted away from him, laughing. 'Go home, Luke.' Would she have done that if Rose had not been there? She looked splendid in red today and Rose felt herself to be colourless beside the big woman. How could she compete with such a large personality? But it wasn't supposed to be a competition.

'Nay, what she doesn't know won't hurt her.' Jim appeared behind him and Luke glanced at his friend. 'You won't tell her, will you?' He turned to Maeve again and Rose thought his face was flushed. 'Here, sweetheart, let's have a drink. I've been without seeing you for too long.' He threw an arm round her shoulders and planted a smacking kiss on her cheek.

Maeve hissed at him and flapped her hands, but Luke didn't seem to care. It was too much to bear and Rose slipped out of a side door, leaving her basket behind. She wanted to get away from them all, to go home and forget what she had seen. So this was how her husband behaved when she wasn't with him. Unless, which was even worse in a way, he had seen her and was doing it to annoy her.

A little way along the track, Jim caught up with Rose. 'Don't you fret, honey,' he said quietly. 'Blokes talk to barmaids and pub women like that all the time – it means nothing. You'll maybe not have been in many pubs, have you? It's a sort of joke – we all pretend to make love to Maeve even though she is the owner and could buy and sell the lot of us. But we're careful not to go too far, you know. She can fetch you a swipe round the ear that would fell an ox.' His dark eyes were kind; Jim could tell how she was feeling.

'Have you felt it, then? Thanks, Jim,' Rose laughed, with an effort to sound normal. Perhaps he was right; she would ignore it. She rather hoped that Luke would get a box on the ear – it was just what he deserved. He'd been a cheeky child at school, but she had thought that he had grown out of it. 'But maybe Maeve encourages the men, up to the point when she swipes them? Some women flirt a lot, I know, and I suppose Luke would fall for it.'

'No, the only one Maeve really likes is a big chap they call Lordy.' Jim went on, as if trying to divert her from the subject of Luke. 'They say he's a real live lord. Funny, isn't it? And he's very keen on her, but they don't seem to make a go of it.' Rose smiled; Lordy and Maeve were an unlikely couple.

They walked on in silence until Jim said, 'But you know, all the women here have plenty of choice – there's scores of men looking for a wife. Tell that to Luke sometime, will you? A pretty girl like you would have no trouble finding a good man, if you weren't too particular about being married to the one you were living with. Of course, a lot of folks don't worry; it's a bit different out here in the wilds.' He paused. 'But I expect you would have standards.'

Rose blushed. 'I know you're trying to cheer me up, Jim, paying me compliments, but you're right, I'm not likely to go off with anybody else.' He had made her feel a little less rejected, less worthless.

Jim stopped walking and looked at her. 'Well, I think you're a very good catch for Luke, you're not easily scared and you'll turn your hand to anything. A lot of women wouldn't stay here on their own. He'd better look after you. Honest, Rose, I envy him. I won't mention it again, but if ever you're in trouble, you can depend on me.' This was very serious talk from a man like Jim and a long way from his usual joking self. She thought that perhaps he meant what he said.

'I hope I can keep out of trouble, Jim.' The water in the creek was shining in the sun, the bush was fresh after the rain and trouble seemed very far off.

After a few minutes Luke caught them up, carrying a fish in Rose's basket. 'She sent me home like a puppy dog,' he grinned. 'Fish for dinner, lass! As it happened, we had two, so Maeve got one. And Jim can join us.' Perhaps that was to avoid being alone with Rose to face her anger, if he realized she had seen him with Maeve.

As they neared home, six young cattle walked to meet them and stood in a group, waiting for something to happen. Luke said sourly, 'My cattle! They must ha' got out. Didn't you move them, Rose? You should be more careful.' It was evidently her fault that they had escaped from their badly fenced paddock. The only way Luke could keep them at home was to move them often on to fresh grass, but Rose was hoping the fences would soon be finished properly.

Jim's mouth tightened but all he said was, 'Well, we'll soon get them in, there's three of us.'

'I threw them some grass ... the gate was too heavy to move,' Rose explained. The animals seemed to want a game. They capered about, throwing their hind legs in the air and snorting and it took Luke, Jim and Rose half an hour to round them up again.

When it was all over and the cattle were rather sulkily penned in a fresh paddock, Luke lit the cooking fire while Jim cleaned the fish, to Rose's relief. She went to the hut to get some plates and found a bunch of roots on the step. They looked like pale young carrots to Rose. 'Who could have left these?' she wondered.

Jim looked at the plants carefully. 'These are yam daisy tubers, they grow round here. I've never tried them but the Ganai eat them, they say.'

'Calling blackfellas by a big name?' Luke scoffed. 'Well, I don't suppose they left them so it must have been Martha, or your friend Erik that's so keen to help you. We'll find out next time we see them.'

The fish was good, cut into fillets and cooked over the fire, and they ate it with the yams, which were sweet and rather like carrots. Rose thought she would gather some for herself. Jim showed her where the small yellow flower grew and they seemed to be everywhere after the rain. She was sure that the shy women had left the plants for her. What could she give them in return? This little act of kindness eased the hurt of Luke's indifference. She was sure now that he would never love her, but she would survive.

When Jim had gone, Rose decided to ask Luke a question that had been in her mind for hours. 'When you walked into the pub, did you see me there?'

'Of course I did! I was carrying on with Maeve for a joke, just to see what you would say! But you've got no sense of humour, have you?' Luke laughed. 'Never mind, lass. It was all in fun. Don't be so serious – you're always worrying about something.'

'Don't you think I should worry? About fencing the land, for instance?'

Luke moved restlessly. 'Nah. Drives a man mad, to have a wife that's always nagging. I'm beginning to see why some men stay single.'

'And I'm beginning to realize why some women aren't keen to come to Australia,' Rose said quietly. Several of her neighbours in the village had warned her against it. Perhaps it was wrong to marry someone you didn't really love? She was ashamed to think that she was here partly because she wanted to get away from home. It would have been easier to take a living-in job with a family somewhere in Yorkshire – as a nanny or a housemaid. The other reason to come here was the hope of a loving husband.

As autumn turned to winter, Rose wondered whether it would be anything like a Yorkshire winter. They could see snow on the mountain tops of the Great Dividing Range, the Victorian Alps as they were called, but lower down at Haunted Creek there was the odd light frost, no snow and sunny days were warm and pleasant. Geraniums still grew outside against the fence and with a heavier dress and sometimes a shawl, Rose was warm enough for most of the time. Days of fog and rain were worst, when the wind blew cold.

Luke had managed to clear a little more land and he put up yards of fencing so that Rose could buy a few sheep with the money she earned from the eggs. He seemed to accept that Rose was in charge of this money, although he was always looking for ways of earning money himself. There was no mention of building a better house and Rose knew that the farm came first.

Up on the hill, the Carrs were making much faster progress. The thin cow that walked in with them behind the cart was fat now and had produced twins. Charlie and Peter now had a calf each to care for and they told Rose that this would be the start of their own farms. Bert Carr had bought sawn planks from the tree fellers and the house was to be finished before the worst of the winter weather. He was earning money by carrying goods with the bullock cart and was now known as an honest carrier who treated his cattle well.

Then came a shock. 'You're looking a bit peaky, love,' Martha told Rose one day when she called to see Rose with a gift of cabbages. 'Not in the family way, are you?'

Rose sat down suddenly, facing the reality she had been pushing away in her mind. 'We'll have a cup of tea,' she said weakly to Martha and raked the fire together. 'I might be …'

'You're a funny one. It's the first thought in most lasses' minds, either way, whether they want a baby or not,' Martha laughed. 'It would be a blessing, a little lad to help his dad on the block. Anyway, when the time does come, remember I'm a midwife. I was trained before we were wed and I've delivered a lot of babies.'

'So – you could tell me what to do? I don't know much about it, you see.' Rose's head ached and she felt confused.

'Of course I'll help you, love!' Martha seemed to relish the idea of a baby. Luke was making his way up from the paddock and so she added, 'Come and see me, say next week. We can have a talk and see whether a baby is likely, or there's something else. You can go to the doctor, of course, but he's down in Moe. We can manage between us if all goes well.'

'I won't say anything to Luke,' Rose whispered. 'Not yet.'

Martha nodded. 'It wouldn't do to disappoint him, if it's nothing.'

For the next week Rose wondered whether her unwell feeling was due to pregnancy, or something else. She had helped Luke with getting in wood for the fire and lifted pieces that were too heavy for her, which had given her pains in the back. The monthly flow had not happened, but this was not too unusual in her case.

What would Luke say about a baby? They had never really discussed the subject; Luke was not one for serious talks. He might be pleased, or he could resent having more responsibility. The hut was hardly the place to bring up a child.

Rose wondered how to find an excuse to see Martha, but the problem resolved itself. Tom Appleyard rode in one day on a sturdy horse and asked Luke to go to work for him. 'I reckon a young couple can always do with a bit more cash,' he said, with a wink at Rose. 'I've got a big stand of mountain ash to clear and limited time to do it. My lads have cleared off to Melbourne, so I'm calling on you and Jim Carlyle to help me. Only problem is, we'll be working away from home. It's more than twenty mile off, over by Noojee.'

'That's no problem,' Luke said immediately, as though he was itching to be off. 'Rose can manage on her own, can't you, lass? She likes it.' He had probably planned this since they had met the Appleyards at Easter.

Winter was very different, with short days and long nights to listen to the shrieks and groans in the bush. 'How long for?' she asked Tom.

'Not for long,' the woodman said cheerfully. 'We'll not be gone above a month. Or maybe two, if weather holds us up.'

They might be gone until the spring.

EIGHT

ROSE PERSUADED LUKE that he intended to improve the fencing before he left, especially for the sheep paddock. He was so pleased to be going that he did everything she asked and chopped a huge pile of wood for the fire.

'The pay's good, and if I do well I might get a regular job with Tom,' Luke said happily the night before he left. 'Sorry about leaving you, but ...' He did not look very sorry.

'This place needs two of us, Luke,' Rose told him quietly. 'You can't leave it too often. If you want to be a woodman, maybe we should sell the land.' He had said that she liked being left alone and she was proud that she could manage the farm by herself, but her strength was not up to some of the heavy work and with a baby, life would be hard.

'Never!' Luke was quite certain about that. 'If I earn a regular wage we can buy more land.'

You can't manage the land you've got. There was no sense in quarrelling just before he left, so Rose said nothing.

Luke and Jim were to travel to their destination in a cart with Tom and the big saws and axes. Rose packed up as much food for them as she could and a spare set of Luke's clothes. When the little clearing was quiet after they had gone, there was time once more to count her blessings. There was no meat left but the goat had kidded at last and was now milking well, so she could make cheese, and with eggs and the vegetables they had grown, she would manage quite well. There were plenty of daisy yams in the bush.

There would be no time to feel lonely and, in any case, she had good neighbours. Erik and Freda had kept in frequent contact with Rose and when he and his mother called, he always had something new to tell her or show her. Luke tolerated the visits, probably aware that Rose needed to know there were friends not far off.

Rose walked over to see Martha the week after Luke had gone, feeling certain that a baby was on the way and Martha agreed. 'You'll be carrying through the heat of summer, too,' she lamented. 'Well, we'd better set to and make some clothes for him.' Of course it was going to be a boy.

The advice Martha gave was just common sense: good plain food, plenty of sleep and exercise, but not too much heavy lifting. Martha said settlers' wives often worked too hard before the birth, not like town women who put their feet up. 'It's too bad that Luke's gone away, but in one way it's good – you'll have peace and quiet,' she said.

Keeping busy, Rose harvested all the potatoes and put them in sacks and then realized that there were many more onions than they could deal with. The surplus could be sold.

The twenty ewes they had bought were to lamb in spring and the cattle had settled down. Coming back to the hut from the creek, you could hear the cockerel crowing and the cackle of a hen that had just laid an egg. They were homely sounds. Once the bush was tamed and the trees retreated, civilization would come to Haunted Creek and they might have a little village there in the future.

Freda Jensen came to see Rose one Saturday when a light drizzle dampened everything and made working outside unpleasant. Rose was sitting at the door of the hut, making a patchwork quilt for the bed. She enjoyed sewing and was thankful that she'd brought plenty of material in the big trunk. Soon she would make baby clothes, but the baby was hardly real to her as yet.

'Luke's gone off again? My dear, you do have a hard time of it!' Freda's face was concerned. 'I've come to ask you for help, as it happens.' She looked at the work on Rose's lap. 'And I can see that I've come to the right place. The school needs a sewing mistress and now the Board of Education has put up a little more money, I can ask you if you would like to take the job. Mrs Brown used to help us out, but she's gone to live in Moe.'

'To teach the girls sewing?' Rose asked uncertainly. Was she good enough? She had made her own clothes for years, but teaching other people was a different matter. You would have to know exactly how each stitch was made, how each stage was done.

'To teach both boys and girls, Rose, although the boys might not like it much. It's always useful for a man to be able to sew a button on.'

Rose thought for a while. This would be a good chance to earn a little money, but ... 'I seem to feel more shy now than I used to do,' she confessed. 'I would be nervous with a whole class of children.'

'That's probably because you are alone too much,' Freda said firmly. 'This is just the thing for you, Rose. You could start off with a small group at first.' As she talked, Rose realized that the teacher was right. She was good at sewing and would be able to share her skill.

'The group could grow in time and the school is getting bigger. All the children in Haunted Creek and Wattle Tree come to our school. I suppose you know that Victoria was the first state in the world to introduce free education? It's something to be proud of. It's also compulsory, so families that live near enough have to send their little ones to school.' She smiled happily; Freda believed in education for settlers' children. 'I think it will help to make the place more civilized, in the end.'

'There is one problem,' Rose said hesitantly as they sat at her scrubbed table, eating gingerbread she had made in the camp oven. 'I think I'm going to have a baby.' She smoothed back her dark hair nervously.

'Are you pleased? Of course you are!' Freda was looking at her carefully. 'Well, we can try it for one term to start with, but you'll probably be able to carry on until the birth. The school is not very public, after all.' She picked up the pieces of quilt and then looked at the curtains Rose had made. 'And afterwards, too, if you like the job. A baby's not the end of the world, you know.' She looked round. 'I admire the way you've made the very best of this hut.'

Rose was startled. Was this a sort of Scandinavian freedom? In England, women were supposed to hide away when they were pregnant.

As Freda left she asked Rose to have lunch with them the next day, to see the school and get some idea of the work the children were doing.

Wearing a new dress she had made and a thick winter jacket, Rose set out the next morning with a list of questions for Freda and Erik. On the way, she looked over the sheep. They were going to have babies, too, and it would be good to double their flock when they lambed in the spring.

Freda's welcome was warm and soon the new teacher was happily sitting beside a wood stove while mist swirled outside. Erik came in and she blushed a little, but that was all. As usual, the Jensens wanted a report on farm progress.

'We've twenty sheep to lamb in the spring,' Rose said proudly. 'They're a sort of cross breed with black faces, nice and fat.' Not many, but a start. Luke had said he could shear sheep.

The school was quite small, but there were two rooms and Freda said the sewing class could use the small room while she taught in the larger one. 'Can you start tomorrow?' she asked and Rose nodded nervously. 'There will be no need for preparation. I have the materials ready for hemming some squares to make handkerchiefs. Come and look round.'

When they got back to the house after a tour of the school, Erik was sorting through some papers. 'I've got some old copies of the *Weekly Times* – you can have them if you like,' he offered. 'It's printed in Melbourne, but mainly for the country areas.' Erik beamed at her, pleased that he had thought of it. 'And now for lunch, we've got roast pork from one of our own pigs. Most of it was salted down for bacon, but this is fresh.'

Rose had an unreal feeling as she sat at the table with a lace cloth and silver knives and forks, eating a civilized meal with good conversation. Civilization was slow in coming to her hut, but in time they might achieve it, if Luke was willing to stay at home and build. It was August; in a month it would be spring and the baby would be one month nearer.

Well before dark Rose protested that she must go home, but Erik wanted her to see his sheep. She went out with him into a pale sunshine that had replaced the mist and they walked the paddocks, talking all the time. There was always so much to talk about and it was so good to have human company – Freda was right about that.

As they turned back to the house Rose said, 'I love your farm, but for one thing. The ring barked trees … they look so ugly and sad, standing there dead in the paddocks.'

Erik smiled. 'I was thinking the same thing. I'm going to cut them down next week.' He paused and then said, 'I'm so glad you're going to help Mother in the school, Rose. It will relieve the burden for her a bit. She has a lot of pupils and I think it will be good for you.'

'Why good for me?' Rose asked demurely. She thought he meant the money would be useful. But Erik turned on her fiercely, his blue eyes blazing.

'Because you're all alone down there by the creek and it's not right! It worries me, Rose. I was concerned enough before when Luke was on his own there, but he went off to see … other people quite a lot. But for a young woman straight from England, it's – well, I shouldn't say this, but I think it's criminal of Luke to leave you there. I intend to speak to him when he gets back.'

Rose gasped; that would cause all sorts of trouble. Luke didn't like Erik, for a start. Erik added, 'I won't let him think that you've complained, you never do. But I'm glad we will be seeing more of you, girl.' Luke might not like that, either.

Rose left for home, thinking about Erik. He had been so intense, more so than usual. No doubt he too was lonely, but he should go out and find himself a wife. He was such an attractive man. He wouldn't guess, but she was still trying to fight his attraction. Even allowing for the shortage of girls, you would think he at least could find one when he went to town, she thought. Luke thought he was 'tied to his mother's apron strings' but Rose could see that Freda and Erik were independent people who got on well together.

The sun had dropped below the western ridge and as she went along the track it seemed dark under the trees. An owl called, then gradually Rose became aware of faint noises in the distance. She stood still and listened. She shivered as the sound she dreaded most seemed to float up the track to meet her.

It was the howling she had only heard at night and from the safety of the hut. The howling that haunted her dreams. Wild dogs, and she was walking towards them. There was a faint noise some way behind her. Going back might not be possible; there were probably dogs on the track she had just walked down.

Shakily, Rose broke off the branch of a small tree. Armed with a stick, she should be safe from dogs. They were usually shy, people said. The dogs lived deep in the bush and they were often a cross between the dingo, the true wild dog, and domestic dogs that had run wild. Bert Carr had said they hardly ever attacked humans. They would probably go into the bush if they saw her coming.

As the track wound down to Haunted Creek, the sounds grew louder. There was a mixture of howling and barking; several dogs seemed to be coming and going, to judge from the noise.

Then there was another sound: the frantic bleating of sheep. The sheep were being attacked! It rose to a crescendo as if they were running, then died away.

There was no time for fear. Rose ran down the track towards her sheep, grasping the stick tightly. There must be several dogs to make so much noise … In a few minutes she was level with the sheep and peered into their paddock. The ewes had stopped running; they were all lying in the grass, being savaged by dogs.

Five dogs, red with blood, tore at the poor ewes as though they had not fed for days. There was blood and guts everywhere, dark on the ground in the fading light. The dogs were large and of various colours, some with the reddish tinge of the dingo.

White with fury, Rose opened the gate and rushed in. She would beat off the dogs with her stick and even if she saved only one ewe, it would be something. The sheep lay together in a corner, where they had run when attacked, and Rose went straight in to the thick of the slaughter. 'Get out!' she shouted. 'Those are my sheep!'

The dogs left their meal and turned on Rose, snapping and snarling. Too late, she remembered that their old sheepdog at home had been quite savage if you went near him when he was eating. She should have left them alone.

They were all on to her, surrounding her. The biggest dog leapt up at her face and she put up a hand to shield herself. A fierce pain shot through her arm and she knew then that the dogs would kill her, possibly eat her as well as the sheep. What a stupid way to end your life! Rose screamed at the big dog but it had no effect. Snapping and growling, it leapt and she dodged, desperately trying to hold it off with her stick. The other dogs were snapping at her heels.

A shot ripped through the night, echoing among the trees, and the big dog dropped to its belly with a bloodcurdling howl. It rolled over and lay still. The others hesitated, then howled and ran off, going in different directions. There was an unearthly silence for a few heartbeats. The massacre was over.

Erik threw down his gun, strode across the grass and gathered Rose to him, holding her tightly as though he would never let her go. 'Did you realize what you were doing? Risking your life? Oh, Rose!'

It was heaven to be in Erik's arms, safe after a dreadful ordeal. She leaned against him shivering, feeling his warm strength and the pounding of his heart. He stroked her hair, murmuring as if to a child: 'You're safe now, my darling. You're safe with me.'

How wonderful it would be to be safe! He bent his head and kissed her, gently at first and with increasing passion. Rose tried very hard not to return that kiss. In the deepening dusk she lost the struggle and in that moment, she realized how much Erik meant to her. She reached up and kissed him again. The world stood still. *This is how life is meant to be, how it could be; with a loving sweetheart.*

They stood together in the darkness with no need for words, understanding each other perfectly, making the moment last because it could never come again. He held her close until the shivering stopped and the passion subsided a little. Then reality set in and with an effort, she gently pulled away. 'I'm sorry, I shouldn't have—'

Erik interrupted. 'It was my fault, I took advantage of a weak moment … please forgive me, Rose. But I was so afraid for you.'

'I should never have gone near them. Oh, Erik, thank goodness you were here!' He had saved her life, she knew that. The dogs would have pulled her down in another minute or two. Rose was feeling guilty, but the less said, the better. 'We'll forget about … the last five minutes, shall we?'

'Let me see the bite,' Erik commanded and she rolled up her sleeve. Her arm was bruised, but luckily the skin was not torn through the thick winter jacket. 'Thank goodness. Dog bites are serious,' Erik said, almost shakily. 'It's a good rifle, isn't it? I shot him with the last of the light. Any darker and I'd have been afraid of hitting you. Then I'd have had to shoot one of the others, but it might have been too late …' He broke off.

'You are a very good shot, Erik,' Rose told him, trying to stop shivering. 'But why are you here?'

'Because I followed you, of course. But not closely enough. I should have stopped you …' So that was the movement she had sensed behind her tonight. And on other nights, too. She'd been shadowed without knowing it, protected by a man who had never let her know. The thought was humbling, and also alarming; this was a type of generosity she hadn't known before.

'But why did you worry about me?'

Erik laughed, a little exasperated. 'I just wanted to make sure you reached home, where at least you can lock the door. I've always followed you when you came to see us alone. Freda and I decided that we should try to look after you if we could. But of course it wouldn't have been proper to walk beside you – you're a *married woman*.' There was bitterness now in the deep voice. 'You wouldn't have allowed it.'

'Oh, Erik, how kind you are!' Rose's knees were weak and it was not just the effect of the dogs. Erik was still holding her hand and she had to fight hard not to sink back into his arms. 'But you shouldn't – we shouldn't …'

'But don't worry, Rose, Freda knows, it's not a secret or anything.' He sounded embarrassed. 'I suppose it's rather upsetting for you to think you've been trailed, but it was for the best, as we found out tonight.'

It was darker now but the moon had risen, lighting the bush with silver. Erik's face as he looked down at her was full of emotion. 'Rose, you've got to be more careful. We should have let you go earlier. It was my fault you were so late.'

In her head Rose heard Luke's warning. *It's not like Kirkby, you know*. 'Usually, I am careful, but I have to move about. I can't stay in the hut for ever!'

'I'm not blaming you – many women wouldn't stay there on their own.' Erik sounded grim. 'We didn't like to frighten you but it can be dangerous – there are lots of things to go wrong. Some of the miners are very rough, and then there are the eucy men who don't like settlers … the dogs of course … even wombats can be savage at times. I know you're brave, Rose, but you're a woman and quite a small one. You …' He turned away. 'Oh, it's nothing to do with me. You belong to Luke.' His voice very low, he added, 'Worse luck. If you were free, things would be different.'

She had just realized how different things could have been. Rose put out her hand and touched his. 'Please don't worry about me, Erik.' Her own emotions were bubbling over again, just as when she first met him. But shock was no excuse for being unfaithful to Luke.

'Somebody should,' the man said savagely.

No doubt it was shock that had affected Erik too, and broken down the proper distance between them. This was far deeper than her conversation with Jim. Luke's mate had been kind and concerned, had told her she was a pretty girl, but with a lightness that made it easy. With Erik she felt that they were getting into deep water.

'Luke will soon be home and you will soon have a wife to look after.' She tried a laugh; it was rather wobbly. 'I don't know why you haven't been married years ago, Erik. A man like you....'

Erik gave her a look that would linger in her memory, a long look. 'I will never forget tonight, but I promise you it won't happen again. I will always remember that you are a married woman, and so will you.' He held her hand warmly in his. 'Brave and beautiful dark Rose.'

So this was what it was like to love someone. Too late, she had found out what love could be. As she walked with him down the track, Rose knew she would have to be stronger than ever. The best thing she could do for Erik, the test of real love, would be to keep away from him, to keep barriers between them. Eventually, he would find a girl of his own.

NINE

ERIK INSISTED ON going home with Rose, right to the door, swinging along beside her, disturbing and reassuring at the same time. Little was said. The nightmare of the dog attack and the emotions that followed had left her drained, numb with shock.

The sheep were all dead and Rose's dream of a farm was fading, but she had survived. It was strange to realize how near to death she had been for those few minutes. The bush was hostile, beautiful but deadly, no place for a woman. The forest where she lived was dangerous – and so was thinking about Erik.

Lying sleepless in bed that night, nerves twanging like piano wires, Rose thought about her situation. This was why it was wrong to marry a man you only hoped to love, because there wasn't much to hold you together. If she had really loved Luke she would never have felt this devastating emotion, this secret delight that Erik seemed to care for her. She mustn't make too much of it because he was kind and thoughtful with Freda and everyone else – even Luke. It was just the loneliness, she told herself, for both of them, and the emotion of the night, but she would have to keep her distance from Erik. Luke had often made sly remarks about Erik talking to Rose; he must have sensed some sort of bond between them.

It was vital to make sure that their marriage worked out for good. Once they got the farm running, she and Luke would have their memories to share and also their children to bind them together. The baby would be something they had in common and he might think more of his wife if she produced a fine son for him.

Immature village lads grew up to become proud fathers often enough.

Before she slept, Rose remembered that she had to take a sewing class at the school the next day. It did not seem quite so frightening as before. She would have to face Erik again, but the sooner she did it, the better. She thought it might be hard to get back to the easy friendship they'd established, but there had always been undercurrents of emotion. Now she knew he had felt them too.

The next morning Rose dressed wearily, but with care. There must be many people in the world who fell in love with the wrong person and had to forget about it, to pretend it was never there and to deal with it every day. Of course it was worse in a small community, where you had to keep on meeting.

In time you would get used to that hidden part of yourself, the possibility that never had a chance. Once again, strength was needed. It would stay hidden for the rest of her life. Rose concentrated on the job ahead as she walked up the track to the school.

Six little girls and a boy sat waiting for her in the school sewing room, none looking very keen. The boy was Charlie, Martha's son, and he obviously resented being in the sewing class, especially as the girls were laughing at him behind their hands, tittering like little birds. Rose took her time in getting out the needles and thread, working out her approach to the class. When everything was ready, she looked calmly round. 'Let's just talk for a while about what you'd like to do when you grow up,' she began and the class sat up with interest.

'You're not going to make us sew?' Little Lottie peered up at Rose. 'Mrs Brown made us sew all day and rapped our knuckles. It hurt. We hate sewing lessons.' Her mouth was set in an obstinate line, ready to hate the lesson.

Rose had arranged the small tables so that the class sat in a circle and she was part of the group. She had helped with teaching back in England and had some practice in the village school, but it had never developed into a real job. 'What would you like to do when you grow up, Lottie?'

The child fluffed out her golden ringlets. 'I want to go to concerts and play the piano, in a beautiful dress. I'm taking piano lessons,' she said proudly.

Rose smiled at her. 'If we work hard, you will be able to make your own beautiful dress,' she promised. 'In time, of course. We can start with smaller things and work up to a dress. But by the time you need it you will be really good at sewing and you will be the best dressed girl in Wattle Tree!'

There was a silence. Would she have a rebellion on her hands? 'Miss, I'll do it,' said Lottie after some thought and the other girls eventually agreed that they wanted to make pretty clothes, but did not want to be rapped on the knuckles. They were promised there would be no knuckle rapping, no punishment at all if they did their best. They would get as much help as teacher was able to give. They thought about this.

'But, Miss, I always prick my fingers and get blood all over the sewing,' another girl moaned. 'It hurts, too.'

'Some people learn more quickly than others,' Rose explained. 'It took me a long time to learn to sew. Just give yourself time and don't be impatient, or afraid if you make mistakes.'

To convince them, Rose showed them some illustrations of dresses that Freda had cut out from magazines. She told them that her own dress was made in several evenings and they admired the fine stitching. 'If you're not careful enough with the stitching, it might come undone. The stiches might all unravel and then your dress would fall down.'

The little girls shuddered theatrically, but Charlie sniggered. 'Then the boys will laugh at you,' he said. Charlie was not quite with them, as yet.

The atmosphere gradually changed to that of a working party. Lottie was going to have competition as the best dressed young woman in Wattle Tree and the girls set to work on their handkerchief squares to show Mrs Teesdale that they could hem quite well, really they could, and they were ready for the next stage.

Charlie Carr sat with his arms folded. Every line of his young body let teacher know that he was not going to sew hems to please anybody. 'Charlie, what would you like to do when you're a man?'

He looked at Rose suspiciously. 'Why d'you want to know?' Then he relented. Mrs Teesdale would tell his mother if he gave her a hard time in class. 'I'm gonna be a drover, take cattle all over Victoria. I'll have two horses and three dogs. I've got one pup now, as a start. My dad says it's a good way to see the world.'

'Well, Charlie,' Rose said thoughtfully, 'you will be camping out under the stars, far away from the towns, I suppose?'

'We will. I'm not scared,' Charlie agreed.

'Just suppose your trousers got torn while you were working … your spare pair got wet in the river. You'd feel a bit silly without trousers, wouldn't you, if you couldn't do repairs? A good drover can round up cattle, mend a rope and maybe shoe a horse and he can sew up his shirt or pants if he needs to. It happens all the time,' Rose told him, speaking as a great authority on bushmanship. 'But you've got to know how to do it.'

Charlie looked away. 'All right. But I want to sew a shirt, not a silly bit of lace. Please Missus.'

Mrs Jensen was consulted and an old shirt of Erik's was sacrificed to the cause of education as Charlie got to work, frowning in concentration.

At lunchtime, Rose was eating her bread and cheese when a large figure loomed in the doorway. Erik came in and looked round, but the pupils were all outside. He sat down beside her and gave her his heartwarming smile. 'Can we still be friends, Rose, in spite of my bad behaviour?' His shirt was blue and exactly matched his eyes; Rose saw him in a shimmer of light. This man had saved her life and was apologizing for it. How like him.

The teacher brushed crumbs from her dress, wondering what to say. Her heart was thumping. The low winter sun was slanting through the windows and turning Erik's hair to gold. She would be stronger than ever before.

'I'm not sure. We must … stay apart. We both know the … situation. We have to ignore it. For ever.' Rose faltered at that and she saw by his face that Erik was with her, feeling just as she did, but devastated.

'I'm so sorry … I should never have let you know that I love you.' Erik's low voice was almost a whisper. 'And now I've lost what little I had of your company.'

'It's not your fault, I … don't blame you at all. And remember, you saved my life. Thank you, Erik.' She managed a smile.

Erik heaved a huge sigh. 'You're a brave woman, Rose. I didn't sleep last night, thinking of how badly I had treated you. My dear, I won't do it again.'

They sat for a while in silence as Rose's pulse rate slowly subsided and excitement gave way to a deep depression. She was going to lose a friend. Her whole heart went out to him, longing to comfort him.

'You know, I think Luke should teach you to shoot,' Erik said as he stood up.

'Not much point, is there? He takes the gun when he goes away.' Rose bit her lip. 'But he knows I don't like guns.'

'I can't believe it. All the sheep are dead? How could you be so careless? I hope they didn't starve or run out of water?' Luke paced up and down the little room.

His homecoming, long awaited, was less than happy; there were so many things to explain about the two months he had been away. 'Here am I, slaving away at the hardest job known to man, and you let the breeding ewes die. I give up.' He slumped on the bed. 'They were the start of a good flock.'

Luke had guessed immediately he saw her that a baby was on the way; it was beginning to show. They had both changed. Luke was thinner and grimmer than before, with taut, hard muscles. Rose would have liked to cook him a good dinner to welcome him home, but she had no notice of his coming. In fact, she had been at the school when he arrived home that afternoon. It was not a good start.

'Wild dogs killed the sheep, Luke. They've been a menace here for some time, people say. They go for small calves, of course, and cows when they're calving and helpless. And they go for sheep.' Rose paused. 'You must have heard them howling at night, although you've never mentioned them to me.'

'Well, you must have done something different. They never came close when I was here. Did you throw some meat out in the bush or something that attracted them?' Luke was evidently determined to blame her, but Rose had decided not to tell him the full story. He would not like to hear that Erik had been involved.

Without meaning to, Rose sighed; she was feeling weary. 'Luke, I have had hardly any meat since you went away.'

'Sounds as if you're sorry for yourself. Well, let me tell you cutting wood is harder than sitting here. So this baby – when is it due? I suppose it's mine, then?'

Rose felt her heart sink, a physical feeling; his words were like a blow. Luke was so hostile she wondered whether they could ever be happy together. 'I don't think you mean that.'

'Maybe not, but when a man goes away he wonders sometimes what his wife gets up to. I've heard the others talking....'

Rose's patience suddenly snapped. She had always tried to turn Luke's bad temper away with soft words, but not now. 'A man has no right to go away and leave his wife to fend for herself in a place like this! I will not put up with it any longer, Luke. You must stay at home and build a house, and let's be sensible and make some progress.'

Luke flung on his coat and went to the door. 'You won't tell me what I must do! I'm going down to the All Nations for some decent conversation and maybe a better meal.' All she'd had to give him was cheese and potatoes.

Luke came back the next day with a sore head and apologized and Rose managed to get him to give her the money he had brought home. He also shot two ducks and they had roast duck for dinner.

The next week, Luke made an effort to be pleasant and Rose thought she felt a hint of spring in the soft breeze, a sense of hope. She watched a parrot with a scarlet head and bright green body pecking seeds on the ground with the hens, so different from an English bird and not so shy. 'It's time to go to the sewing class,' she said to Luke and he nodded.

'You enjoy it, don't you?' he said affably. 'Just as long as you don't spend too much time with big bad Erik.' He still harped on about Erik, but she was used to it now and ignored it. She pushed away the thought that he was partly right.

Erik and Rose gradually managed to talk to each other again, but warily, not quite as before. Rose felt the danger and she was determined to fight it. There was plenty to talk about and ideas to share with Freda, and Erik sometimes joined in. The shaky, excited feeling gradually gave way to a calmer one. She had to stay calm, for the baby.

Sometimes the Jensens lent books to Rose. It was a new world and her mind grasped it eagerly. Only sometimes when Erik looked at her with laughing eyes, or saved something special to show her, she felt a fierce longing for something that could not be.

When Freda told her casually one day that Erik was interested in a girl in Moe, Rose felt a stab of jealousy. It soon gave way to guilt. She had hoped that the onion selling trips would pay off for him, hadn't she? He was not hers, could never be hers and she was glad that he might be on the way to finding a wife. It would ease the feeling of tension she sometimes had with him. She hoped that his wife would be good enough for him, but his private life was nothing to do with her. This must be how he felt about Luke.

Rose was very proud of her garden that spring, and the little orchard she was starting. The fruit trees blossomed and the vegetables were a welcome addition to their diet. Sometimes when mist hung in the trees near the creek she thought about the dark people and wondered whether they would come back. Life was good, Rose felt well and it was even better when Luke started to make foundations for a new building. The long-awaited house was on the way and he took advice from Bert Carr, who had just finished building their house on the hill.

One day when Luke had gone over to Carr's to borrow some tools, Rose went down to the creek for water. It was warm and the trees were shimmering in the heat. She bent to the water and when she straightened, two Aboriginal women were looking at her. She thought it was the same ones she'd seen before, but the baby was not with them.

'Good day,' she said uncertainly, not wanting to frighten them. 'Are you fishing?'

'Yabbies,' one of them said, and they both laughed at her puzzled expression. 'They're crayfish, you know? Yes, we speak English. We were at the mission over there,' the younger one continued, 'but no good. Too many rules! So we went walkabout.'

From what she had heard of the mission, its intentions were good but if she'd had to live there, Rose thought she would have gone walkabout too. 'So where do you live?' There was so much she wanted to know. 'My name is Rose,' she added.

The older woman sat on the creek bank and patted the ground beside her. 'Sit down, Rose. I am Auntie Mary and this young niece of mine is Sal. Mission names, easy for you! We move about, but mostly in winter we stay in one place where it's warmer, down in the valley.'

'You will have a baby?' The younger one, Sal, smiled shyly. 'We thought you will still be here; white folks don't move like we do.' She brought out something from her bag. 'Wattle seeds. They're everywhere at the right time of year. Grind them up and make damper.' The wattles had flowered at the end of winter, yellow along the tracks like shafts of sunshine. Their seeds would ripen in time and she would collect them.

Rose sniffed the large, sulphurous seeds. 'Thank you for the yams you left for me before.'

'You like them? Good. There is plenty stuff in the bush if you know where to look ... Rose, we will tell you about it.' Auntie Mary settled herself more comfortably against the bank. 'Mr Bulmer at the mission, he wanted to know all about what we collect.' She grinned. 'Didn't tell him everything, did we, Sal?'

Sal laughed. 'Nah. Just said we eat kangaroo and possum all the time. But Rose, if you can catch yabby, it's good ... and ducks ... down east we eat swans' eggs a lot in spring. Big eggs! You seen the swans? Big black birds, you know.' She made her neck long and looked around and for a second Sal looked just like a swan.

Auntie Mary bent down and picked a mint-like plant at the water's edge. Rose had wondered whether it was like English mint, but hadn't tried it. Now she felt as though she had been blind to all the wonders around her; there were herbs everywhere here, just as there were at home. 'You know this?' the woman asked. 'It will make food taste better – and treat your cough as well. Mint warms your belly.'

'What about when you are sick?' Rose wanted to know. 'You have plants you use?'

'Now, that's secrets!' Auntie Mary's eyes widened. 'There's things you will know already, Rose. If you get a sting or a bite, rub it with bracken ... everybody knows.' Rose nodded. 'And *Yanun*, that one.' She pointed to a blackwood tree. 'Boil up the bark for pains in the joints ... you know. And for a cut or when your man bashes you.' She looked at Rose sideways. 'Then you chew up some gum leaves and put them on and the place don't go bad. All sorts of gum leaves will do.' She reached out and broke off a spray of eucalyptus leaves, crushing them in her hand.

'Rose wants to know what's for babies,' Sal suggested, looking shyly into the creek. 'You know the soft bark on some trees – paper-bark you call them? You can wrap your baby in that ... and a possum skin in winter.' She laughed. 'And the stuff you get when you cut the gum tree is sticky gum, good for when the baby shit too much.'

There was a rustling in the bushes and Luke appeared with a bag of tools on his back. The dark women shrank down lower on the creek bank and Rose stood up and went to meet him with her bucket of water.

'Here, I'll carry that,' Luke offered. He hadn't noticed the women and Rose didn't mention them. She knew what his attitude would be. That evening she went down for water again and found the wattle seeds tucked into the bank.

As she grew heavier, the time seemed to go more slowly for Rose. She made some loose-fitting dresses and continued her work at the school, but everything was an effort, especially when the hot weather came. Thunderstorms swept the hills and the air was humid.

Luke continued to work on the new house, but Rose could still not see how big it was to be because he decided to finish off one room first. 'Just for the present.' He clad the walls in slabs of thick bark, so it was very much like their present hut, except that it had a timber floor. 'This is what we can afford,' Luke said whenever Rose asked for something a little more permanent.

TEN

MARTHA EXPECTED THE baby to be born at the end of January and she was very well prepared. Rose was to give birth in Martha's new house, with all the attention that a midwife could provide. 'No child should be born in a hut like this one,' she said to Rose, watching That Spider make his way down the wall. 'You'd better come over and stay with me, so I can keep an eye on you.'

The summer wore on, hot and dry or hot and wet, and Rose was increasingly uncomfortable. Christmas came and went, marked by a carol service at the school and a nativity play from the children, in costumes made by Freda and Rose. Rose enjoyed the distraction. The parents said they had never seen such a good play and the young actors were ecstatic.

Luke thought Rose should eat meat and bought beef from the Haunted Creek butcher, but otherwise he made no allowances for her condition. The farm was going reasonably well and Luke was happy enough, but it would have been better if he'd been more excited about the baby. He made a cradle because Martha told him it was needed, and that was that. He showed no interest in choosing a name, or wondering what the baby would look like. At times Luke found a few days' work helping various settlers with fencing, which meant that their own was not done, but at least they had money coming in.

The school was due to reopen after the summer holidays, but Freda told Rose not to worry about the sewing class for a few weeks. 'We'll manage until you can come back,' she promised. Freda had knitted several little bonnets for the baby and Martha had made pillows and blankets for the cradle. Rose herself had sewn cool cotton garments and knitted a few woollen ones, thinking as she worked about the child and how it would grow up. What would the future hold for a child in Haunted Creek?

Rose was looking forward to a few days of rest in Martha's pleasant house, which was built well enough to keep out the worst of the heat. A few trees grouped round the house gave shade and a green coolness; Bert said it was mad to cut down all the trees, as some settlers did.

One day the Teesdales would have a house like this. There was even a spare bedroom with pretty flower-patterned curtains and a bedspread with a frill to match. Rose hadn't seen a frill for a long time. 'We brought a lot of stuff from our house near Melbourne,' Martha explained.

Rose never got to that pretty bedroom. The day before she was due to go to Martha's, the pains began. Luke had gone out to catch some fish for dinner and she dare not undertake the journey to the Carrs' house now. Try not to be alarmed, try to relax, that's what Martha had said. Rose deliberately made her preparations between the pains: newspaper on the bed under a clean sheet, water … but the buckets were empty. *Luke, where are you when I need you*? He could fetch water and then go for Martha when he came home.

Hours passed and no one came. Rose felt the baby moving downwards and wondered how long it would be before the actual birth; she'd heard that sometimes babies came quickly, unexpectedly. The pain intensified; Martha had given her a few drops of laudanum for emergencies, but what if she was unconscious – and by herself?

Rose tied her hair back from her sweating brow and tried to remember the stories she'd heard about births. Women who lived on the high moors in Yorkshire had sometimes, when they'd been left alone, delivered their own babies. Could she do it? There may be no alternative.

This was the low point; all the things that had happened here were nothing to this. *Here I am in a hut with an earth floor, giving birth to a baby that the father doesn't want.*

Desperately, she tried to work out a plan. When she felt the baby's head in the birth canal she would squat down, that might help, and she'd heard that it was traditional in the old days to sit on a birthing stool.

She turned away from the thought that the birth might be complicated, that she might need help. *It's natural, having a baby, I've helped cows to do it scores of times.* Yes, and when the calf was the wrong way round, they'd had to call the farrier to help them. Rose took a drink of water from the jug they kept in the house and found that her hand was trembling.

Pain came and went, washing over her in waves. Long shadows were falling across the little clearing as the afternoon wore on. Rose found the kitchen scissors and cleaned them on newspaper; she felt strangely calm. She looked at a chair Luke had made and realized she could take out the seat. It might make some kind of birthing stool. She put padded newspapers under it.

Now it was urgent, the baby was coming, the pain was like nothing she'd ever felt before. Why hadn't they told her how bad it was? Sobbing, Rose lowered herself onto the chair. She could feel the head. At least the baby was the right way round … At that moment Luke walked in.

'I've got two fish—' he began, and then gasped as he realized what was happening. 'Oh Lord! I'll go for Martha.' He was about to disappear when Rose called him back.

'Stay right here and help me!' Rose gasped. 'It's too late for Martha now! Here, see if you can …'

Luke's tan had turned yellow. 'I couldn't. I don't know anything about it!' But he shut the door and turned to her, shaking.

Rose summoned all her strength. 'It's your baby, you help! Surely you ...' She stopped as another wave of contractions hit her and she pushed with it, pushed with all her might. She felt like screaming, but that would only upset Luke more. The head would be the worst: get that through and the rest would follow... In a haze of pain, Rose pushed and pushed.

Her husband was retching as he bent down to help the baby and Rose prayed and pushed, holding on to the foot of the bed and biting on a handkerchief to stop herself from crying out. Agonizingly, inch by inch, the little body passed through – surely it must be tearing her apart? Rose could see blood. Then there was a rush of liquid and with a soft plop, the baby was out. The father laid it on the newspaper under the chair and went outside to be sick.

Rose lay back exhausted, but after a few minutes she knew that something had to be done. She cut the cord with the kitchen scissors and wiped the baby gently with a towel. It was covered with after-birth and blood, but it was breathing and soon set up a thin wail.

The little body was perfect; Rose held it to her breast, passed her fingers gently over the little mouth and soon it was sucking happily at the teat. The baby had arrived.

'Get some water and heat it up. We need to wash baby,' Rose said when Luke came back. 'What's the matter with you, man?'

'I can't stand the sight of blood,' Luke muttered. 'The whole thing makes me sick.' He couldn't even look at her and Rose looked down at herself, covered in blood and sweat. No wonder. 'I hated it at home when they were killing pigs and calving cows. I like working with wood – something clean that doesn't scream.'

So much for their farming ambitions, but Rose was in no shape to argue. 'Fetch me water, put a big pan on to boil and then go for Martha,' she said. 'Tell her – tell her it's a girl.'

'Hell! A lass, that's the last thing we need.' Luke brought the water, but still didn't look at the child.

Mother and baby fell asleep until they were woken when Martha bustled in. 'Why wasn't I sent for? What possessed you to do it alone?' Anxiety made her voice rough.

'It happened too quickly … and Luke wasn't here to fetch you,' Rose said quietly. Martha's face relaxed a little as she took the baby. 'You've done very well, Rose, I'm proud of you. She'll be a lovely little girl when she's cleaned up.' She delved into a bag and brought out clean cloths and towels. 'I've brought some of her clothes with me.'

Luke did not reappear. Thinking of his reaction to his daughter's arrival, Rose said when she and the baby were both clean and cool, 'Haunted Creek is a rough world, Martha. How will my poor little girl survive?'

'All the more need for some good women, to soften it a bit,' Martha said briskly. 'This little lass will be right at home here and by the time she's your age, Haunted Creek will be joined with Wattle Tree and we'll have a little town with shops.'

Rose smiled sleepily. She had agreed with Freda and Erik that they all disliked big towns and loved the bush. But in the end, the best place to be was a prosperous, well-fenced countryside with farms dotted across a rolling landscape framed by plenty of trees, and small towns where people could know each other.

There was something pitiless about the untouched forests. They were too big, too inhuman and dangerous. The trees were on a gigantic scale and the overwhelming feeling in those dark places was of sadness and loss. Australian woods did not lose their leaves in winter and the forest was dark and brooding all the year, a strange, alien background to their lives. The bush was lonely.

Perhaps Ada would live to see this landscape tamed. 'Yes, she's Ada, after my mother,' she told Martha. Luke had no name for the baby, but had never considered that it might be a girl. Ada would change her life, Rose knew; she would have someone to love and care for. She felt ready for the task, more confident now than when she first came to Haunted Creek. She was on the way to becoming strong.

*

The young chestnut horse was going well. The buggy moved along as smoothly as the road allowed and with a small vehicle Erik was able to avoid the worst potholes. 'Do you like him? Vulcan's his name. He's stylish, but quite sensible,' he said to his companion, to see whether she liked horses.

The lady sitting beside him nodded, but said nothing. Harriet had never been to Wattle Tree before and Erik wondered what she would make of it. He had been visiting Harriet Sinclair's father for some time for advice on legal matters connected with buying more land. Harriet had smiled at him and offered drinks of lemonade and he had gradually begun to spend a little time with her when he went to town.

Erik was taking Freda's advice and was at last looking for a wife, but it was hard to muster much enthusiasm. Was there something wrong with him? Underneath, he knew very well why it was hard to take an interest in ladies from town.

The reality was that it was time Erik Jensen found a girl of his own, a good farmer's wife – but would a lawyer's daughter like the bush? He would soon find out.

At first the visit went well. Freda had prepared lunch and Harriet, although rather overdressed for the warm weather in large skirts and an elaborate bonnet, was gracious. After lunch, Freda and Erik showed the visitor round the little school. 'And I suppose the church will be somewhere near the school?' Harriet asked, standing near to Erik and looking up at him with large grey eyes.

'Er – yes, actually, it will be. But the church isn't built yet. Wattle Tree is just beginning … the post office is at Haunted Creek, but as more people settle here, there will be a church.' Erik thought he'd better not mention that the social centre of the district was the All Nations hotel, which was lively but not very godly. 'We hold church services here in the school, for the present.'

'Goodness me! No church? I had no idea I was so far from civilization!' Harriet was perhaps joking, but Erik felt uneasy; she thought that Wattle Tree was backward. He had not mentioned marriage, but she must know what he had in mind and she was probably working out whether it would suit her to live here. Perhaps she had seen herself as a leading light in a little church in the hills.

With the sun beating down from a brassy sky, Erik borrowed a parasol from Freda and offered to take Harriet on a tour of the farm. But the lady looked down at her kid shoes. 'I think not, thank you. Farms are so dirty, are they not? Of interest to men, but not to ladies.' So they walked round the garden, of which Freda was proud, but Harriet was not very interested in plants. Erik by now was desperately trying to keep up a conversation and feeling inadequate. This woman must have spent all her life in the town; strange, in a young country like Australia.

They sat on a shaded wooden bench that Erik had made for his mother to sit with her sewing, looking out over the forested hills. Wattle Tree was on a ridge between two river valleys, a beautiful, peaceful spot.

Harriet arranged her dress prettily around her, but made no comment on the spectacular view. What could they talk about? What on earth did they have in common? She looked at her spotless kid boots.

Over the grassy paddocks at the edge of the trees, Erik saw a magnificent wedge-tailed eagle taking off with a rabbit in its talons. He loved to watch their powerful flight, but when he pointed it out to the lady, she was horrified. 'Do you mean to tell me that you live so very close to the forest? How dangerous it must be! Eagles are huge, terrifying ... and there may be wild dogs and snakes in there under the trees – and even blacks! You must never feel safe!' She shivered and he could tell this time that she was serious.

So that was it; Harriet did not like his farm. Perhaps she'd heard some of those stories that went round, sensational tales embroidered every time they were told. You heard them all the time in Moe. *This great big tiger snake come at me and when I turned round, by golly there was another behind me....*

Disappointed, Erik escorted Harriet back to the house, where she seemed to feel safer.

'Of course, an educated man like you could easily find employment in Moe, or better still, Melbourne.' Harriet smiled as they had an afternoon cup of tea before he drove her home. To his mother she said, 'Did you not tell me he trained as an engineer? What a waste, to bury yourself up here in the hills!'

Freda raised her eyebrows at her son. *This woman thinks we are buried*, the eyebrows seemed to say.

'As a matter of fact I like farming – it's as much a challenge as engineering,' Erik told Miss Sinclair quietly, guessing the direction of her thoughts. 'I think it has a good future here as the population grows.'

'Oh, but you would soon get used to city life, and then you would realize all that you had missed!' Harriet was quite eager. 'I will ask my father if he knows of any openings ...' Her little face was much more animated than it had been.

'Please don't worry Mr Sinclair,' Erik said as smoothly as he could, and turned the talk to the new buildings in Moe, about which Harriet held definite opinions.

'Of course, once the railway comes through, we shall have a fine town,' she said hopefully, as though she wanted him to change his mind.

By the time Harriet was delivered to her father's house again in a rather sombre mood, Erik was wondering how he could get out of developing the friendship further. She would have certain expectations of him, now that she had met his mother. On the other hand, she hadn't been impressed with his farm, so she might be getting cold feet herself.

Erik plodded home, the buggy pulled by his older and heavier horse Prince this time. The evening light fell softly on the mountain ranges and the sunset filtered through the trees on either side of the track. It was strange how little interest Harriet had shown in the countryside. He now realized that she was afraid of the wild hills beyond the boundary of the town. Would she ever settle down on a farm?

They swung into the Wattle Tree track and Erik sighed. He knew one woman who appreciated this place as he did, a small dark-haired girl who pulled him like a magnet, all the time. He thought of Rose very often, but he knew that he had to forget her. Harriet might have been a diversion. He had hoped so, but after a day in her company he hadn't been able to get rid of her quickly enough. 'Rose, Rose, what have you done to me?' he muttered and the horse wandered to the wrong side of the track. It was Rose he wanted, no other. A married woman.

Something would have to be done. Erik had looked after Rose from a distance when Luke was away, but now the baby had arrived and Luke was at home. Of course Luke would see they came to no harm. Any interference from another man would be – well, it would be immoral. He must keep right out of their lives. Heavily, Erik worked through his problem and reached a conclusion. He would have to go away for a time.

To leave the farm would be painful and it would also put a burden upon Freda, who already worked very hard in the school. But to see Rose with her baby, Luke's child, would cause him even more pain. His mother had said she was radiant. 'Rose will be a wonderful mother,' she'd said. No doubt she would love her husband and now they had a child, they would be a happy family. Jealousy was a bad feeling, but it couldn't be helped.

Just a few weeks away would give him a respite from thinking about Rose, Erik decided as he stabled the horse.

ELEVEN

A SPELL OF droving would be the answer to Erik's problem, as it had been for many a man with difficulties. He would be fully occupied with moving cattle along the Gippsland tracks, making sure they were fed and watered and not stolen or strayed. Droving cattle was something he'd enjoyed from time to time. It wasn't a case of running away….

Erik leaned on the stable door watching the moon rise, thinking about it. He had been offered a trip that would take him to Melbourne and back over a few weeks, moving cattle and working with a couple of experienced men. Freda would look after the farm, the fences were in good order and he would arrange for a man to do some of the work. He'd be home in time to harvest the autumn crops.

Distance and time, the distractions of the road, would surely dull the ache he felt whenever he saw Rose or even thought about her. In time he would find a wife and he and Rose could be like brother and sister – when they were old, perhaps.

If this was the pain of love, then you were better off without it. It must be better to found a marriage on respect, friendship perhaps, but not this gnawing obsession. It would wear you down if it went on too long.

A trip away might also give Miss Sinclair time to find another beau, if that was the word she used. 'Miss Sinclair's not the girl for Wattle Tree, is she?' Freda commented when Erik walked in after stabling the horse. 'But I suppose if you love her, it might work out in the end.'

'You never know, Mother.' Erik sat down wearily in his chair, not willing to discuss the girl.

Freda handed him a glass of lemonade. 'Good luck, Erik. Harriet's intelligent and quite pretty – she might settle down.' She was probably disappointed that Harriet showed no interest in the farm and so was he, but those little black kid boots were meant to stay in town.

Some mothers would have wanted to keep their sons for themselves, but Freda was obviously hoping he would marry the right girl. Harriet was not the right girl. Even if she'd liked the farm, he found her brittle conversation tiring. You couldn't relax with Harriet.

The next week, Erik went to Moe with vegetables and called on Duncan Black, the stock agent who arranged cattle sales and sorted out the mobs of cattle for drovers to move across the country. The most usual job was to take beef on the hoof to feed the growing population of Melbourne.

Duncan said he was just in time and could start a trip in a few days. 'Three of you will be enough. You start with fifty or so, head from here and pick up all the way down the track to the Newmarket saleyards,' he was told. 'A steady trip, don't rush 'em. They need to hold their weight or, even better, fatten along the way. You know the drill.' He looked at Erik. 'You fit enough?' Duncan himself was built like a jockey, lean and wiry with shrewd, far-seeing eyes.

'Of course, Duncan. A Wattle Tree farmer can't be anything else. Quick or dead, that's us. The only thing I ask is – if we get a real rogue that upsets the mob, what do we do?'

'Shoot the bugger and note the brand,' Duncan said briefly. 'No doubt you'll take a gun with you – you might need it. Wild dogs are bad round the Bunyip, I'm told. The money will be here when you get back. George knows all the pickup points.' He grinned. 'And say goodbye to the lady friend for a while – you'll be bringing another mob back so it's a slow trip each way.' Erik nodded. At ten miles a day it would take them several weeks to go to Melbourne and back again. Thank goodness Freda didn't mind.

Next he called to see Miss Sinclair, not sure how to proceed except to say that he was going away. No doubt she would disapprove of droving as a very low occupation, not fit for a gentleman, so if she was not discouraged already this might finish her off. In Erik's experience drovers were steady, skilled men, but the popular view of them was of drinking, swearing, fighting cowboys.

A drover, even part-time, was not the kind of man for Miss Harriet Sinclair the lawyer's daughter. Erik never worried about differences of class, or of race. He wasn't afraid of 'the blacks' and knew some of them quite well. And that could be another barrier between the lady and himself. She was a little person of fixed opinions.

Harriet kept him waiting for over fifteen minutes, listening to the slow ticking of the dining-room clock. At last she came in, all smiles and with every hair perfectly in place. *Oh dear, she seems pleased to see me*. Erik stood up.

'Dear Mr Jensen – Erik! I have news for you. I hope you will not be too hurt.' Harriet looked coy. 'But I have just become engaged to be married. To Dr Maitland of Sale – do you know him? We have been friends forever, you know, but only yesterday he persuaded me to marry him.' She looked up at Erik to note his reaction. 'I do hope you don't … mind too much.'

Erik stood holding his hat, searching for the right words. A shocked silence seemed to be the proper reaction. *Thank you, Dr Maitland, I'll be eternally grateful* … 'Well, naturally, I'm disappointed that our friendship must come to an end.' He tried to look suitably sad. 'But I wish you well, Miss Sinclair. I do know Dr Maitland. I'm sure the best man has won.' Was that a little too gallant? Maitland must be about twenty years older than Harriet but the lady loved it and they parted with words of goodwill.

Thank goodness that was over; one look at his farm had been enough to send Harriet into the arms of the doctor. Sale was a flourishing town, doctoring was a respectable profession and the marriage would suit her very well. *Goodbye, Miss Sinclair, good luck.* He left the house with a weight off his shoulders.

That week Erik made his preparations for the journey. He took out his stockwhip of plaited kangaroo hide and it reminded him of the trips he'd been on before, several summers ago. He unrolled the canvas swag, a bedroll that was carried behind the saddle, and found it needed a few repairs. As he repaired and oiled the swag to make it waterproof he thought about Rose and wondered how she could go about, now that she had a baby. An idea began to form in his mind.

'The first couple of days are usually the worst, until the cattle settle down to the routine,' Erik told his mother. He knew Freda was trying to hide the fact that she worried about him when he was on the road. 'It's not as if we'll be in the bush. We go straight down the three-chain road to Melbourne, round the edge of the swamp, grazing as we go, with overnight stops along the way.'

'Sleeping in ditches, I suppose?' Freda said casually.

'Not on this trip – it's civilized! We stop at places that have cattle-holding paddocks and mostly we can sleep in a bed at night. Places like the Cobb & Co. stop at Toomuc Creek, that has a sort of lodging house. The Bunyip, Brandy Creek – they're strung out at intervals all the way to Flemington, places where the mail coach changes horses and there's plenty of water for travelling stock. You could do it yourself, Mother, it's not too hard.' He laughed at her.

At the back of Erik's mind he knew that once the railway came through to Sale, cattle would travel to Melbourne by train and trips like this would be over. The only droving jobs then would be overland, bringing cattle from remote places across mountains and bogs to the railhead – much more difficult than this route. 'There's very little to go wrong.'

'Pity I can't come, but somebody has to teach in school and stay on the farm,' his mother said ironically. 'I'm going to ask Rose to come back soon, to take sewing again. She gets the best out of the children, she has a talent for teaching in her quiet way … but I don't know how she'll carry that baby up the track, even though it's quite small as yet.'

Erik nodded. 'She'll grow. I thought of making a sling for her. I've got some canvas left. A baby carrier to fit on the back; that's the best way to carry a load.'

A few days later Erik swung into the saddle, trying not to see the tears in Freda's eyes. He rode the young horse Vulcan and led another. His two collies, Dan and Sim, trotted at their heels. Prince, the old horse, was left for Freda's use.

It was a relief to be on the road again. It was not quite a holiday, you had to be always thinking ahead, but it made a change from farming. Several neighbours had promised to help Freda if she needed it, including Luke. It would do that youth good to help someone for a change. Rose didn't know he was going, unless Luke had told her, and he didn't want to see the expression in her eyes when she found out. But how could you trot over and kiss a married woman goodbye?

The other two drovers were on time. They had worked together before and knew each other well. George was about fifty, with a grey beard and a gentle way with cattle. Sep was younger and he seemed rather nervous, fidgeting with his girth and adjusting the stirrup length, anxious to be off.

The first batch of cattle was collected without too much trouble, although at 200 head it was a much bigger group than they'd been promised. They were a mixed bunch, three and four years old, some of them red and white Herefords and others darker Longhorn crosses with sweeping horns.

Erik looked the cattle over critically from the back of his horse and his older dog Dan did the same. They were in good condition, quiet already, and after a few days on the road they would be like old friends. The part of droving he hated was when, having got to know the animals and been with them for weeks, he had to hand them over to be killed. But you didn't mention that thought to anybody else; tough men were not supposed to think of droving except as a job, although they were good with the animals.

There was plenty of grass at the side of the wide track after recent rain and they drifted slowly west, the cattle grazing quietly as they went. A little traffic passed them on the road, farmers in buggies, bullock carts with supplies and once, the coach from Sale rattled by in a cloud of dust.

The dogs trotted along, looking around them with interest. Dan looked up at Erik from time to time and wagged his tail. 'It's good to be back on the road,' he seemed to be saying. Dan loved tailing cattle, keeping them in a neat group, and he never seemed to get enough of it at home. Collies were bred for the work and they were happy working. It was a pity men couldn't be the same.

As the afternoon shadows lengthened the animals slowed down, although thirst kept them moving: they wanted a drink. They would settle down quickly in a fenced paddock at Steve's Creek after being watered and Erik looked forward to a quiet night.

A cloud of dust swirled ahead as another mob of cattle came swiftly to meet them. As they got closer Erik could see that they were probably youngsters intended for breeding, bound for settlers' farms. They were travelling east and on the right of the track, a bit faster than George would have allowed.

Erik watched for the drovers in charge of the other herd to turn aside on a smaller track, to let them through. That was the rule of the road: if you can turn aside, do so. But not this mob. They kept coming on, at the same brisk pace. What on earth were they thinking of? Erik began to sweat as he saw what would happen, but there was nothing he could do. Their own mob were on the left and were running out of room; they had nowhere else to go because there were no side tracks and a fence ran along the edge of the road.

'Here we go,' Erik groaned and George, the older man, swore quietly. They watched helplessly as the two groups met and mingled, with much bellowing and dust raising in a sea of tossing horns. The cattle seemed to enjoy the drama and made the most of it. Coughing, Erik couldn't see which was his group for the choking dust. What a thoughtless lot the other drovers must be. 'They can't have looked ahead at all,' Sep grunted.

George had evidently seen this sort of thing before. 'We'll turn them into yon paddock, the whole blooming lot,' he called to the others above the din. 'You stand by the gate, Erik. We'll draft the young 'uns out.' He pointed to a small grass field belonging to some hapless farmer who had the bad luck to live next to the road. They would borrow his field for an hour or so. Watched by the other drovers, Erik and his mates herded all the animals into the enclosure.

Round and round in the small paddock the cattle circled, kept on the move by George, Sep and his dog. Every time one of the yearlings came near the gate, Erik pushed it through back on to the road, with his dog Dan holding back the others. It was the only way to draft them out and it was slow, but in time they had their 200 cattle in the pen and about 100 young ones back onto the road again. The men and the dogs were thirsty and covered in dust. The grass in the paddock was trampled into the earth and George would have to offer some cash to the owner.

'Next time, look ahead, think what you're doing! You could've turned off down the track yonder and saved us all that,' George growled at the other team as they lounged by the gate. 'What's your name, lad?'

'Sorry, boss,' the young drover said with a grin. He and his mate had done nothing to help with the drafting. 'John Smith.'

George growled, 'Well, John Smith, I've got your description and that'll be good enough for Mr Black to make a note of you. You'd better mend your ways or you'll be out of a job. You can't go on like that and get away with it.' The young men went off, muttering about greybeards telling a man what to do.

By this time, the cattle needed to rest and so did their drovers. 'We'll never make Steve's Creek stock paddock tonight – we'd best stop as soon as we can,' George decided and the other two agreed. They soon came to a spot where the grass verge widened out, with a small creek for the cattle to get water. The herd drank gratefully and then they gradually sat down to chew the cud in a fairly tight group. They were settled for the night.

Breathing a sigh of relief, Erik tied up the horses to trees. When all the horses were fed, the men rolled out their swags by the side of the road and ate bread and cheese to save cooking. Erik lit a fire to boil the billy and as they sat round it, drinking strong black tea, he found that he was looking forward to the trip. The setting sun lit the track ahead to a blood red and then sank to an orange glow, promising more fine weather.

It was uncomfortable on the ground at first, after months of sleeping in a bed. As he looked up at the stars Erik listened to the puffing and blowing of contented cattle. They were all lying down, dark shapes with white faces glimmering in the faint light of the fire. There was the occasional gurgle as an animal regurgitated its cud. The men would take turns to watch them, but they were not likely to stray, tired as they were. Sep took the first watch.

Far off Erik could hear the croaking of bullfrogs in a waterhole and the hoot of an owl. The night was cool and fragrant with the scents of the bush, the aromatic, sharp eucalyptus mingling with the bottlebrush flowers' perfume. He imagined as he drifted off to sleep that you could bottle this essence of the bush, to give to Rose as a present....

A sudden bellow woke Erik with a start. Several steers were on their feet and soon they were roaring through the rest of the herd, which had been dreaming peacefully. Sep was obviously taken by surprise as the terrified cattle jumped up and took off in all directions. The night was full of frenzied bellowing, mounting to a roar as the whole 200 cattle joined in. George jumped up as Erik did and Sep yelled to them, but they couldn't hear what he said above the noise.

Erik shrugged on his coat and ran towards the horses. He had slept in his boots in case of emergency and here it was, on their first night. The cattle had been tired and he thought they wouldn't go far, once the first rush of panic was spent. Something had scared them; it could be a wild dog. They would have to be rounded up again.

The next moment a huge steer rushed straight at Erik in its mad panic. It was a dark Longhorn with wild eyes, foaming at the mouth. He was knocked off his feet and lifted as the terrified animal tossed its head. There was sharp pain as the steer's horn pierced his skin and then he fell down, down into the soft earth and darkness.

TWELVE

THE HARDEST PART of caring for a baby turned out to be the incessant crying. Ada cried a lot, sometimes screaming and sometimes sobbing, but never quiet for long. Often she was too hot. The summer was declining into autumn and there had been rain, but the heat persisted. Flies were bad that summer and it was impossible to keep them out of the hut, so the baby's cradle was swathed in muslin all the time, Ada cocooned in a strange white world of her own.

Rose could hear the sobs and cries in her mind even when the baby was quiet, a discordant background to her days and nights. If only the child could tell her what was wrong! Martha suggested gin as the cure-all for babies, but they had no gin. Even though Martha had more experience, how could gin be good for babies when it was bad for adults?

Ada's crying was tiring for her mother, but Luke said it was worse for him. He could not bear it. After a few nights he suggested that he move into the new cabin he had built and Rose suspected that this was why he'd that day finished off one room.

'I think that I should sleep there with the baby, not you,' Rose said, keeping her eyes fixed on his face. 'It's much cleaner and better for little Ada.' Without waiting for his reply, she moved the cradle and the baby's bath into the cabin, put up fresh curtains and wondered why she had not claimed the room immediately. 'Could you buy some glass and fit the window? To keep the flies out, and mosquitoes at night.' She inspected for spiders before Ada was allowed inside; a spider bite would be serious for a baby.

Luke was a little happier once he was able to sleep through the night, but he never offered to help with the baby. He did as Rose asked, fitted the window and then put up some shelves. He had made a big wooden bed and stuffed a mattress with dried bracken. Looking round the cabin when Ada was sleeping, Rose thought that it was a great improvement on the hut. That Spider seemed to have been left behind.

One day Luke came home with a borrowed cart, bringing an iron stove with a metal pipe for a chimney. Over the next week he installed it in the cabin, cutting a hole in the roof for the chimney. 'You can cook on it in winter when it's raining outside,' he said as though it was all for her benefit. It was a relief to know that she'd be able to keep the baby warm in winter.

As soon as she could, Rose had taken charge of the poultry again and Luke delivered the eggs for her. They were getting along together reasonably well, although they seemed to live separate lives. Luke never came to the cabin and Rose never joined him in the bed in the hut. Thinking about him, Rose decided that Luke didn't like women very much. He'd never courted a girl in Kirkby that she could remember. He'd only come to see her and talked her into marriage because he thought a settler needed a wife, but he seemed to prefer a bachelor's life.

How could a woman with a baby move about in the bush? While Ada was very small, Rose carried her everywhere tucked in a shawl, but she couldn't carry baskets of eggs or buckets of water at the same time. She couldn't leave the baby alone and there were no near neighbours who might mind her. This meant that work at the school was out of the question, in spite of Freda's wish to start the sewing class; again. Rose missed the class, she missed the talks with Freda. She tried not to think about Erik.

One Saturday after the school term had started Freda came to see Rose, carrying a parcel. After she had cooed over the baby and drunk a cup of tea, she gave the parcel to Rose. 'This could help you,' she said and sat back in her chair.

It was a kind of rope harness, attached to a canvas bag with holes in it. What could it be? Freda laughed and slipped her arms into the harness. The bag fitted on her back. 'Baby can ride on your back, Rose. It's strong enough to hold her, maybe until she can walk! You can move about, carry things and little Ada will be safe. Women in several countries carry their little ones this way.'

Freda admitted under pressure that Erik had made the baby carrier. 'He likes to work with his hands,' his mother said. 'But he doesn't want you to know that he made it. You might think it's not proper, or something. I can't think why. I thought you'd just be grateful!'

Rose grasped her hands. 'I am so grateful to both of you! Thank you so much for thinking of it. I've been trying to work out how to carry her ever since she was born.' Erik was still thinking of her, caring for her, although they never met. A warm feeling, mixed with guilt, spread through Rose. She couldn't even thank him. 'It will make all the difference to my life. Please tell Erik that, won't you? Tell … tell him how pleased I am.'

Freda nodded, smiling. 'So as soon as baby settles down a little and sleeps more often, you can walk to school.' She paused. 'If you agree, the baby can sleep at the back of the room while you teach the sewing class.'

'Thank you. The problem is, she doesn't sleep much and she …' As if on cue, Ada gave a long wail. 'She cries, Freda. I wish I knew why.' Rose reached out and rocked the crib automatically and after a while, Ada slept.

Freda was brisk. 'It could be colic, that's the most likely. There are several things we might try – dill water, for one. I have some dill seeds, Rose, I keep them for digestive problems.'

Rose's memory went back to her grandmother's garden and the 'gripe water' she'd made for the village babies from the feathery dill. Of course! Why had she not thought of it herself? 'I'd forgotten about dill, Freda.'

Freda returned to her theme. 'Once Ada is more settled, I'd like you to come to school. Lydia, the eldest girl, can walk her out a little – we have an old baby carriage. Lydia wants to be a nursemaid and will be pleased to get experience.' She smiled. 'There are more ways of learning than copying exercises into a book.' Rose discovered much later that the old baby carriage had been found by Erik in Moe and completely refurbished for little Ada's benefit, and that his Moe acquaintances had teased him about fatherhood. Erik had told them he believed in being prepared.

Before she left, Freda said gently, 'Erik's gone off for some weeks, Rose. He's droving, helping to take cattle to Melbourne.'

Erik gone … Somehow Rose had never imagined that Erik would go away. But in one way, it might be easier for her if she could go to the school without running into him. She looked down to hide her expression. 'That will be … a nice change for him. He might come back with a wife!' Her voice trembled slightly, but that was all. The pain of loss came back, with an overwhelming sadness. 'He'll evidently make a good father!' *And a wonderful husband for some lucky woman. Bless you, Erik, and good luck.*

'Not many young women on the droving routes, I would think, but you never know. He might meet a damsel in distress. He's rather good with them, isn't he?' They both laughed, but Rose thought that Freda might have guessed how she felt. Of course she knew about the wild dogs. Would he meet attractive women on his travels?

Rose wondered why Erik had gone off so suddenly and was surprised to hear that Luke knew about the trip. 'Luke has promised to help me on the farm, if I need it,' Freda told her. 'If he's here, that is,' she added doubtfully. 'That's what he said.'

Feeling almost deceitful, Rose told Luke that Freda had given her the baby harness, but not who had made it. There were now quite a lot of things that she did not tell Luke, but he took little interest in her doings. He and Jim were still trying to work out how to make money.

Rose was glad to hear Luke and Jim had decided not to go

prospecting for gold any more. One evening the men talked together for a long time and afterwards, Luke told her that they had decided finding payable gold was a gamble. 'We're just dabbling in the creek and turning over the old mullock heaps, it's boring,' he said. 'To do the job properly you need a crusher – all the machinery they used to have and plenty of men to work it.'

He didn't tell her what they planned to do instead, but when Rose said she was going back to the school Luke said, 'Good. You'll earn some money, which is just as well. I've got to go away again. Tom Appleyard – you remember the bloke with the tree house – has another timber contract. I meant to tell you before.' He looked slightly guilty.

'Oh, Luke, I thought you were staying—'

Luke cut in. 'This time it's a big one, opening new tracks through the bush round Noojee. They've surveyed a road – there's tin mining there.' He grinned. 'We've fenced the cattle and there's no sheep, so it will be easy for you.'

Rose sat down suddenly, feeling giddy. What about clearing their own land? So that was why Tom had visited them one evening and why Jim was uneasy when he spoke to her. Jim Carlyle had the occasional meal with them, sometimes bringing a duck or a rabbit to be cooked, but lately he'd seemed to have something on his mind.

'Why would they need tracks out there in the bush where nobody goes?' Erik had gone away and now Luke was going. She would need to be strong, as Maeve had said, especially with a baby to care for. There was no point in protesting; Luke's mind was made up, as usual, but it was a pity he couldn't discuss his plans with his wife.

'So that people can go there, silly. To carry out the timber, that's why, and to open up farming land. There's a demand for building timber, but it's locked up, they need to pull it out. It will open up this country, Rose. There'll be more settlers soon. They might build a railway through here in time. Then you'll get your shop and church and everything, just like Kirkby.' Luke made it sound as though the tracks were being cut just to make Rose's life easier.

Freda brought some dill water the next day and they gave the baby a few drops. 'Only what I expected,' she said when she heard that Luke was going away.

The change in the baby was noticeable; in two days she had almost stopped crying and slept much more, or gurgled to herself happily. The belching had lessened, although as Martha said, babies have wind because they are bound to suck in air with the milk.

Perhaps because of the quiet in the cabin, Luke came over to join Rose one night. They sat in the twilight and talked about what he would need to take with him to Noojee. He looked down at the sleeping child. 'I haven't been much of a father so far, have I? Or much of a husband, I suppose.' He sighed. 'I'm sorry, but I can't stand the noise she makes, or the smells at times, poor little devil. I should've helped you more, but … well, Rose, I'll go with Tom this one more time and then I'll settle down and be a real family man and farmer.' He smiled at her and Rose saw a hint of the young man who had made himself so agreeable that she'd come to Australia. 'You sorry you came here?' Luke asked her.

Rose was not sure. 'There are so many contrasts, Luke. I love the country, the look of the valleys and mountains, the space and the beautiful trees. And then, there's so much opportunity, the chance to buy land that we would never have been able to afford at home.'

'That's why we came,' Luke agreed. 'I like the freedom – you can shoot and fish more or less anywhere you like. There's plenty of room between the selections. You certainly can't do that in England unless you're a poacher, and most of 'em get caught in the end. And there's nobody lording it over you, no gentry to put you in your place.'

'And yet in dry, hot weather the place is ugly.' Rose decided not to mention the hut, the spiders, the flies, or the hazards of wild dogs and eucy men. 'Everything's grey and brown, everything's covered in dust, the trees droop and the grass crunches under your feet. No wonder the older people look stringy and dried out. We'll be like that one day.'

Perhaps the hardest thing to bear was that they were so shut away. Sometimes Rose felt the sadness of the bush weighing down on her spirit and adding to the hardship of isolation. These trees, this mile upon mile of dark forest, was not on a human scale. Ada would have no other children to play with until she went to school, unless Rose had another baby. But it would be too hard to cope with two small children, especially if Luke went away so much. She would try not to get pregnant again.

Rose looked up and found that Luke was still smiling at her. 'You're very quiet, lass,' he said. 'You know, I'm proud of the way you're managing out here. It isn't easy for a woman.'

It was the first time he had ever seemed to notice what she did. Luke said he was proud of his wife! She could hardly believe it. He took her hand. 'Let's go to bed.' Tonight, things seemed more friendly between them.

Luke went off two days later with his pack on his back to meet Tom. He kissed Rose and looked down at her. 'Look after yourself and the bairn.' He sounded more Yorkshire than usual. 'We'll have a better life when I come back, a proper house … I'll make it up to you, lass. You've had it hard, I've begun to see that, and Jim let me know about it the other day. Called me a selfish devil, he did.'

Rose smiled at him; she was not going to tell him the truth about himself just as he was leaving. 'We'll both try harder when you come back, Luke.' She had hardly ever criticized him, but her silences must have felt hostile. 'Why do you like to work with Tom so much?'

'The money, of course! But I like to be with the lads, I don't like working on my own.' He grinned apologetically. If Rose could only arrange things so that some of the settlers helped each other – this might be the way forward for Luke. 'See you in a month or so.'

He strode off abruptly as usual, but where the track disappeared into the trees Luke looked back and waved. Framed by the bush, young and vital, he looked like a portrait of an ideal settler. Then he was gone, but afterwards that image stayed with Rose. Luke had his faults, but so did everybody; he had good points too, and he was very likeable if you didn't have to depend on him. When he came back they must start again; she would try to understand him better and encourage him. If she had talked to him more he wouldn't have felt so lonely.

Rose toiled up the track a little later with Ada on her back to take the Wednesday sewing class. Her hair was tied back neatly and she wore her blue teaching dress with a white collar. The baby seemed to like being carried in the harness and fell asleep, soothed by the motion. Thank goodness for dill water! Rose decided to plant some of the seeds in her garden.

The pupils filed into the sewing class and there was the usual chorus: 'Good morning, Mrs Teesdale.' Ada was put into the baby carriage, which was overflowing with fresh new pink and white cotton covers. The class waited to see Rose's reaction.

'What pretty pillows and covers!' Rose looked round at the eager faces. 'Who made these for baby? They are so well done!' The hemming was neat and there had even been a spidery attempt at embroidery.

'We did!' Lottie jumped up and down. 'While you were away. Mrs Jensen told us what to do and we worked all by ourselves, except when she came to see us.'

Rose met Freda's eyes above the children's heads and saw that she was laughing with pleasure. 'We like sewing!' Lottie announced. 'We want to do some more.'

The sewing class worked happily all morning, making cushion covers for home, and when Lottie started humming to herself, Lydia asked, 'Can we sing, Mrs Teesdale, if we keep working?' So the class sang, and Rose with them, some nursery rhymes and songs they had learned from Mrs Jensen. They loved 'Twinkle, Twinkle Little Star' and sang it several times, and followed it with 'Little

Boy Blue' and 'Jack And Jill'. Then they sang 'Little Snail', a Swedish song that Rose guessed came from Freda's childhood.

'When children are learning, they enjoy it much more if they do a real project with an end result, rather than an exercise. That's my way of teaching,' Freda explained at lunchtime over a cup of coffee while the children played outside. 'Sewing for Ada was a big incentive.'

They were quiet for a while, resting after the effort of teaching, and then Freda said, 'I heard you singing with the class. Do you play the piano, Rose?'

'Not since I came here,' Rose said ruefully. 'I used to play at home, though.' The thought of a piano in a bark hut was ridiculous. 'I've been singing to Ada lately – she seems to like it.'

'I'd be grateful if you could take the whole school for singing. You have a true voice,' Freda said. 'I can pay you for extra hours, if you can spare the time.'

Rose felt herself blushing. 'Thank you, I would like it very much.' There had been little music in her life in Australia, and she missed it.

'You'll have noticed that Charlie's not in the sewing class this term,' Freda went on. 'He sewed to his own and my satisfaction, so that he can do basic repairs. And then he asked to learn farming. So he goes off to Ben Sawley's farm one day a week. Of course he has to keep a journal and let me read it.' She laughed. 'The other boys brought in sewing too, so now they work in the garden on Wednesdays and learn botany and arithmetic. They have to measure and calculate, I make sure of that. Erik set up a little garden area for them.' There was a pause. 'I haven't heard from Erik since he left.'

'It will be hard for him to write a letter if he's travelling all the time,' Rose said to comfort her. 'I'm going to deliver eggs tomorrow – I can call at the post office if you like.' If only Luke thought of writing a letter! Rose never knew how he was faring, or when he was coming home until he appeared.

Freda's normally serene face was worried. 'Thank you, Rose, there may be a letter tomorrow. Erik usually writes to me … there are plenty of post offices on the Melbourne road.'

THIRTEEN

THERE WAS A quiet routine to Rose's days as the heat of summer cooled into milder autumn weather. Instead of being an effort, it was a pleasure in cooler weather to carry the basket of eggs down the track to the All Nations hotel. Maeve was always pleased to see her and to play with Ada. 'Reminds me of when I was young, with my little Paddy on my knee,' she said with a laugh that shook the big shoulders.

Of course there was no word from Luke, but Rose didn't expect it. Erik was another matter and the last few times she had been to the post office, she had asked in vain for a letter for Mrs Jensen. Rose believed that bad news travels fast, as they said in Yorkshire, and that they would have heard about it if Erik had come to grief, but she felt a nagging uneasiness about him.

Although Freda said little, Rose understood that droving could be dangerous. Luke had assured her it was one job he wouldn't take; he'd talked to drovers and heard their stories. 'What with sleeping rough, wild cattle, the Ganai clans on your tail and duffing down the track, a man wouldn't have a minute's peace by day or night.' He'd told her that sometimes cattle came in from the big runs that had hardly ever seen a human being, let alone a Cobb & Co. mail coach flying along to make up for lost time. 'Those cattle are toey,' he'd said and Rose could imagine what he meant. 'Duffing' must mean cattle stealing.

'And some of the Ganai are partial to a leg of beef, although they might not take the whole steer. They're good hunters, too.' If something had gone wrong, surely the agent would have let Freda know? Perhaps he had no news, either.

Early one misty morning Rose fed and dressed the baby with her usual care and took to the track along the Haunted Creek. Wisps of vapour curled up from the water to disappear in the blue sky and high in the tree canopy, magpies warbled. It was good to be alive. The air was still; not a leaf moved.

The road was so familiar now that she was able to enjoy the morning as she walked and Rose was watching two lyre birds with their plumed tails spread when a slight movement made her turn round. The dark women were standing on the track where she had just walked, the ghosts of Haunted Creek.

'We follow you for a mile! Did you see?' Sal giggled and Auntie Mary beamed. They both wore cotton dresses and carried their soft grass bags. Rose shook her head; they had startled her a little. 'Haven't been here since long time. We come for berries,' the older woman told her. 'What a lovely little white baby you got!' Both women laughed again and Ada chuckled up at them.

'The first time I saw you, there was a baby with you,' Rose said. 'Is it yours, Sal?'

The girl's eyes were sad. 'My little baby died … got sick. There was nothing could save him. He's gone to heaven now, buried with a cross on his little grave.' She held out thin dark arms to Rose. 'I like to hold your baby for a while.'

'You shall … her name is Ada.' Rather reluctantly, Rose took off the harness and Sal took the baby gently, rocking her. She began to sing in a strange, faraway voice. She sang a lullaby, but it sounded like a sad song of farewell. Rose felt all the sadness of Haunted Creek, of the wider country, in the simple notes that rose and fell. It was a lament for the dead child but she felt that Sal sang too of other sorrows – the passing of a way of life, the loss of country. Sal knew about loss.

Past and future blended as Rose looked down at long grasses, weeping into the clear waters of the stream. Was it old sorrows, or was there sadness in store?

Auntie Mary wiped away tears and then it was over. As she handed Ada back, Sal looked earnestly at the child. 'This baby is strong. She will live.'

Ada chuckled, the spell was broken and the women laughed at her. When they were walking again Rose asked quietly, 'Which are the berries you gather?'

'*Garawed*'s the best – look here.' Sal pointed to a shrub under the trees as they walked along. She turned aside and picked a cluster of berries.

'It looks like an elderberry, only it's white. I never noticed it before!' Rose tried the berries and found them sweet; she must have been blind to miss them. 'Do you eat those little raspberries?' Those she had seen and eaten herself, this last week.

'*Yalaban*? Course we do and quite a few more, some here, some there. You should try them.'

They came to the wider track up to the hotel, where not far away a couple of men were loading food supplies onto a donkey. When they saw the men, the women quickly turned to go, but Rose stopped them and gave them some eggs from her basket. Smiling, they thanked her and put the eggs carefully into their bags. 'See you after,' they said. 'We need to tell you …' And then the track was empty and Rose was alone with the baby. Perhaps she would see them on the way back, or perhaps they meant next year.

Maeve insisted that Ada be left with her while Rose went to the post office, but once again there was no letter from Erik. It was too bad of Erik not to write to his mother. Perhaps the stock agent who employed the drovers would know something; she would ask Bert Carr when next he was going down to Moe. He might be willing to see the agent.

Maeve was holding Ada on her knee when Rose went back to the All Nations, but she handed over the baby quickly as four men came in, demanding bacon and coffee for breakfast. They had obviously been living rough for days. 'Give us plenty of bread with it, missus, we're starving.' Maeve rang a bell and Boris the cook appeared to take the order.

As Rose slipped into the harness again she caught a whiff of eucalyptus oil and realized that the men at the bar were the dreaded eucy men. The tall one was Lordy, the polite Mr Barrington, leaning on the bar looking at the landlady. He took off his hat and bowed to Rose, then went back to gazing at Maeve. She recognized a large hat with a beard under it as Joe and there was the rat-faced Benny and his mate.

As she was turning for the door, Joe caught sight of Rose. 'You again, you bitch. Still bloody here? It's time you left this country before something bad happens to you.' The hoarse voice echoed round the room.

'Here, Joe, can't you be civil in my bar? Everyone is welcome here and you know it.' Maeve brought a fist down on the bar with a crash. 'You can all leave right now unless you apologize – no breakfast for you. I won't have my friends insulted.' Maeve looked magnificent, blue eyes flashing fire. 'Boris, come here!'

The big Russian appeared in the doorway and stood there, silently glowering at the men.

'Please, Mrs Malone, do forgive Joseph. He is extremely hungry and thirsty. We offer no insults to Mrs Teesdale, she has as much right to be here ...' Lordy's cultured voice was lost in a shout from one of the others.

'Push off back to England, you English bitch!'

Boris lumbered forward. There was much noise and confusion, but Rose did not wait to hear any more. She picked up her empty basket, slipped the baby on her back and went off down the track as fast as she could in case Ada heard any more bad words. The eucy men were dangerous, but Lordy – was he one of them? His smooth manner with her might cover up a dangerous streak. Maeve had Boris to keep order and you could see why she'd chosen such a big, brawny cook.

Half a mile from the pub, Rose found the dark women sitting by the creek eating berries and waiting for her. 'Lunch, better than mission tucker.' They smiled, giving her some of the elderberries. She sat down with them, thankful to be among friendly faces after the scene in Maeve's bar. Why did people warn her about Aborigines? But of course she had not met any of their menfolk ... they might be different. There seemed to be a bond between women, a desire for peace and harmony.

'We tell you message now, we should have told before,' Auntie Mary said seriously. 'The drover is safe.'

Rose started. 'Drover? You mean Erik?' Her heart pounded.

'I think so. My cousin said, tell this Rose that live up here somewhere. He didn't know, but we thought of you.' Sal handed over some more berries. 'The drover spoke in his sleep, they thought he said "Rose"... he has been sleeping long time. But he ...'

A shot shattered the peace from the far side of the creek and the dull echo of the shotgun rumbled through the trees. Sal moaned and clutched her chest. Before Rose could move, Auntie Mary jumped up, put her arm round Sal and they limped into the forest. In seconds they were out of sight.

Rose cradled the baby protectively; would they shoot her next? Wild thoughts flashed through her mind: if she were killed, would Maeve take care of Ada? Rose kept her head down low, over the baby. There was a little blood on the bag the women had left behind. Poor Sal had been wounded.

'Winged one. That should teach 'em,' said a rough voice. With horror Rose saw three eucy men were ranged by the water, looking across at her. Lordy was not with them.

'How dare you fire at people!' Rose was so angry that she forgot to be afraid. 'Defenceless women and a baby!'

'Them's not people,' Joe sneered, lowering the shotgun. 'Let it be a lesson to you. Just because of you, we gets thrown out of our pub. And then we find you talking friendly with blacks, that's bad. Don't come down here no more or you'll get bloody shot the next time.'

'Blacks won't come back here again,' said the one called Benny as Rose turned away. 'Not ever. They can't stand lead, y'know.' The others laughed, a pitiless laugh almost like that of the kookaburras.

The homeward trail for Rose was blurred with tears. It was quite likely that she would never see Auntie Mary and Sal again. It was even worse because they obviously knew something about Erik, they could have told her where he was. They'd said that berries were easy to find everywhere, but they'd come up here again to see her. To see Rose, and look what it had brought them.

The gulf between black and white was not surprising, if people of either colour behaved like this. Perhaps the eucy men had been attacked by Aborigines in years gone by. But it sounded as though an Aboriginal man was looking after Erik; Auntie Mary's cousin.

Erik … he had called out her name in his sleep. A surge of love washed over Rose and with it came a glimmer of understanding. Erik may have gone droving because of her, because she was married to Luke and he'd decided to keep away from her. He'd always seemed to put her interests before his own.

Stopping at home only for bread and cheese and to feed the baby, Rose went on to Wattle Tree to see Freda. There wasn't much to tell and perhaps Freda would not believe Auntie Mary, but it was the first news since Erik left.

Rose explained briefly that she knew the women and that they had passed on a simple message – *the drover is safe* – before they were fired at and ran away.

'Thank you, Rose,' Freda said. School was finished for the day and they were sitting on the veranda that Erik had built, Freda with the baby on her knee. 'If he's had trouble, Aborigines would help him if they knew of it. He's always been a friend to them and they tend to remember … I'm very glad to have the message, though I wish we knew more.'

If they hadn't been shot at, the women might have been able to tell Rose more. 'But why are those eucy men – and other men, even

Luke – so against dark people? They are different, of course, but I can't see why there shouldn't be peace between us and them.'

Freda sighed. 'For many reasons, Rose. It was natural for the original people to resent the arrival of white men. So sometimes they tried to get even, and so … the conflict was there from the start.' She thought for a while and then said, 'There's also, if you'll forgive me, a belief – not with people like you, of course – that the British, or perhaps the English, are a superior race. They do the rest of the world a favour by imposing their way of doing things. That's how the Empire was built, but not all the Aborigines want to be loyal subjects of Queen Victoria.'

'We were always taught to be proud of the Empire … but I see what you mean,' Rose said slowly. 'Weren't you?' She had taken her nationality for granted.

Freda smiled. 'I'm looking at it from the outside, in a way. Erik and I are officially British subjects, all Victorians are. I suppose we're loyal to the Empire and the Queen. But I was born in Sweden, so I tend to take a more detached view.'

Rose went home thoughtfully. Victoria was not just an outpost of England, like a remote Yorkshire parish with the same traditions. It was a different identity, a mixture. All Nations was a good name for the hotel. Her little Ada would grow up speaking English, but not Yorkshire, and she would join a community with people from all sorts of backgrounds.

By the time she arrived at her hut, Rose was very tired and it was a shock to see a man sitting in her chair on the veranda. She needed to feed Ada and a visitor was the last thing she wanted. The crickets were chirping in the garden and the birds were singing undisturbed, which meant he must have been there for a while, silently waiting.

The man unfolded long legs and stood up. 'Good evening, Mrs Teesdale,' he said and she saw that it was Lordy, cleaner than usual and wearing a fresh shirt. 'Forgive the intrusion. I am most concerned that you were fired upon by those ruffians today. As soon as they told me, I came to see whether you need any assistance. Where is your husband?'

'Thank you, Mr Barrington,' Rose said faintly, subsiding into the chair next to him. 'Luke's cutting a tree down somewhere,' she said evasively. It was probably true, unless he was in a pub. She didn't want the eucy men to know that he was away.

'The police should hear about this, of course. But one hesitates to rock the boat, as it were.' Lordy lounged in his seat, chatting away, and Rose put the billy on to make tea. 'I do hope the young woman is not badly hurt.'

Barrington told her he had a house down by the Tangil River and had been looking for gold, but had not been successful. He had sent for money from England and when it came he would buy some land, but until it arrived he wanted to work with the distillers and understand the process. 'And a rough crowd they are, as you have seen,' he admitted. 'Joe said he didn't really intend to hit the native women, just to fire over their heads. But he's a lousy shot, y'know.'

'In that case, he is even more dangerous. I wonder how you can put up with them,' Rose admitted, while one half of her mind wondered what they could have for supper. She had no meat and she'd sold all the eggs, but if her visitor didn't go soon, she would have to feed him. It was the rule of the bush: anyone there at a mealtime was fed.

'I'm so glad you are unhurt. I brought you a gift,' Lordy said as though he had read her mind. 'Three blackfish from the creek … *Gadopsis marmoratus*, if you wish me to be exact.'

Rose smiled at Lordy's way of talking. 'Thank you.'

'Shall we eat together, if you don't mind? I will cook them, of course. And we can save one for your husband.' He took the fish out of a large bag by his side, packed in wet ferns.

Rose went into the cabin to feed the baby and put her to bed, while Lordy cleaned and cooked the fish. He asked for a little fat, coated them with flour and sizzled them in Rose's large frying pan over the fire. She felt quite safe and in any case, there was nothing she could do about the visit; he had decided to stay for supper and in a way it was good to have his company. He'd even brought a lemon in his pocket.

'Thank you, Mr Barrington,' Rose said politely after the meal. She had provided bread and a small salad from her garden and the fish had been tasty.

'Please call me Jasper,' the tall man said humbly. 'And may I call you Rose? I fear English convention would not approve, but then I would not be sitting alone with you by your fire if we were on our native heath, so to speak.'

Rose decided to ask a question; it was usually considered ill-mannered to question people too much, but she wanted to know more about the man. 'Someone told me you're a lord … is it true? Perhaps I should call you Lord Barrington.'

Lordy sighed. 'Alas, it is true and that is why I prefer my Christian name. It is a great impediment here to bear an English title, especially if you wish to impress the Irish.' He looked at her solemnly but with a twinkle in his eye. If it were not for the scar, Lordy would be quite handsome in a big-boned way. His beak of a nose made him look like an aristocrat, but he could easily be an actor.

Rose considered this. 'The Irish? You mean Maeve?'

'Maeve Malone, the most beautiful woman in the world,' Lordy said dreamily. 'I wish to marry her, but she scorns me!' He paused for effect. 'Well, not absolutely, but she will not commit herself. Now, if my inheritance were to materialize, I would be able to offer her much more. I think she would overlook my – um – unfortunate background, were I to present her with evidence that I could support her.'

'But Maeve likes her independence, she told me so,' Rose objected. 'And I don't think you could buy her with money. Wealth would be useful, of course, but maybe you need to impress her in some other way.'

'I fear you may be right, Rose. I shall have to think of some other way to her heart. And now, I must leave you. Thank you for your gracious hospitality, and compliments to your husband. I hope he enjoys his fish.' Placing his hat on his head, Lord Barrington stalked away, leaving Rose feeling as though she had spent an evening in high society.

FOURTEEN

'MRS TEESDALE, COULD you leave the class for a while?' Freda's careworn face appeared round the door of the little room. Rose drew a deep breath; there must be bad news about Erik. A feeling of panic rose, but she fought it. 'Of course, the girls can manage on their own quite well.' The sewing class nodded energetically, gathered round a low table where they were practising cutting out dress patterns from newspaper. Little Ada was sleeping peacefully at the back of the room.

'Now remember, girls, don't put pins in your mouth,' Rose reminded them on her way to the door. It was traditional for dressmakers, but dangerous. Joining Freda, she braced herself to hear the news.

Freda had tears in her eyes. She led the way out of the building into the noonday glare to where two men were sitting with bowed shoulders in the shade of a tree. 'It's more private here,' she said. 'Please sit down, Rose. I'm afraid the news is bad.'

Rose sat opposite the men. They were covered in dust, unshaven and with red eyes. They stood up as she approached, then sank down again and picked up their glasses of water. Two horses with heads down stood in the shade by the fence, covered in dust and sweat.

With a stab of horror, she realized who the men were: Tom Appleyard, Luke's employer, and Jim Carlyle. They were bringing bad news to her, not to Freda – unless by chance they knew something about Erik....

A kookaburra laughed harshly once, and was quiet. Bees buzzed in the garden flowers as Tom said gravely, 'We came as soon as we could. Mrs Teesdale … Rose, I'm afraid your husband has had an accident.'

The world seemed to spin for a while and the garden tilted, then righted itself. Rose found she was breathing fast. 'How badly is he hurt? Where is he?' Her mind was working frantically; where was there a hospital? She'd heard that they were going to build one in Warragul, to service the area between Melbourne and Sale, so there was no hospital yet for over 100 miles in either direction. Only Martha and people like her, trying to help the sick and wounded. Oh Luke …

'He's dead, lass. We hate to have to tell you this.' Tom passed his hand over his face wearily and she saw that Jim, haggard, pale and wretched, could not meet her eyes. 'It was a big tree … it was nearly sawn through, ready to come down, and of course we have to get out of the way.' He sighed heavily and fumbled for his pipe.

Rose held her breath but she knew what was coming next, could see it in her mind's eye.

'The tree fell a bit different to how we thought and Luke … he was running, but he tripped on a root and the tree got him. He died on the spot, he wouldn't have known anything … no suffering. That's a small mercy.' Tom puffed on his pipe desperately.

Luke was dead. That bright, careless laughter she would never hear again. All her plans for a better understanding of each other were gone. She crumbled a leaf in her fingers and the sharp smell of eucalypt surrounded her.

Rose knew she should have thanked them. They had obviously ridden straight here to tell her, but she was numb. No words would come and she felt faint.

Freda took one of Rose's hands and held it. 'Rose will need to come to terms with this,' she said quietly. 'Can you tell us where is he now? Did you bring him home for burial?'

Jim said with an effort to control his voice, 'He's buried at

Noojee, in a little cemetery there. It was all they could do, Rose. We thought you'd understand, it was what he would have wanted. They say the name Noojee means the valley of rest.' He gulped for a moment and then went on, 'Luke was full of plans for the future. He was going to make life better for you, Rose.'

Tom added, 'Please accept our sympathy. We know how hard it is for you … not long come out from England and all. And with a little baby.' He shook his head. 'It beats me why these things have to happen. We all did our best to be safe …'

She found her voice. 'Thank you.' Luke was not coming home. A fierce emotion went through Rose, a mixture of pain and black anger. Fate had let them down. Ada would grow up without knowing her father, Rose would go on being lonely and the farm would never be created. Nothing mattered any more.

They sat for a while in silence, thinking of Luke. Freda moved eventually and said to the men, 'Please come into my house and have some food. You too, Rose.' She looked older, more grey since they heard the news.

Rose stood up shakily and remembered her vow to be strong. She was going to need strength as never before. 'Thank you for all you've done,' she said to Tom and Jim. She had no tears yet. 'Is there anything that I need to do?' Jim took two steps towards her as if to comfort her, and stopped. Pulling her shoulders back, Rose went into the house behind the men.

They sat round Freda's table with cups of tea and the men accepted bread and cheese. Tom handed over a damp envelope. 'Death certificate,' he muttered. 'Doctor on his way through to Sydney. It was lucky he was there.'

After a while Rose went back to her class, but she found it impossible to concentrate. Her pupils looked at her with wide eyes, aware that something had happened. She took Ada into the house and mechanically fed and changed her.

The day wore on slowly; time itself seemed to have slowed to the pace of grief. Gradually, anger was replaced by a devastating sense of loss. Rose knew she would always remember Luke as he stood at the turn of the track, waving goodbye. They had just begun to understand each other a little; there was so much more she might have done to encourage him, so many things they could have done together.

Life was cruel. It hadn't been easy for either of them in those first months when the pattern of their lives was being set. It wasn't the lack of money, although more money would have made it easier. But at first, Rose had needed to concentrate on surviving, getting used to the shock of the new environment. Luke had probably been trying to adjust to thinking about a wife and family, instead of looking out for himself. The baby's crying had been hard for them both to bear. With more time, things could have been different.

For that week and for several more, time passed in a haze; the world felt unreal to Rose, like a bad dream. 'I'll take you to see Harriet's father,' Freda offered. One day when the school had a half-term holiday, they yoked up Erik's oldest horse in the four-wheel buggy and trundled down to Moe.

'I think Erik might marry Miss Sinclair,' Freda said as they jogged along. They still had no more news of Erik. 'She's not used to the bush, but most unmarried women he might meet live in the town and they do seem to adjust to farm life, once they marry. He hasn't mentioned her to me recently, but …'

'I hope so,' Rose replied sadly. Harriet Sinclair would come to a much better farm and environment than the bark hut among the trees that Rose called home. But Erik was still missing.

Rose was not at all interested in legal matters, but Freda was determined to help her to sort out Luke's affairs. Mr Sinclair was quietly sympathetic. 'Fortunately, Mr Teesdale's papers are with me,' he told Rose. Freda had expected as much as he was the only lawyer in the area that she knew. He scrabbled in a tall mahogany cabinet and brought out a box file.

Rose learned that Luke had taken out a joint title on the block of land in both their names, so the patch of forest and the two huts now belonged to Rose. The bad news was that the government's conditions of sale included a clause that directed them to 'improve' the land and, of course, to clear it. 'Some of it's fenced, and there is a house,' Rose said defensively, not looking at Freda. On her knee, the baby gurgled as though she understood the deception; house was a grand name for their dwelling.

Mr Sinclair pursed his lips. 'Your best course will be to sell the land, Mrs Teesdale. Let someone else worry about improvements.'

'It's too soon to make any changes,' Rose said quietly over the baby's head and Freda nodded. Freda had warned her against making decisions while she was still badly shocked. Time would heal the hurt a little, she'd said as one widow to another, and then it would be easier to think clearly. She had also said, 'You will feel anger at first.' It was true.

Luke had signed a will leaving everything to Rose. There were no debts, thank goodness, but no capital either apart from the cattle. All the money they had was in Rose's tin trunk. A memory stirred, of Luke saying that he'd owed money to Jim and was working for him to pay it off. She must ask whether the whole debt had been paid.

Mr Sinclair was still shuffling papers, peering through rimless spectacles on the end of his nose. He came to the bottom of the box and found a bulky sealed envelope. 'There's this, though. It's for you.'

Luke wrote badly and it was difficult to read the words: In the Event of My Death, Please Give This To My Wife Rose Teesdale.

Rose opened the envelope with trembling hands. There was no letter inside, but a heavy object fell out. It was a gold nugget, gleaming with a dull shine. Luke had left her gold. Ada reached out her baby hands to it.

'He came in one day, not so long ago,' the solicitor told them. 'Said he'd been prospecting and thought he'd better put it away for you as a sort of insurance.'

Tears began to fall as Rose realized that she'd judged the lad too harshly. He and Jim had not spent all their gold on drink, after all. He'd thought about the risks he took and had done this to safeguard her. If only he'd told her what he had done, if only she could thank him! What a strange mixture Luke had been: thoughtful and indifferent by turns.

When she looked up, Mr Sinclair was talking about the gold and offering to get it valued for her. Weighing it in her hand, Rose wondered why Luke had not continued with his search for gold. This success should have made him want to go on. Had he been trying to impress her by working hard to earn money? She would never know. 'I would like to leave it here with you, for now,' she told the solicitor.

It was several weeks before Rose had recovered enough to take eggs down to the hotel. Meeting her at the door, Maeve swept her into a huge, perfumed embrace. 'Rose, mavourneen, we heard about Luke and what a shock it was too. But I know you're a brave girl, you'll keep going! You won't be off to England at all? Not now you've had a little time to be thinking. New widows now, they panic, they often scuttle back home on the next boat, God bless 'em, and us needing more females in the country!' She stood back and looked at Rose with shrewd, kind eyes. 'You've lost weight and no wonder it is.'

'You talk as though there's a lot of widows about,' Rose told her. There was something comforting about Maeve's soft voice.

Maeve shrugged. 'Young men get themselves killed, more's the pity, but so it happens. For the rest, there's no doctors for miles and miles and never a priest, and so you take your luck as you find it.'

'It's all luck,' Rose agreed. 'Ada was lucky to be born … the birth could have gone wrong.'

Maeve nodded. 'Well, now, and folks can die from lack of care, you know that. There's mud fever sometimes down the river, the men come in here with yellow eyes and very sorry for themselves they are … but I reckon women are tougher than men, when it comes to surviving. If men had the babies there'd be a fine to-do.'

Rose felt her stiff face moving in a smile, the first for many days. 'There would.'

Maeve led the way into her sitting room. 'And now, Rose, we will have a cup or two of Boris's coffee and you can tell me your plans.' She smiled happily, plumping up cushions in the chairs. 'I dearly love a plan and it'll help you to clear your mind. I'm glad you're back – we've been short of eggs for weeks and the boys are getting restless. But they don't complain, not when Boris is in the kitchen.'

In the face of so much cheerfulness, Rose felt her mood begin to lighten a little. Ada was taken out of the harness and put on the sofa, where she went to sleep. 'I haven't really started to plan,' she admitted. She had got as far as realizing that waiting for an absent husband to come home was far different from sitting alone, knowing that she had only herself to rely on. 'I'm not sure whether to go home or not,' she admitted. 'My father has a nice farm, but I don't care for my stepmother.' That was putting it mildly.

Maeve sipped her coffee with eyes narrowed, thinking, while Rose's mind strayed to Kirkby. Should she go back? There could be more support for them in Yorkshire, but no real place. Luke's parents would be sad, no doubt she would hear from them when the English mails came. But their loss was cushioned by the fact that they hadn't expected to see their son again when he went off to the other side of the world. They'd already faced their loss. There were two younger brothers to give them grandchildren eventually. Her father would write too, but he'd never had any real suggestions for her future.

A noise erupted in the bar and Maeve went through to see what was happening. When she came back Rose was half asleep, worn out by the sorrow of the last few weeks. Rousing herself, she said, 'There are so many things to decide ...' Perhaps Maeve would help her. She was an experienced woman.

'And of course you are the only one in the world that can decide them,' Maeve said, waving her hand for emphasis. 'Nobody can make you a plan, tell you what to do. But I can suggest how you might be working on it, for sure.'

Maeve wasn't going to tell her what to do. At the back of her mind Rose had expected Maeve to take charge. But she didn't want that, although part of her longed to be given no options, just a straight course to follow. 'Tell me,' she said.

'It's better with pencil and paper, but you can be doing it in your head. Take your time, there's no hurry, take a week or two.' Maeve paused, emphasizing she was in no hurry. 'Make a list of all the good things, the strengths you have, your assets, even friends.'

Rose thought hard, but couldn't come up with many assets.

Maeve went on quietly, 'Then a list of the weaknesses. The obvious one is no man in the house and too many trees to chop down, I would reckon. Isn't that right? The problems, there's never a lack in this world. But after all that, you can look into the future a little – what chances are there of improving your situation?'

There was too much darkness in the future; Rose felt weary.

After a while Maeve went on, 'On the other side of the coin, what might threaten you – and for all love don't say the eucy men! They've gone over Port Albert way for a while and good riddance to them.' Maeve's black hair shone as she shook it back.

Rose thought about all this. Little Ada was a strength and a weakness, a reason for living but a brake on Rose's activities. What would be best for her child?

'I suppose,' Rose said slowly, 'I could look at going to England the same way … for and against, whichever adds up the highest, taking feelings out of it and just looking at facts.'

Maeve nodded. 'You can do that, macushla. But then, whichever way it goes at all, you follow your gut feeling in the end!' They both laughed.

On the way home Rose looked out hopefully for the dark women, but she met nobody. Perhaps the eucy men had gone away for fear of revenge. Sal had been injured and the men in her group might be after Joe and his horrible friends.

Jim Carlyle called to offer practical sympathy. He was very quiet, grieving for Luke, no doubt, and he said he'd been unwell. She was tempted to let him help. Jim was big and strong, he could do work that she could not, and he had seemed to understand her situation better than Luke at times.

'There's nothing I need help with at the moment,' Rose said. 'I'm just living from day to day.'

When he had gone she thought about his offer, using Maeve's system. It would be a great advantage to have someone finish the fencing, maybe even clear the land. She could offer a share in the profits perhaps. But there would be disadvantages: it would put her in his debt, at least for a time. He might be planning to court her, after a decent interval of mourning. Rose was not vain, but Jim had once told her that women were scarce in Haunted Creek and he'd said he envied Luke.

Rose realized that she was certain of one thing: she was not going to marry Jim or anyone else. Erik's future was with Miss Sinclair, supposing he came back safely, and she wasn't going to come between them. It would be too selfish. She knew that she was not the same person, not the woman Erik had known.

The way she felt now, it might be years before she was fit company for a man. Rose was grieving for Luke with an intensity that surprised her, guilty that she hadn't appreciated his good qualities enough. Given just a little more time, they might have loved each other. She would be faithful to his memory.

Then there was the child: she would rear Ada according to her own ideas and with no interference from anybody else, however well-meaning they were. That was point number two.

There was a third aspect. Rose didn't want gossip about her to circulate among the settlers. Even in this remote spot, single women couldn't have visits from men without eyebrows being raised. She would have to be very careful.

'Right!' she said to Ada when all this had been thought through. 'We've got some things straight already, my girl.' She often talked to the baby; how else would Ada learn to talk herself? Already she seemed to be listening and was gurgling replies.

Jim offered to take Rose to visit Luke's grave, but fortunately Tom Appleyard had offered too and in the end Tom and his wife and Jim all went with her in Tom's cart to Noojee. Rose was entranced by the stands of tall mountain ash and the brilliant green tree ferns under them, the little bubbling creeks and the undulating country, with small clearings here and there.

Standing at Luke's grave with its simple wooden cross, Rose made a silent promise. She would bring up Ada to the very best of her ability and would make sure that her father was not forgotten. Jim and Tom took off their hats and Tom read a prayer for the dead. Mrs Appleyard took Rose's arm in sympathy.

Leaving him in that peaceful spot with the breeze whispering through the trees, Rose felt slightly comforted. Luke was at rest, he was better there than being maimed by the terrible accident and living a life of pain and frustration.

On the way home they were all quiet and Rose was able to think with no distractions. What could she do to make it clear that she had not forgotten Luke, that she was not looking for another husband? Under the canopy of the tall trees it came to her: she would do what the Queen had done. Over fifteen years since Prince Albert's death, the English papers reported that she still wore black.

Rose remembered she had some plain black cotton to make dresses and she could buy a black shawl. Wearing black would save any explanations; anyone who met her would know her situation straightaway. All the colour in her life would be saved for Ada. Now she understood why widows she had known in Kirkby had worn black. It was the perfect answer.

FIFTEEN

THERE WERE FEW sounds, just the soft lapping of water and the mewing call of wood ducks in the distance. The sky was enormous, a great bowl of blue with small white clouds moving slowly across it. From where he lay on a springy bed of dried grass, Erik idly watched the clouds.

After a while, or maybe after a day or so, he raised his head and now he could spot ducks among the reeds, black ducks and little teal, swimming and dabbling. A heron stood patiently on one leg, watching for fish. Dragonflies danced above the water, rising and falling with the breeze. Erik moved and his muscles protested. His whole body ached.

Where was he? Erik propped himself on one elbow and a black face appeared. Was he a prisoner? The Ganai had got him; this must be their camp. In his present state, there was nothing he could do about it.

'You right now?' The face looked anxious. 'You been sick, we thought might die.'

'Ah.' Erik's brain felt sluggish and he digested this for a while. He knew who he was ... but there was something he should be doing. 'What happened?' That was the safest question. He might be a prisoner. The Ganai man looked friendly enough, but you heard some bad stories. Delving into his memory with difficulty, Erik had the feeling that the Ganai were his friends. There was a big sad face, back in the past....

'You wait.' The face disappeared and a woman brought water,

which Erik drank feverishly. After a while she gave him a broth made of some kind of shellfish; it tasted good.

Gradually he felt more normal and Erik pieced together the facts of his situation. It would be so good to lie back on the grassy bed and sleep again, but he must think. Painfully he rearranged his aching limbs.

To begin with, he was on the Great Swamp. The three-chain road skirted this huge area of wetland, keeping clear of the water and the fogs. The swamp covered many miles of ground and Erik thought it stretched about half way to Melbourne, unless there was more than one swamp. He'd often watched the birds as he rode by, but white men rarely went into the swamp because of snakes and mosquitoes.

Where was home from here? It was afternoon, the sun was moving to the west. It would be too far to walk home; it was a few hours' ride from the swamp to the foothills of the mountains.

How did he get here? He'd been riding, that was it, with a mob of cattle. With George and Sep, probably not far from here. They had been surprised in the night and – and then everything was blank. He remembered shouts, the bellowing of the herd. A huge steer with horns came out of the dark at him, crazed with fright … and nothing more.

The man came back and squatted beside him. 'We talk now. I am Lewis.'

'Erik is my name.' They looked at each other and Erik sensed a great goodwill. 'Thank you for looking after me.'

Lewis looked down and then said, 'Very pleased you come good. Erik is a friend of Ganai – remember little Toby?' He grinned.

The memory, that sad face, came back to Erik now. Little Toby, a huge man by Ganai standards but very gentle, had been in trouble some years ago, through no fault of his own. Erik had intervened as he was about to be locked up, having seen the brawl that caused the trouble.

Lewis was hard to follow, but Erik pieced together the story of what had happened to get him here. The Ganai group had heard the cattle stampede, so this camp must be quite near the road. They had naturally gone along to see whether there was any stray beef for them to pick up. It sometimes happened. Lewis had almost fallen over Erik as he lay unconscious by the side of the track. 'If big thunder mail coach come by, you might be in little pieces now,' he said seriously. It was true. Cobb & Co. drivers were perched up so high and went so fast that a body lying in the road would never be seen.

The hunters had picked up Erik and brought him back to their camp, not knowing who he was until one of the women said he'd helped Little Toby. 'You are a very heavy man, Erik,' Lewis told him.

'You seem to know a lot, Lewis. What happened to the others – and where are the cattle now?" Erik rubbed his stiff limbs. It wasn't often that cattle spooked badly once they had settled in for the night. He hoped the Ganai hadn't disturbed them.

Lewis looked shocked. 'You think we took them steers? Nah! It was white men, they took half the mob, went away fast in dark towards the sea.' He pointed south. 'Your mates got back the rest and then they look for you, Erik, think you gone home. One horse missing, see, we got it. Our Lenny heard them say horse was gone. *The bugger's gone home to his mammy and left it all to us*, the old one said. He was swearing and stamping about, that one.' Lewis grinned. 'You much safer with us mob.' He sauntered off.

Ganai hunters had been out that night and the drovers had never known it. In this swamp country, on the rivers and by the sea, hidden eyes might be watching you at any time and hidden ears listening to your conversations. Erik tried to concentrate on the information. White men? Were cattle duffers out that night too? So George and Sep went on down the track; they had to go on, to pick up the other consignments.

Erik staggered to his feet and went away from the shelter. When he got back there was water waiting for him in a large shell and he washed. He could now see the bruising, particularly on his ribs. Breathing was painful, so he must have broken ribs.

The sun went down and the camp fire was lit; something was roasting. Erik was too weak to do anything but sit by the glow, watching the light on dark faces, listening to the laughter. He was given roast meat – had they in fact bagged a steer? – and a kind of damper. It was better not to ask where the meat came from. After the meal came the stories, a soothing murmur of sound in the tribal language that chimed in with the moving lights of stars, reflected in the water.

These people had saved his life and they were taking pleasure in it. 'You right now?' One by one they came up to him, shyly smiling, and touched his shoulder, the firelight flickering on their smiles.

'Thank you, I'm right.' Erik's head was clearing. 'Thank you, the meat was good.'

The next day Lewis showed him his horse Vulcan and the two dogs, tied up and waiting for him. Dan was nearly hysterical, his whole body wagging a greeting. Lewis grinned. 'We could have ate the horse, but there's plenty of meat.'

Thinking of riding home the next day, Erik found he was too weak yet for the hard ride into the hills. He couldn't even climb onto Vulcan's back in this state; he would have to rest and get his strength back.

For the next few days he went fishing with the men, ate the fish in the evening and slept soundly all night. But time was going by and he had responsibilities.

Had the stock agent told his mother he was missing? 'I'm worried that my mother doesn't know what has happened,' he told Lewis as they sat under a tree one day. Erik had promised to send a letter from a post office on one of the early stages. How long ago had they set out?

'No worry.' Lewis spread his hands in a gesture of calm. 'My cousin told Rose you're safe. She'll tell your mother.'

'Rose? How do you know her?'

Lewis laughed happily. 'Sal and Auntie Mary, they got to know her. And you Erik, you shouted out, like. When you were sick – you said the name two, three times. Before you woke up. So then I thought she's your woman, but Sal says she lives with another bloke. It's not good, ay?' His expression changed to a serious frown. 'But anyway, this Rose was happy when they told her. She must like you.'

'She's ... a friend of my mother's,' Erik said quietly.

Lewis chuckled. 'Oh, ay. You want her, you should ask for her, real loud. Good woman, Auntie Mary said.'

Erik sighed. She was a good woman. The less he said about Rose, the better.

'But there's more. Same day them bad eucy men took a shot, they hit Sal. And then – and then she died, after.' Lewis was quiet for a time.

'I'm sorry, that is very bad.' What more could Erik say? *Sorry we can't all live in harmony, that we've never tried to understand each other. And now it's too late, the patterns have been set.* He sighed.

'So we're after catching them eucy men but they gone away.' Lewis stood up and stretched. 'One day we find them.' He looked out over the water for a long time. 'Anyway, you want to come on a duck hunt?'

Each evening a flock of ducks came in at dusk, circling down to a small stretch of open water near the camp. Tonight, hunters would be waiting. During the day nets had been spread in the shallow water, big nets made from tough creeper stems. Erik took his place in the group but he had no weapon. He expected to see spears but the seven or eight other men carried only curved sticks.

As the ducks came in, the tension grew until the leader gave a signal and the men shouted. The ducks took off again, swinging out in a wide circle over the swamp. It seemed an odd procedure. After a few minutes the birds came back, returning to the lake in a tighter group. Down, down they came and just before they touched the water, a rain of sticks beat down on them from above, pushing them into the nets. The ducks rose again and came back to the men's feet; some of them were caught in the hand. Wading into the shallow water, Erik helped to pull the strings that drew the nets tight. 'Goodness!' he said.

The man next to him chuckled. 'You never seen this before?"

Erik shook his head. He sometimes shot ducks to eat in the autumn, as well as other game. He always felt regret, a sadness that the game had to die. The dark people seemed to express this feeling, standing in silence for a few moments before carrying the harvest home.

The ducks were prepared by the women and roasted in the ashes of a fire, wrapped in wet bark. Hours later, they were eaten with damper made from yam daisies. After supper the songs began and Erik leaned back, content. He would worry about going home in a day or two. Apart from his injuries he could feel himself slowing down, adjusting to a different way of life.

How strange it was that white men had died of hunger in the bush, while these people lived so well. Of course, the swamp was a rich source of food but Europeans probably ate too much. These people were slim and seemed to be fit but they ate much less than he was used to. Perhaps, though, their way of life didn't call for hard, regular physical toil, as farming did.

A few days later, reality came back with a thud when Erik saddled his horse, collected his dogs and departed for Moe. Now he could feel how stiff and sore he was and for the first time he noticed a lame leg that made riding difficult.

'Where the hell have you been?' The cattle agent scowled at him from behind the big desk. Duncan Black's face was well formed for scowling although normally he wore a pleasant expression, being all things to all people as an agent needed to be. 'You deserted on the first night out. I couldn't believe it. I thought you were steady. Been on the grog ever since, by the look of you. Well, I won't be employing you again, Jensen.'

Erik faced the hostile man across the desk, but he felt lethargic and the timeless influence of the dark people was still with him. There was no point in quarrelling. He had tried to clean up, not very successfully. The baggage roll was still on the horse, but he'd given most of his clothes to the Ganai men who had saved his life, which had pleased them. His shirt and trousers were in rags and his beard was clean but unkempt. No doubt he looked like a drunk. Outside, the horse and two collies waited, looking just the same as he did, but in better condition. Erik had lost a lot of weight.

'Duncan, I've been ill,' Erik said quietly. 'Got knocked unconscious the first night. Can you tell me what happened to George and the cattle?'

'The men have gone down the track, of course,' Black said shortly. 'Somebody has to get the job done. Sent me a note from Shady Creek – said they thought you'd gone home. They were angry with me for sending them out with a dud.'

'I was knocked out,' Erik explained patiently.

The agent was not listening. 'Sep saw you go down. They thought half the herd had trampled you but when they went to look for the body, you'd gone.' He shuffled papers irritably. 'You managed to lose half the first mob between you and George knows what he's doing, so you're to blame.'

'I suppose George is not back yet to tell you the tale?'

'No. You lost a hundred head, prime steers they were. That's a big loss and I'd bought them, I stand it. What possessed you to camp on the road that night instead of making for the stock paddock at Steve's Creek? That's what we agreed – you should have stuck to the plan. You had plenty of daylight to do it.' Black glared at him.

Suddenly, light dawned and the facts fell into place. 'We met a couple of young blokes a few miles out from Moe, bringing cattle this way,' Erik told him. 'They didn't turn off down Moe River track as they should've and we couldn't turn off at all, so the mobs got mixed up. It took hours to sort them out and those lads just stood and watched us draft them. You know how long that can take.

It would have been worse but the other mob was young stock, so we could tell the difference.' He looked at Black, willing him to understand.

'So?' The agent was shuffling papers impatiently.

'I realize now what they were up to. They did that on purpose to delay us, so we couldn't get to Steve's Creek before dark. The steers were out in the open but they were well fed and watered. They bedded down quiet enough, so we thought it would be safe. We were set up – it was easy to rush them on the road.'

At last the agent was listening. 'So you think the duffers delayed you.'

'Yes. I think John Smith and his mates came back and stirred them up and managed to run off with half of them before George and Sep could get going.' He paused. 'I heard sudden bellowing … I don't remember anything after that. I woke up in a blackfellas' camp. You surely don't believe I would have left them the first time anything went wrong?' Erik sat down on a chair, feeling rather weak. 'How long is it since we left?'

'Six weeks, man.' Duncan Black stood up and came round the desk. 'George would have been back with the full tale by now, but he took another mob along the coast. I don't know whether he worked out what happened. Well, it seems I owe you an apology, Erik.' They shook hands. 'Where are my cattle now, do you think?'

'Lewis, the Ganai man that looked after me, thought they'd gone south. Maybe they'd run them down to Port Albert and ship them round the coast, change the brands on the way so they couldn't be traced.' Erik thought a moment. 'The young stock they were driving might have been stolen, too.'

Black sighed. 'We'll never catch them now … cattle duffers are getting worse all the time. You'd better give me a description of these young thieves. Now, come to my house and clean up afore your mother sees you. If you go home like that she'll never let you out again.'

Freda was startled, even after Erik's 'clean up', when her son rode into the yard that evening and climbed stiffly down from the saddle, landing rather heavily. She held him tightly and he tried not to wince; the ribs still ached. Looking down at her, he thought she had aged while he'd been away.

'Oh, Erik, you're so thin,' she said, leading his horse into the stable. The dogs played around her, happy to be home. Erik felt so weak he leaned on the stable door and watched his mother look after the animals.

In the house, Freda lit the kerosene lamp and pulled a pot of stew on to the stove. 'I've made some bread today … now, sit down and tell me about it. I heard you were safe, but no more. What kept you?'

Under the shaggy hair Erik could still feel a large bump on his head. He'd been lucky to live, but the headaches still persisted. 'Give me a glass of something strong and I'll tell you.'

It had been a long ride and Erik wanted to go to bed, but he had to talk to Freda. The collie Dan, the only one allowed in the house, sat on his feet as though willing him to stay at home and no doubt his mother felt the same. When he'd told the story, Freda gave a sigh. 'What a good job the Ganai were there … but I can't understand how they knew to tell Rose that you were alive, even when they didn't seem to know your name. *The drover is safe*, that was the message.'

Erik suppressed a yawn. 'It's surprising what those people know, Mother. They must have known where we live – I'd seen some of them before in Moe – and they probably gave the message to the only person they could talk to up here. Most of the settlers are afraid of them, you know.'

'It's a pity. Rose asked me one day why we can't be more friendly with the Ganai. I suppose, on both sides, the gulf is too wide.'

'I felt quite at home with them, you know.' Erik was already half asleep. 'I suppose it's a good life in summer, but I wouldn't want to be living outside in the cold winter months. Lewis and the rest … they were so genuine, somehow.'

SIXTEEN

IT WAS THE next day before Erik asked his mother for her news. They sat at breakfast in the sunny kitchen and Freda ladled out porridge as she told him what had happened on the farm. Then she said, 'There's bad news, I'm afraid. Luke Teesdale was killed. Rose is taking it badly, which is not surprising.'

Erik felt anger rising, threatening to choke him. Luke had never deserved a girl like Rose; he'd let her down all along the way. 'What did the young fool do? He should've taken better care of himself … leaving a wife and baby. Irresponsible to the last, obviously.'

'Now, Erik, don't speak ill of the dead. Luke was killed by a falling tree. It could happen to anyone. He'd made provision for Rose – the land is hers and there's valuables in safekeeping …' Freda looked at him uneasily. 'My dear, has your accident affected you? You seem a little – angry.'

'Of course not, Mother,' her son said crossly and saw her wry smile. Was it a normal reaction? Poor Rose! She would remember the youth's perfections but not his faults, of course. People often did that when someone died. She'd always been very loyal to Luke and now she'd be devoted to his memory.

In spite of his first reaction to Luke's death, over the next few days Erik began to feel a spark of optimism, growing from a tiny seed. Of course Rose would be grieving for Luke. He would leave her alone, give her time to get over him. But … in time, his memory was bound to fade. She would be free and he would wait for her, years if necessary. He remembered that night of the dogs, the way they had clung together. It had been a reaction to the fear and horror, but there was more to it than that.

Erik made up his mind. He would work hard on the farm, increase production, build another house – the very thought of marriage to Rose gave him energy. He would exercise the lame leg and make a complete recovery.

'Will you cut my hair, Mother?' Erik asked that night when school was over. He needed to get back to normal, to overcome the lethargy of the past few weeks.

Rose had given up the sewing class and so Erik didn't see her for some weeks. One Sunday the vicar came to Wattle Tree for a service and as the congregation filed in, Erik was shocked. The new widow was thinner than before and looked smaller, all in stark black without so much as a white collar. Her face was strained, she was nothing like the glowing girl of his memory, but she greeted him with a ghost of the old smile. Mourning black was the convention, of course, but wasn't it a little bit theatrical? She seemed to be emphasizing her loss.

Erik took her hand gently after the service. 'Rose, I was so sorry to hear your news.' Thank goodness, the baby looked well and had grown. The baby would keep her going; with Ada becoming more mobile, Rose would have little time for grieving.

'Thank you, Erik. I'm glad you're back, your mother was worried. Yes, losing Luke is hard to bear.' She was pale and composed, but there was a slight tremor in the low voice and Erik had to bend down to hear her. 'I feel worse because I could have done more to help Luke. It's too late now.'

Oh Lord, she's feeling remorse. That makes it much harder. Erik sighed.

Rose looked up at Erik and he felt a surge of the old feeling; this woman affected him as no other had ever done. He loved her as she was, wrapped in mourning; he would love her when she was old and grey. This was the woman he'd called for when he was unconscious, giving himself away. There was no hope for him with anyone else. 'Dear Rose,' he said quietly. 'Live for today, not for yesterday.'

At that moment Freda came up and invited Rose to lunch. There was never another chance for Erik to get a private word with her and his mother walked with her back to the hut, the little black figure looking pathetic with the baby on her back. He knew that it was going to be a long, long wait.

'Can't you persuade Rose that she did everything she could for Luke?' Erik demanded that night as he brought in wood for the fire. 'Heaven knows, his shortcomings were not her fault.' He'd been turning it over in his mind since she went home.

'How can anyone outside a marriage know how it worked – or it didn't? I can't interfere in Rose's private life.' Freda put a piece of wood on the fire. 'When will you see Miss Sinclair again? Perhaps if she visits here a few times, she'll get used to the bush.'

Erik sighed. He hadn't yet told Freda that Miss Sinclair was married. 'I'll go and feed the dogs.'

It might be better if Rose didn't know what Luke had been up to, even if it could have helped her to get over his death more quickly. It would be cruel to tell her; he would just have to wait.

Winter was mild that year, a damp season. Rose borrowed some books from Freda and once the baby was asleep, she read every night. It was a strange feeling to read about Charles Dickens' London in the depths of Gippsland. The hut was quite cosy with a warm glow from the iron stove that Luke had fitted; there were far worse places to live. In the intervals of reading she gazed into the fire, wondering what to do with the land.

Her first plan was to increase the poultry flock again. Poultry were easy for a woman to manage. She bought some ducklings to rear after the butcher at Haunted Creek told her his customers would buy ducks, and a few geese for Christmas. During the summer the hens had hatched out more chickens and they would come into lay next year.

The cattle were another matter. They were big and needed stout fences. Rose liked cattle, but reluctantly she decided to sell them. Bert undertook to sell them for her and she made a profit. They were females and the farmer who bought them wanted them for his breeding herd. That had been Luke's plan – to breed beef cattle.

The sale of the cattle left a lot of land producing nothing except tall gum trees. It was pleasant open woodland and she loved it, but the land had to be improved by order of the government and it also had to earn her some money. Erik would know what to do, but she had to keep her distance from Erik. It was part of her loyalty to Luke's memory.

Over the winter, Rose was given some empty kerosene tanks by a miner who was leaving the area. Maeve had arranged it, of course. Scrubbed out, they were set to collect rainwater. It saved time bringing water from the creek and would help to keep the garden alive in the summer.

Rose had been surprised at how often her garden needed watering. Even when the rainfall was good, the warmth of the sun dried the ground up quickly. She was getting used to the Haunted Creek conditions; someone had told her that the Victorian climate was like that of Italy and she knew it was a lot warmer than chilly Yorkshire.

The egg money was spent as fast as it was earned, but it was being put back into the farm. It cost Rose very little to live, although she was often tired of goat's milk cheese.

One spring day Rose took Ada to visit the Carrs up on the ridge. She felt guilty of neglecting them when she saw how pleased Martha was to see her. After Luke died Martha had called to see her several times, but Rose had never made the effort herself. She felt that she was not fit company for anyone, pale and sad as she was, but now she realized that it was a selfish notion. Going to see Martha might be good for both of them.

They sat in Martha's new kitchen and admired her splendid kitchen stove; she didn't need a camp oven any more. Bert was at home that day and over a lunch of soup and bread, he talked about the demand for fresh food. Folks were sick of living on damper and pickled beef, he said. Looking at him, Rose had an idea. 'You're a vegetable man?' she said.

Bert looked surprised. 'So I've always believed,' he said drily.

'I have some land that's not being used. Would you – would you like to grow some onions or potatoes on my land? We could come to an arrangement and I could weed them for you.' Rose blushed a little; it seemed rather forward. She pulled her black shawl closer to her chest.

Martha nodded in approval. 'But you could grow your own crops, Rose. It's not that we don't want to help, but you've your own living to make. Bert could tell you how to go on and give you the seed.'

Bert held out his mug for another cup of tea. 'She could, but turning the soil's far quicker with my team than with a fork.' He grinned. 'You've got your eye on my grand plough, eh, young woman?' He ploughed with six bullocks yoked to a large three-furrow plough; Rose and Luke had watched him one day and admired his skill.

'Well, that is a consideration,' said Rose, who had not thought that far. 'But I know you need to grow crops on a different patch of land every year, rotate them, and that would be easier if you had my land as well. We only grew a small patch of potatoes for ourselves … of course, we did grow onions.' We should have done more, she thought, I should have encouraged Luke. It was a constant buzzing in her head. By the time Rose left for home they had a rough plan of action. The available ground between the trees would be divided into sections and the vegetable crops would be rotated round them.

'It'll be easier when it's cleared, of course,' Bert told her.

The land needed fertilizer and it was time to buy some more sheep to provide it. There had been fewer wild dogs of late and the farmers shot them on sight, so it was worth trying again. 'We'll be proper farmers, Ada,' Rose told the child, who tried to agree. Ada would soon be talking.

To learn what she could, Rose helped Martha with the weeding at the Carrs' farm, now called Carrs' Hill, in the weeks that followed. 'There's a lot of weeds we didn't expect, English weeds coming in,' Martha told her. 'Bert says they come in the bags of seed. But I reckon some blow in from Wattle Tree. They've been working the land there for years and they've got thistles, all sorts.'

On her knees working among the onions, Rose suddenly let out a cry of delight. 'I can use these! I've been missing them!' The weeds Martha hated had been useful herbs to Rose's grandmother. There was dandelion, self heal, plaintain, nettle … and at the side of the track she found yarrow. Martha was not convinced, so Rose promised to make up some remedies if the weeds were allowed to grow in one corner.

At over a year old, Ada was making good progress. She walked rather unsteadily round the clearing and she was almost too big to be carried on Rose's back. A donkey was the answer, Rose decided; a donkey would carry Ada and also it could be used to deliver vegetables. She had seen donkeys over the fence at Ben Sawley's farm near the Wattle Tree school. He might sell her one.

Mr Sawley turned out to be a donkey enthusiast. Ten or eleven animals were grazing in a small paddock and when he called, they all came running over to him. Surrounded by gentle donkey faces and long ears, Rose held up Ada to stroke their soft necks. 'Treat them right, missus, and they'll carry aaanything,' he drawled. Mr Sawley spoke very slowly and it took a long time, but in the end Rose knew quite a lot about donkey care. 'If you take one and don't treat it right, I'll be aaafter you,' he threatened. 'There's a laaat of folks have no i-dea.'

The farmer had a brick-red complexion and sparse fair hair; he was middle-aged, a careful man with a tidy farm. He thought that Rose's vegetable venture was a good idea. 'They've found more gooold down in the diggings … mooore folks'll be up here sooon,' he told her.

Rose went home with a young male donkey called Dougal, leading him on a borrowed halter. Ada sat on his back and so their progress was slow, especially as Dougal stopped to browse on tasty bushes at the side of the track. He might get on well with the goat for company, but Mr Sawley said it depended on whether they took to each other. Dougal would need shelter from extremes of weather, so it would be good if Gertrude allowed him to share her shed.

A few weeks later, Ada said her first clear word: 'Dougal!' The two were friends, very gentle with each other. Gertrude the goat had not yet made up her mind about admitting a donkey into her life. They stood in adjacent pens, getting to know each other gradually and Rose let them out in turn. Being bowled over by Gertrude would not be a good start for the newcomer.

By early summer there were potatoes, cabbages and spring onions ready to sell and Rose had bought panniers to strap across the donkey's back. Mr Sawley had told her what sort were the most comfortable; they were made of light wicker work. With Ada perched on top of the load they made their stately way down the Haunted Creek track to the store.

'Well, isn't this grand! And the baby riding on top! My, Mrs Teesdale, you'll do well with your veggies now.' Mrs Thorpe gave Ada a biscuit. The storekeeper and his wife looked at her with sympathy and didn't haggle over her price, although Rose herself thought the price Bert had suggested was high. But business was good, more folks were coming to the Tangil goldfield and so more vegetables and eggs were needed.

'Will the ducks be ready soon?' Mr Thorpe asked as they left.

'It depends whether you want duckling, or older ducks,' Rose called back over her shoulder.

On the way back they called at the All Nations with the last of the eggs and Maeve came out to see the donkey. Wiping away a tear, she said it reminded her of bringing home the peat as a child in Ireland. 'I can just smell the peat smoke and feel the soft rain,' she said, stroking Dougal's nose. 'And you in the black shawl now, that's pure Donegal. Did you not have an Irish granny?'

Rose smiled. She'd seen pictures of poor Irish folk with their donkeys and only now did she realize that she looked just like them. Perhaps that was why the storekeeper had treated her so well. He may have had an Irish granny.

Rose sat down on a bench outside the pub and looked around warily for eucy men, but there was no one else about. Maeve brought out coffee; Ada was given a drink of milk and said 'tank you' which impressed Maeve very much. 'I can see the plan's going well and good luck to you, Rose.' She smiled. 'You're surviving without the husband, God rest his soul. I was always thinking you would.'

'Just. All the money I earn has been needed to set up,' Rose confessed. She had not gone back to the sewing class. Their diet was very plain, mainly eggs and goat's milk cheese with vegetables and bread. The new potatoes were a great treat, but Rose wanted to sell most of them.

Martha and Bert sometimes killed a pig and gave Rose some meat and once or twice, Charlie brought rabbits for her. Jim Carlyle walked over to visit Rose from time to time after his work was done and he offered to cut firewood for her, but there was plenty of dead wood lying under the trees, so she was able to maintain a wood pile near the hut.

Rose had never before seen trees that dropped their branches so often and she was careful not to walk under them in a high wind. You never knew what was coming down next. For weeks she practised with axe and splitter and was then able to manage the bigger branches. As Martha told her, it was a knack, not just brute strength. Martha was a good wood chopper and she told Rose that most settler women were. 'You need wood all the year for cooking and of course you can't rely on the men to fetch it in,' she said.

'Their work's more important. But they'd soon notice if they didn't get fed.'

Jim didn't call often, and when he did his attitude was respectful and rather formal. Perhaps the black dress made her look like a nun. Rose didn't invite him inside, but sat with him on the veranda or by the cooking fire outside. He told her on one of his visits he had nearly finished building his house, a grand affair with three bedrooms and a corrugated iron roof to catch the rainwater. He looked across at Rose's hut and added, 'My house will be good but I feel guilty, you know. I shouldn't have taken Luke off to Noojee like that, and you with this hut and a small baby.'

'Don't blame yourself,' Rose told him gently. 'Luke loved to be off. If you hadn't been there he'd still have gone with Tom Appleyard. He was doing what he loved to do, that's a bit of consolation.' Although at first she'd thought that Jim was a bad influence, she had since decided that Luke's friend was the steadier of the two.

One evening they'd been talking for a while and Jim said, 'Did you ever think of getting wed again, Rose?'

Rose shook her head, but didn't explain. Her guilt and sadness were receding, but she felt bound to Luke still. 'I was going to ask the same of you, Jim. Have you found a good young woman yet?'

'Well, Ben Sawley has a daughter, Ellen … do you know her? Nice girl, she's a teacher in Warragul so she don't come up here much.' He gave her his cheeky lopsided grin and added, 'But I wanted to find out whether you're … er, well, whether you would be likely to consider matrimony … some time in the future, maybe … before I made a move. Didn't want to upset you, before. But it's a year ago now, since we lost Luke.'

Rose was shocked. Real love didn't work like that, she knew it now. Real love meant one person only, no second choices. 'Now, Jim, you're trying to cheer me up again, talking nonsense. I met Ellen once – she's just the type for you. Invite me to the wedding!'

There was another surprise; Jim's face cleared and he said, 'Well, I'm glad that's settled, then. You see, Rose, I thought maybe you expected me to … well, offer for you, after we've been friends and all. Luke would've expected me to look after you, a woman on your own. And … I've tried to help, but you're very independent. There's nothing I can do, it seems.'

Rose smiled at him. 'You're a kind lad, Jim. But to think of marrying me out of kindness! That's daft. Bring your Ellen here to see me when you can – and forget all about any duty to me. I'm doing very well.' The hut didn't matter any more, she welcomed visitors. Was she getting used to living in poverty? Maybe it was just that people were more important than possessions. She should have known that when she first joined Luke.

They had a cup of tea and as Jim was leaving he said, 'It wouldn't be too much hardship for a man to wed you, Rose. You're still a bonny young woman.' He kissed her quickly on the cheek before she could move away, and was off.

SEVENTEEN

'WE'RE WATCHING OUT for you, these days. When we see the donkey coming we know the eggs and stuff are on the way – and we need them. But where's the bairn?' Emily Watson was new to the district, very friendly and determined to succeed. She and Sam had put all their savings into their new retail business. 'WATTLE TREE GENERAL STORE PROP S WATSON', a large sign in fresh paint, advertised the shop to all passers-by.

Rose laughed as she tied the donkey to a rail outside the store. 'Ada's started school. I can hardly believe it myself. I've been here six years now ...' She brushed the flies from her black dress, unloaded a bag from the panniers and followed the woman into the shop, which had been enlarged by the new owners. The population of Wattle Tree was growing and so was Rose's business.

The years had flown by for Rose, as she watched her baby grow and struggled to earn their living. She supplied Haunted Creek and Wattle Tree with vegetables, herbs, eggs and just recently, goat's milk. There were three goats in the clearing now, with Gertrude very much in charge. The donkey plodded up and down the track three days a week and Rose was kept busy on the farm for the rest of the time. It was a little farm now, although nothing like she'd imagined it would be. The proper house was still a dream, but she had no time for serious housework, so it was just as well.

Rose had kept away from Wattle Tree for a long time because she thought Bert Carr sold his produce there, but one day Martha had told her about the new people at the store. 'They're set to get bigger, you should go and see them,' she advised. 'Get in at the start and offer them good stuff for a fair price.'

'Doesn't Bert sell there? I thought ...' Rose frowned. 'You've been good to me, Martha. I didn't want to get in his way.'

'You've had your head down, Rose, working so hard you don't know what's going on. Bert's got Charlie helping him now. They've bought another wagon and they cart our vegetables to Moe and bring stuff back – they're carriers, you might say. They go for large loads, you see. Charlie does the mail run twice a week as well, on his pony.'

'So Wattle Tree's too small for Bert. Well, that's a good thing. I'll go to see them.' So Rose had another customer, who also supplied the little hamlet of Fumina. She could sell all that she was able to produce.

Things hadn't gone smoothly all the way. A spell of warm weather with hot north winds killed off Rose's first carrot seedlings and she had to start again. She would never forget the day she came back from the vegetable round and found all her plants flopped over, wilting before her eyes. Most of them recovered in the evening, but by the end of the day the carrots were gone.

The beautiful brightly coloured parrots and rosellas happily ate the fruit from her apple and plum trees before it was ripe – and this was after several years of waiting for a crop. Some creature made holes in cabbage leaves; was it rabbits or birds or even caterpillars? It was nothing at all like Yorkshire.

'Growing vegetables is harder than you'd think,' Rose lamented to the Carrs, who laughed and agreed. Haunted Creek was slow to warm up in spring, but the hot summer sun was too much for some of the plants from milder climates. Rose learned to watch the weather, to water often and to be ready to shelter tender plants from the sun or the wind and even from hail or heavy rain. The next summer she wrapped the fruit trees with net curtains and managed to save some of the crop.

Gradually, she learned the secrets of growing things and the last few years had been tranquil and quite satisfying for Rose. She was at peace, partly because she had learned to accept the setbacks.

Luke was by now a distant memory, although his daughter sometimes looked at her with the same brown eyes and mischievous smile. As soon as she could talk, Ada was a wonderful companion; they explored the world of the creek together, learning the names of the plants and animals. There was no time for regrets, no time to feel lonely.

From cuttings Freda gave her, Rose had grown beds of perennial herbs and they proved to be very useful. They needed very little care and she was amazed to find that they grew through the winter.

Sometimes she dried herbs to make creams and tonics, but most of them could be sold fresh, in bunches. 'You can take cuttings from these and grow your own,' she told her customers, even though that would eventually lose her a sale. Herbs were for everyone, Grandmother had said. Rose told her neighbours from her own experience that rosemary and lavender would thrive here, as would sage. You had to keep mint damp or plant it near a pond.

Even with Rose's advice, some of the settlers found it hard to get plants to grow in the variable conditions of Haunted Creek, where it was often too hot or too wet or too dry. This worked in her favour, as many people gave up the struggle and bought her produce instead.

The February sun was hot on her head as Rose walked back with empty panniers from Wattle Tree one day, passing the site for the new church on the way. She planned what she would do with the next few hours before she toiled up the path again to collect Ada from school. She would do some washing and then pick some flowers to take for Freda. It was a pity that they were both so busy that they hardly saw each other, although the teacher had told her that Ada was a good pupil. 'Not many children can read before they come to school. You've made my job much easier,' she said one day.

Erik was seldom seen. His mother said he'd bought more land

and was busy building a house on it. Miss Sinclair must have agreed to marry him, Rose decided. The Jensens had given a small plot of land for a church and the skeleton of a wooden building was already there. Everyone hoped it would be finished for Easter.

Wattle Tree would soon be a centre of civilization, although the settlers had already decided that they didn't want a pub. Drinkers could make their way down to the All Nations and try not to fall in the creek on the way back, they said.

Rose hoped that the drinkers wouldn't pass too near her house. The hut now had a fence covered in climbing plants to screen it from passers-by. Over the years a few people had called in, but not many because there were other, wider tracks to the Haunted Creek settlement.

When she got back to the hut Rose ate some bread and cheese and then put on her oldest dress to do some work. A row of carrots needed attention, but first she picked some beans. Her basket was full and as she straightened up to ease her back, she heard a moaning sound from the bushes fringing the vegetable plot. Was it an animal in pain? Rose set down the basket and listened again. Something or somebody was in trouble and it couldn't be ignored.

Rose trod among the bushes carefully, holding up her skirt in case of snakes. The noise had stopped. Had she imagined it? The next moment she nearly fell over a large body lying on the ground, one arm flung out.

'Lordy! What happened?' Rose knelt down beside the man and touched his hand; it was feverishly hot.

Lord Barrington opened one eye and groaned, then shut it again. 'Benson, bring round the horses,' he commanded hoarsely. 'There's not a moment to lose.'

His wits were wandering and Rose tried to rouse him without success. What should she do? Her mind went over the things Martha had told her about first aid in the bush. 'Water's often the problem. Folks can go very strange without water,' she'd said. Then Rose saw the blood and bruising on his face and hands. His lips were dry and blackened and the livid scar stood out in the bony face. She would try water.

A few minutes later Rose knelt beside Lordy again with a mug of water. He was heavy, but she managed to prop him up a little. 'Lordy, please drink this.' No response. 'Jasper!' she said in a loud, commanding voice and the blue eyes opened. He drank some water obediently and then flopped over.

Several times Rose gave him water; Martha had said that it was better to give little and often rather than all at once. Gradually some life returned to his battered face. 'I'm going to take you home now,' Rose said. 'Perhaps you could try to get up, and lean on me?'

'What a perfectly splendid idea,' mumbled his lordship and fainted again.

Rose stood looking down at the man as the flies buzzed round them. He was tall and well built, but she would have to move him. She would try later. Ada would be waiting for her at the school. Rose brought a blanket and covered the man with it, to keep away most of the flies. 'I'll be back soon,' she promised, but he was not conscious.

Freda's flowers were forgotten as she sped up the track. Not waiting to speak to the teacher, Rose rushed home. She could have asked for help, but there were two little children in her care while their mother had another baby. Freda had her hands full.

Some time later, it was Dougal's patient strength that got Lordy out of the bushes and down to the creek. Rose helped him to his feet and, leaning on the donkey, he struggled along. 'Madam, I must insist on bathing,' he muttered, so Rose left him to it, giving him a large towel and a bar of soap. The donkey waited for him and when he finally fell onto her veranda, Rose thought he looked a little better. The bruises remained but the blood had been washed away. His clothes, she noticed, were wet; he'd probably tried to wash them.

Lordy had more to worry about than a few bruises. He drank tea and ate some soup with difficulty and then he fainted again. 'I am so sorry. It's Rose, isn't it?' he said when he came round. 'The Rose of Haunted Creek. I don't want to inconvenience you … I'll be off now.' He stood up and fell down again, clutching his side.

Rose put Ada to bed and then stood over her guest. 'Jasper,' she said in the strong voice that seemed to get most response from him. 'Jasper, let me see your side. Have you a wound? It might need attention.'

'Not from you, dear lady,' the man gasped. 'You have done enough….'

'I am a herbalist,' Rose said firmly. After all, she had been an apprentice to her grandmother, long ago. 'A medical person. You must let me see.'

A gaping wound in Lordy's side had obviously been washed in the creek, but a few maggots still crawled in it. Rose gagged, but persevered. It looked like a stab wound and it was hot to the touch. Rose thought quickly. What would Martha do? 'I'm going to wash this with water. Please sit down here,' she said.

The billy had boiled, so she poured boiling water onto a big handful of gum leaves, remembering what the dark women had told her. When the water cooled she tore a strip from an old piece of cotton and gently bathed the wound. She got rid of all the fly maggots and eggs. This gash was a few days old but the fragrant eucalyptus oil might stop infection. A wound like this could kill, if it were not treated; the badness could spread through the body.

'You must have lost a lot of blood,' she said quietly. This man was critically ill. Tomorrow she would fetch Martha to see him, but tonight she was on her own. A fresh piece of cloth was spread with honey and she bound it over the wound. Lordy gasped a little, but kept still.

When it was done he looked across at Rose. 'Thank you. I had been staggering about for a couple of days, I think … not sure how many. Confused and all that, you know. I am deeply indebted to you, Rose.'

Well, thought the herbalist grimly, let's wait and see whether you survive. Lordy was hot and sweating in spite of the cool evening air. Rose brought cold water from the creek and bathed his brow with it. She gave him a bowl of soup, but he could take very little. She moved the sleeping Ada into the hut and persuaded Lordy to lie down on the bed in the cabin. There she left him for the night with a mug of water beside him. To ask him what had happened might make matters worse.

By morning Lordy was cooler, but still so apologetic that Rose had to silence him. 'Lord Barrington,' she said very firmly, 'if I were in need of help, I'm sure that you would help me.'

'Of course, my dear, absolutely. Not much use at the moment though,' he said, looking down at his side. 'What exactly did you have in mind?'

'I'll reserve it for when I do need help. Meanwhile, let's have no more apologies.' Rose explained that she was going to fetch Martha, who had been a nurse.

Lordy said he knew her. 'Do bear in mind that I don't need a midwife, my dear.' He was trying to make a joke; that must be a good sign.

Martha inspected the patient and then they had a conference in the garden. She said that Rose had done the right things. 'The wound should heal in time. Keep checking, change the dressing every day and don't let it go bad. But he mustn't go off for a week or two, he's in need of a rest. You don't mind having him here, do you?'

'I don't mind him here,' Rose said truthfully. 'The cabin is separate, he can have it for a while. I don't know whether he'll stay, though. He seems uneasy.'

Martha smiled. 'I won't come again unless it's desperate. He's your case. Well done.'

When Martha had gone Rose informed her guest that he was staying for a few weeks, the cabin was his and there was to be no argument. It seemed best to establish the situation right away and he seemed to respond when she put on the voice of authority. Maybe he'd had a bossy nursemaid as a child.

Lordy had also been thinking about his situation. 'I should go back to my house, but it would be difficult at the moment,' he agreed. His voice, usually melodious, was hoarse and weak, but his brain seemed to be working. 'I will be delighted to stay as your guest, providing you will allow me to pay for my keep. As a paying guest, that is.' He drew out a notecase with difficulty and passed over some money. 'This is for one week.'

Rose looked at it. 'Too much!' she said at once.

'I include medical treatment, consultations and general counselling,' the patient said loftily. 'Not to mention the cost of the *materia medica*, you know. Cheap at the price, I think you'll agree.' They both laughed, although Lordy winced and held his side.

'Of course,' Rose said gravely, 'eucalyptus swab and honey poultice are very expensive items.'

'And then there are your years of experience, Mrs Teesdale, coupled with twenty-four-hour attendance. If we were in London, heaven forbid, you would charge me far more.' Lordy seemed to be enjoying himself.

'Now you mention it, I'll be leaving you on your own from time to time. There's Ada, of course, and I have to deliver the produce. Tomorrow it's Haunted Creek.'

Lordy's face lit up. 'Is it? Will you pass on a message to the delightful Maeve? If I am still alive tomorrow, inform her of it, if you please.' He looked at Rose. 'Perhaps you will be able to tell whether she is happy to receive the information … or not.' He thought for a moment. 'I will do my best to survive. It would be so very inconvenient for you if I – um – *did a perish*, I think the term is – in your house.' He was facing facts; it was still possible that the wound would spread poison through his body and kill him.

The next morning Rose left Lordy on her veranda with a book. She took Ada to school, came back, loaded up the donkey and went down the track.

Maeve was presiding over the bar in deepest black. Her greeting to Rose was subdued. 'Girl dear, have you heard the news?' Her face was tragic.

'What do you mean?'

'That Lordy. Jasper. He's dead, Lord bless him, as far as we know. There was a fight, here in the bar. A miner went for him with a pick. Such a thing was hardly ever seen in my time here before. I saw it, a mortal wound it was, but he went off in the dark … he'll be found dead under a bush for sure, and him only doing what he thought was right.' There were tears in the big woman's eyes. 'I was after stopping the fight but I should have gone after him….'

'He's alive, Maeve, so far anyway, and he wants to know whether you are pleased or not.'

Maeve waltzed around the bar and gathered Rose into her arms. 'The man's alive! Praise the saints! I'm deloited, me girl, and you can tell him so. Maybe I'll go to see him and tell him myself.'

'He might not survive if you grab him like that,' Rose said as she detached herself. 'I found him two days ago … the wound is quite bad but we're treating it and Martha Carr has seen him. He won't be able to travel for a while.' Curiosity got the better of her. 'What were they fighting about, do you know?'

'There was a few miners had been drinking here all day.' Maeve rolled her eyes. 'I discourage drunkenness, but what can you do? Mostly they just fall asleep, but with some it brings out the worst, they turn to fighting talk. That's what happened. They were picking on a poor lad that has just come out to the diggings from Ireland. Poor Sean has only the Gaelic and he still looks half starved. The famine's a long time gone, but some of the parishes are that poor …' Maeve paused to serve a couple of men who had just walked in.

In a few minutes Maeve went on quietly, 'Well, two miners in particular were very cruel. He refused to fight, so they were twisting Sean's arm up his back and forcing whisky down him. They meant to get him drunk but it was wicked – men have died that way. I begged them to stop but they sneered at me. I didn't know what to do and Sean was rolling his eyes at me, pitiful he was.'

'How dreadful! I wonder how you ever cope with a pub, with such unpredictable customers.' Rose perched on a bar stool.

'So then Jasper – that's Lordy, you know – walks in with his head up as usual, looking down that beak of a nose, and he sees what's going on. He goes white with a sort of fury, you know. Lordy gets like that.'

'And he stopped them?'

'Indeed and he did.' Maeve sounded proud. 'He was sober, of course, he don't drink much. Clean and tidy for once, he hadn't been working. Shouted at those miners, Lord love him, as if he was giving orders on his estate. "Stop that at once, you cowardly scum! You should be hanged!"' Maeve attempted the upper-class English accent. 'They only laughed at him, so he waded in. He knocked the drunks down and took poor Sean away to the washroom, made him sick. It probably saved his life.'

There was a silence and then Maeve whispered, 'When he came back to help me, they were waiting for him.' She looked round. 'And Boris wasn't here that night. They'd not have tried any of it if Boris had been here.'

'I see.' A miner's pick was a lethal weapon in a case like that. Rose shuddered.

'Three of them hit him, one stabbed him with the pick. Then I started throwing chairs at them and Lordy got away. The man's no coward at all, but if he'd stayed they'd have killed him.' Maeve sighed and then said briskly, 'Coffee?'

A publican's life was quite dangerous, thought Rose. 'Yes, please, I would love some coffee.' Rose felt quite protective of her patient and she wondered whether the men would pursue the quarrel. Lordy might be safer with her for a while yet.

They drank strong coffee and then Maeve called to the kitchen. 'Come and mind the bar, Boris, I'm going out.' To Rose she said, 'Might you spare a few minutes? We could go to Jasper's house and collect some things for him. He must be needing a change of clothes.'

EIGHTEEN

'PRETTY STRIPES, MAMA! Come and look at him!'

Rose was at the door of the hut when she looked up and saw what Ada had seen. A tiger snake was emerging from the flowers at the far side of the yard and Ada was running towards it with outstretched hands. She liked to look carefully at each new animal, frog, butterfly or beetle that they found and Rose had encouraged her interest.

Ada had never seen a live snake at close quarters before, or admired the pretty stripes. Rose had seen to it that they were kept away; if she saw one she made loud noises and beat the bushes with a stick until it disappeared. Ada had been warned that snakes could bite you, but Rose had avoided making the child too frightened to go outside. Now for the first time she was faced with one and she forgot the warnings.

Rose prayed that it would slide away. They usually did. But Ada let out a whoop of delight and it must have felt threatened; it came on aggressively.

'No! Come back, Ada!' Rose called desperately, but Ada took no notice, intent on the snake. Rose started to run towards them, stumbled in her haste and fell.

The creature was thick and well over three feet long, with vivid stripes. Its head was weaving from side to side, the mouth opening as it came. Rose started forward again but there was a lot of ground to cover. Too much; she could not save the child.

Lordy was sitting on the grass not far from Ada. He had been dozing, or the snake would have been chased off before the girl saw it. Waking suddenly at Ada's shout, Lordy flung himself bodily between the child and the snake, and fell forward at the last moment before it reached her. It lunged and struck him with its fangs, while Ada backed off in alarm. His reaction had been amazingly fast, but the snake was faster.

'Get back, Ada!' Rose shouted.

Lordy twisted round and gave the snake a kick with his stout boot. It took off at great speed, but the damage was done. Rose's mind started to race. Snakebite remedies – what were they? Martha had said that they were not likely to work. Once the poison was in, you couldn't get it out. It had all happened so quickly and in a few seconds someone's life could be taken. It might have been Ada's. It was probably going to take Lordy's.

Lordy lay on the grass where he had fallen, breathing heavily while Rose bent over him in an agony of remorse. She should have been watching Ada more closely; this should not have happened. 'Jasper?'

With difficulty Lordy sat up. 'The nearest run thing you ever saw, as the Duke of Wellington once said,' he drawled. 'Ada, my child, may I suggest that you keep a careful watch for snakes and try to avoid them? Snakes are not friendly, you see.'

'Jasper – you've been bitten.' The striped tiger snake was deadly; they all knew that it could kill a horse. He had saved Ada's life. There were no words to thank him.

Ada was looking at him with concern. 'That pretty snake's gone away now. 'Did it bite you, Lordy? Oh, dear.' She sat beside him on the grass and patted his shoulder.

'Not very much, dear child, don't worry.' Ada was looking very scared.

Rose didn't believe him. She had seen the flickering fangs sink into his side. 'But I saw it bite you,' she whispered. 'Whatever shall we do?'

'Jumping in the creek's the thing, so I'm told. Cold water to slow down the heart rate if you've still got one. But there ain't much anyone can do for a tiger snake bite, you know.' Lordy winced and then smiled. Smiled in the face of death! Rose gasped and then he said, 'Fear not, Rose, I shall not perish – not just yet. The fangs struck the bandage, luckily. Thanks to your extremely thorough bandaging, they didn't reach my skin.'

'Jasper ... what can I say?' Relief was following remorse and a great thankfulness and Rose felt very shaky.

The hero winked at her. 'There's something you can do. Reach into my bag in the cabin, if you please, and bring me the bottle of whisky you will find therein. I think we both would benefit from a wee dram, as the Scots have it.' Rose smiled as she went to the cabin. Maeve must have slipped a bottle into the bag with Lordy's change of clothes.

They sat on the veranda with Ada playing at their feet, drinking diluted whisky – in Rose's case, well diluted. After they had relaxed a little Jasper said, 'But I'm afraid, such a nuisance, the wound has opened. All your good work has gone for nought.' He unbuttoned his shirt and Rose saw that a bloodstain was spreading through the bandage.

'No wonder – that fall and twist could have injured anyone. Your wound was only just healed; it wouldn't stand the strain. Why didn't you tell me before?' Rose went off for the basin and swabs. When she came back she noticed that Ada was playing with a new toy; it was a tiny doll's house made of pieces of bark. Its occupants were twig people.

'Lordy made me a house,' the child said happily. She had forgotten all about the snake.

'Just a diversion. I made it the other day,' Jasper said quietly. 'The young mind needs to be diverted, you understand.' Rose did understand. Ada had been pale and scared after the snake episode, probably because she could see her mother was upset.

That night as Ada got ready for bed, she took the toy house with her. She was thoughtful and then she said to Rose, 'Lordy stopped that snake from biting me, didn't he?'

'He did. Wasn't that brave of him?' Rose was still feeling the effects of the fright they'd had. 'You really will have to watch out for snakes, Ada.'

'Yes, Mama, I will. Lordy is a good man, isn't he? Do you like him?'

Rose pulled the little nightgown over Ada's head. 'Of course I do, we both do.'

Ada snuggled into bed with enthusiasm. 'I'm tired. Mama, are you going to marry Lordy?'

'Heavens, no. What put that idea into your head?' Rose was alarmed.

'They thought so at school.' Ada's big brown eyes looked up at her, considering.

Her carefully preserved reputation was in ruins. Rose spoke more calmly than she felt. 'Now why would they think such a thing? How do they know he's here, anyway?' She hadn't told anyone except Martha, and the Carrs were too busy to gossip.

''Cos I told them he's living here and he has breakfast with us and you are looking after him. So they thought you might be going to marry him.' Ada sat up. 'Please mey I have a drink of watah?'

She sounded just like Lordy; she was picking up his speech. Ada would be the only pupil at Wattle Tree school to speak with an English upper-class accent. But Rose was far from laughing; this was serious. 'Here's your water. Now, Ada, you know that Lordy is here because he's been sick. We've been making him well again and then he'll go home. And do you know, it's a secret – don't tell anyone – but Lordy is going to marry someone else.'

'I hope she's nice,' Ada said sleepily. 'Good-night, Mama.'

It was going to take more time to heal Jasper's wound after this and more care and attention. The patient had obviously worked this out and he suggested the next day that he should move somewhere else. 'I have presumed upon your goodwill long enough, dear Rose,' he said in his formal way. Rose was dismayed. How could she abandon a man who had just saved her daughter?

In one way, it would be better for her if he left, after what Ada had said. But the damage was done by now. Rose knew theirs was an innocent relationship, so what did it matter what the neighbours thought? In any case, she liked his undemanding company. Lordy was a gentleman; she understood what that meant now. He was quite used to ordering people about and he certainly liked his own way, but he was gentle and considerate. He would make Maeve a very good husband, if she could but see it.

'Well,' the nurse said thoughtfully, 'your own house is better than mine and it's neat and clean, I saw it when we collected your clothes. But you need company and treatment for a while yet and we'd like you to stay.' She'd been surprised at the bare cleanliness of Lordy's little wooden house. 'I hope that you would like to stay.'

Lordy looked pleased. 'Of course I would, delighted, my dear, but I am thinking of you. There is a great deal of work here for you, without medical orderly duties. So you like my house? I built it myself, you know. When I first came here I worked with a carpenter ... the poor fellow was appalled at my lack of skill, but we did make progress in the end.' He thought for a while. 'Do you know, I think I could stay at the All Nations. Maeve has plenty of rooms.'

'Dear Lord Barrington.' Rose too was beginning to pick up his style. 'I believe that you should avoid the All Nations hotel in the interests of safety, for some time at least.'

Lordy grinned. 'Maeve told you how I lost a fight. Damned careless of me.'

After this, Lordy settled down; he took Rose's advice, ate everything she gave him and made good progress. The wound healed again with generous applications of honey, following bathing in eucalyptus water as before. Honey was an old-fashioned country remedy that Rose had learned long ago in Yorkshire. She was impressed with the way honey kept the wound clean of infection and it must have also healed, because every day she could see an improvement. More honey was bought at the store; she would always keep some by her in future.

One evening when she was gently dressing the wound, Rose said, 'The Ganai women told me that gum leaves in water stops things going bad, or I might not have thought of it.'

Lordy raised aristocratic eyebrows. 'Really? At one time I thought of going into the eucalyptus business. I understand from friends in Melbourne that surgeons are using eucalyptus oil as an antiseptic these days. And about time, too. The insanitary conditions in our hospitals were appalling until Miss Nightingale took it upon herself to improve matters.'

'You didn't fight in the Crimea, did you, Jasper?' He had a military way with him sometimes. Freda had lent Rose a book about Florence Nightingale and her heroic deeds and she would have loved to talk to someone who had actually met the lady.

'A little before my time, don't you think?' Lordy was shaking with laughter. 'I fought in the third Ashanti war with Wolseley in '74, that's all, and I came here straight afterwards. Decided that I'm a man of peace.'

Maybe that was where he'd got the jagged scar. 'All the same, if you have fought Ashanti in – Africa, was it? – it was rather careless to allow three drunken miners to get the better of you. Keep still while I fasten the bandage,' Rose said severely. 'Jasper, you wriggle too much.' She passed the bandage round his slim body once again.

'How very critical you can be at times, nurse! That was a little hard, you know.' They both laughed. Rose looked up at that point and she thought she saw a motionless figure at the gate, watching them. The next moment it was gone. Had she imagined it? If someone had been there, who could it be?

In three weeks, Lordy was feeling restless. He was mending, but still needed care. 'I want some occupation. Have you a tape measure, dear lady?'

Mystified, Rose gave him one and he measured the floor of the hut. Then he walked slowly off to visit the Carrs. Some time later he was driven back by Charlie in a cart and Rose thought the walk must have been too much for him.

'I thank you, Charles, please unload here,' he instructed and the youth took down boards from the cart. A bag of tools and nails followed. 'I hope to fit a floor in this room of yours ...' Lordy avoided calling it a hut. 'But we will need to remove the furniture.'

Rose was worried that Lordy would injure himself again but he assured her that he would be very careful. A wooden floor would be luxury – but should she allow it? Carpentry was hard work, particularly sawing. 'Can I help you with it?' She found herself being politely overruled and decided that the English upper classes had not bossed people around for centuries without knowing how to get their own way.

Fortunately, Charlie stayed long enough to help to move the furniture. He giggled when he saw Rose's sewing basket. 'Reminds me of those classes we had with the girls at school. Mind, Mrs Teesdale, I can still sew a patch!'

Charlie had also brought some canvas for a makeshift tent. While the improvements were in progress, Rose and Ada should have the cabin and Lordy the tent. While he was sitting on the veranda, Lordy must have planned it all. Rose had never mentioned the trouble she had with the earth floor, the dirt and the dust and the insects. But Lordy had worked out that this was the priority when it came to improvements. If only Luke had seen it.

On the veranda in the evenings, Lordy talked about many things. He had travelled all over the world before he came to Victoria and Rose enjoyed his stories. One night she asked him about the eucy men. 'Joe's a villain and I suspect the others may indulge in criminal activities from time to time,' he said. 'Stealing cattle, that sort of thing, y'know.'

'They didn't look very honest,' Rose agreed with a shudder. 'Was that why they meant to frighten me? Or perhaps they just wanted an excuse to ... assault a woman.' To change the subject she added, 'But you worked with them on the oil distillery.'

'The process is fascinating – do you understand it? I rather thought of setting up a distillery myself one day and that was why I worked with them for a time. The cutting is dirty hard work, of course, but no harder than mining.'

Rose thought back to the first time she'd seen Lordy and the other eucy men. They had been dirty, unshaven and carrying sharp knives, a world away from Jasper's cultivated ways. How had he put up with them? Their treatment of her still made her shiver when she thought of it. They were completely heartless.

'Wouldn't the others be annoyed if you set up in competition with them?' Rose kept thinking of the different ways in which Lordy could be injured and tried to discourage him from taking risks.

'They are currently operating well to the south of us, near Port Albert, my dear,' Lordy said with a smile. 'Took the big tank and all their gear with them. A sensible choice, I feel. One can always leave on the next boat if things get a little too hot. You may not know that a party of black gentlemen was earnestly enquiring as to their whereabouts.'

'I was there when one of them shot a Ganai woman,' Rose reminded him fiercely. 'They deserve all they get.' Because of that action, she would probably never see the Ganai again.

'Unfortunately, the young woman died. I know you will be sad to hear it. The clan is after them and so are the police by now. That makes Haunted Creek a safer place for women and children, of course.'

'Poor Sal ... she lost her baby and now she is gone.' This was another case of bad luck, of being in the wrong place. Rose felt like weeping for Sal. With an effort she asked, 'So you think of distilling?'

'Haunted Creek is the perfect place for a eucalyptus plant,' Lordy said happily. 'Just down there on your land you could fit one in. You have to pack the leaves into the vat with a tank of water underneath it. A fire is lit under the water tank and the steam filters through the leaves and takes out the eucalyptus oil with it.'

By this time Rose was wondering whether this would be a good business venture for her. Once you had a vat, the materials were free, although she would have to employ men for the cutting. 'But why Haunted Creek? There are gum leaves all over Victoria.' She waved a hand towards the vast tracts of forest that lay between them and the mountains.

'Ah, then to get the oil you need to pass the steam through pipes submerged in cool water … hence the creek. An ingenious system … invented by an Englishman, of course,' Lordy finished.

After some minutes Rose said doubtfully, 'Would you really like to start up a plant down there, Jasper, on my land?' It would mean more people, probably rough men, and carts coming and going. The peace would be shattered.

Rose suddenly realized that she didn't miss village life any more. The peace of their little clearing was precious to her. This place had changed her, but what would she become? Ada would grow up and need to go away, to live her own life. What then?

Rose noticed that Lordy was looking at her. 'I think not. It would change the nature of your property. The peace here has been so good for me, Rose. Even though my house is not far from here, it's not a bit like this. The gold field is a busy place, men coming and going all the time. Besides, I hope to marry Maeve and then she will choose what we do next.'

By now it was early autumn and the weather was fine and mild. One afternoon Rose was working among the vegetables and looked up to find a woman standing over her. 'Good day,' she said politely. Was this a new customer for produce? The woman's golden hair shone in the sun and her tightly fitting bodice was cut rather lower than was the custom in Haunted Creek. The way she thrust out her bosom made it more obvious.

'Oh, I – er …' The woman seemed surprised to see Rose. 'I'm

actually looking for Mr Teesdale, Luke Teesdale. This is his property, I believe?' She looked at Rose's shabby black dress and added, 'He's a particular friend of mine.'

NINETEEN

'YOU'RE A FARM servant, I suppose?' The woman looked down her nose, although she was not very tall. Rose looked hard at Luke's 'particular friend'. What did she mean by that? The sound of hammering came from the hut, where Lordy was finishing off the floor, working slowly and cautiously as instructed. 'Perhaps he's in there, is he?' She took a few little steps towards the hut and Rose noticed that her pointed shoes were not going to get her very far down the Haunted Creek.

'I'm afraid not.' Rose stood straighter and pushed back her hair. 'Luke died some years ago … I am his widow. What did you want with him?'

The woman's eyes widened, looking into Rose's stare. 'Luke dead!' She shook her head. 'Widow? Surely … he said he wasn't married, he wasn't the marrying kind. Poor Luke. I don't know why he chose to bury himself up here.' She gave a sob that sounded like acting, but it might have been real. 'He was popular in Moe, a wonderful card player … you could call him a ladies' man. You look surprised, darling. Surely you knew that?'

Were they talking about the same man? Surely there couldn't be two Luke Teesdales in the area. Rose had an unreal feeling as she tried to come to terms with the idea that Luke was not the simple country lad she'd thought him to be.

'Come on, tell me it's not true. You're just trying to keep him to yourself.' The woman looked round as if expecting Luke to step out from behind a tree.

Rose was seething by now but she held herself in. She had never met a woman like this before. There had been women on the ship who were quite openly looking for a man, preferably a husband, but they were good natured. 'Why are you looking for him now? It must be years since you knew Luke.' Six long years since he died, and before that – how had she known him?

The visitor looked her up and down from eyes outlined heavily in black. 'You don't look his type, somehow. Not a very big bust and you're rather thin, that's strange. Luke always had an eye for the plump girls, the devil.' She sighed. 'Well, well. This spoils my plans. I never expected him to go and die on me.' She turned away, patting her fair hair.

'What were your plans?' Rose couldn't help asking, just as she couldn't help looking down at her bust. She was thinner now after her years of work in the sun, but it was still there in a modest sort of way.

'You might not like it, if you really are his wife.' She was good at insults. 'It must be about eight years ago now. Luke was boarding in Moe before he came up here and I worked in the boarding house.' She giggled. 'We spent our spare time together. Had some good times, but then I got pregnant. My name's Maudie, by the way.' She pushed out her bosom as if proud of her charms.

Rose walked over to a bench and sat down suddenly, feeling faint. Could she believe this story? 'So – why did you wait so long to look for Luke again?'

The woman sat down beside Rose on the bench and arranged her skirts. 'Well, we sort of drifted apart for a time. He had plenty of choice, of course. All the girls wanted Luke. When Luke got the land I didn't see him quite so much, only when he came into town. He came when he could and we always had a good time then – he was a bit of a devil, wasn't he? But then the baby happened. Baby was going to be a problem.'

'I see.' Rose looked round at the home she'd shared with Luke, a stranger. She had thought he didn't like women much because he was so casual with his wife. He'd obviously enjoyed himself with women in Moe, until she had arrived and spoiled his fun.

Maudie nodded. 'I did think of getting rid of it, but just at that time another bloke offered for me and he was comfortably off, like – an older bloke, you see. Luke had said he didn't want to wed so I went off with Alfred to Bendigo. I had a little boy, Lucas I called him. Alfred thought the baby was his – right proud he was.'

Rose waited; the story was not over yet. How could Luke do this when he was already married? While she was waiting to join him, then travelling from the other side of the world, Luke had a mistress, or perhaps more than one. This might be why the progress on the house had been so slow.

'We had a good time in Bendigo, but poor Alfred died of a bad heart. My folks are in Moe, so I came back last week. It's a bit of a backwater, you might say, after Bendigo. And then I thought, why not look for Luke? I don't need his money, you understand, just his company in bed at night. Naturally, I won't live out of town, but I thought of persuading him to join me, put a manager on the farm, something like that.' She looked round at the farm. 'Not that it looks that sort of a place, I suppose.'

'So you thought that Luke might want to take up with you again? Rather hopeful, wasn't it? You must be a fair bit older than him, I should think.' Rose thought that might silence her, but the woman only laughed.

'Bitchy, aren't you? Don't worry, Luke liked a woman with a bit of experience. And he might like … he might have wanted to see little Lucas. His son.'

Luke had a son, now living in Moe. Ada had a half-brother. How strangely things had turned out. But Luke had been indifferent to Ada – maybe a son would have been better. Why didn't the woman go away? Rose stood up, hoping to end the interview.

Maudie settled herself more comfortably on the bench. 'Come and sit down, missus. Now, tell me the truth. Are you sure he's dead? I can't believe it. Luke always got himself out of trouble. He wasn't one to lose a fight or have an accident. Did you see him in his coffin? Did you have a funeral? What happened, anyway? You haven't told me yet.'

'I have a death certificate, although it's none of your business. He was killed by a falling tree. Now I think you should leave. I'm not going to tell you anything else.' Rose glared.

The woman laughed. 'Don't look at me like that. It happens here, you know. Blokes, and some women too, they go off and start again somewhere else. Convicts bail out when they've done their time and why not, but many a bloke has deserted after a blue with his missus.'

'You must know some strange people.' This was an underworld Maudie lived in, a place of lies and broken promises.

'It's life, me dear. I expect in England it'd be a bit hard to run off, with all the parish knowing your business. But Australia's a big country, you can lose yourself easy if you want to. Go down to Port Albert and step on a boat, nobody sees you leave. The mail coach – well, that's a bit more public, but if you go east it's easier. There's a lot of country the other side of Sale and then you're on the road to Sydney.' Looking round her she added, 'I wouldn't blame Luke if he got sick of living on the land. It would be just like him to fake his death and go off to the city.' She laughed heartily; Maudie thought it was a good joke.

A dreadful doubt struck Rose like a hammer. She had not seen the body, or the funeral. She'd seen a cross in a cemetery and been given a piece of paper, supposedly signed by a doctor. The death certificate was blurred, almost unreadable because Tom had packed it in his pocket with some bread and cheese. There had been no reason to question either Tom or Jim about the details and at the time, she'd been too shocked.

She had certainly not wanted the details of his horrific injuries.

'You have an evil mind. I think you have made all this up to annoy me.'

Maudie snorted with laughter. 'Made you think, though, didn't

I?' Leaning forward, her bosom nearly falling out of her dress, she whispered, 'I just might be right. Luke might be living it up in Sydney, missus.'

Rose backed away, repelled by the woman's nearness. But she had been clever enough to plant a doubt, a niggling thought in the mind. What if shrewd, worldly Maudie was right and Luke was still alive? In that case, she wasn't even a widow. Just a deserted wife. Why had they not come to fetch her for the funeral? In a few minutes, Luke's mistress had changed her view of the world. She had changed Rose's memories of Luke for ever.

Rose wanted to be alone, to digest this story. 'How did you get here?' She really meant to find out how the woman would leave; she was obviously not a walker.

Maudie smiled complacently. 'I hired a lad to drive me out from town. He's waiting for me up the track. I told him to leave us alone, we might be having a reunion. I'd planned it, you see. Luke would have been so excited to see me. The visit could have taken several hours. What a disappointment it's been! Only you here and this miserable shack.' She stood up and moved off. 'Terrible road, isn't it? I wouldn't live here for quids. Well, I won't trouble you again.'

As she got to the track, Maudie turned back. 'I'll check up your story, just to make sure it's true. You might want me to think Luke's gone, mightn't you?' She cackled. 'Or ... he might have wanted you to think so. You'll have to live with it.'

Silently Rose let her go, the first visitor not to be offered hospitality. The hut, the garden, everything looked shabby to her, tainted by Maudie's view of the world. She sank down again on the bench.

'I say, are you feeling under the weather, my dear?' Lordy was looking down at her with concern.

Rose felt numb with shock, but Lordy's cheerful scarred face reminded her it was time for a cup of tea. She would have to get used to this news gradually. For now, she would live in the present, enjoy the tea and the peace of Haunted Creek.

That night the floor was finished and the huts put to rights.

They all went to bed tired and to her surprise, Rose slept well. The next morning she got up at dawn and bathed in the creek, carefully washing her long dark hair.

Lordy was boiling the billy for breakfast when she got back and Ada was dressing herself, as she had learned to do. Rose went into the hut and shut the door. The sharp smell of new wood met her and she smiled; the place was transformed. She would buy a mat when she next went into town.

The new floor was a sign of her new life. Rose opened the cabin trunk and shook out her old dresses. She chose a blue one and hung it in the sun to get out the creases. In the old black dress she walked with Ada to the school, but when she got back she changed to the blue one.

Lordy seemed not to notice the coloured dress; he was busy making something with the ends of wood. Her choice of black had been practical, after all. Many country folk wore black to work in and she had not stood out as unusual, except that she'd never worn anything else. Rose had been true to Luke's memory, had worn mourning for all these years, and now it was time to take another look at her life.

It was true, I didn't know Luke at all. He loved company, he was sociable. She had assumed at one time that he didn't like women, but now she went back in memory to their village life in Kirkby. Luke was a very good quoits player and helped Kirkby to win matches against Thorpe. There was a standing joke in Kirkby that the Thorpe girls always turned out to watch and that they arranged assignments with the quoits players. It was probably true.

So this Maudie had relieved Luke's loneliness in Moe. No wonder he was surprised when his wife turned up. He'd probably seen Maudie that very day! Rose blushed as she wondered whether her neighbours knew about her.

Even worse than a liaison with Maudie was the thought that Luke might have 'bailed out', left her to fend for herself with a baby in Haunted Creek.

There was no time for sitting and thinking on the farm. The next day Rose delivered her produce to the Wattle Tree store and called to see Freda as she sometimes did, timing her call for the school's mid-morning break.

Freda, as always, was pleased to see her. They admired the garden for a while and then Freda made a pot of tea. Pouring the tea she said, 'That dress is pretty, Rose. It's good to see you out of black at last.'

Rose sighed. 'I thought it was time for a change. Now, Freda, I've got a hard question for you. Tell me, did you know what Luke got up to in Moe before I came out?'

Freda sat at the table and folded her arms. 'We often wondered whether you should be told. It was hard to know, Rose. He had several women friends in Moe, Erik knew that. But we assumed that once you were here, he would settle down.'

'So everybody knew?'

'Not the newcomers, people like the Carrs, although Bert might have heard something in Moe. Poor Rose, somebody has told you a tale, have they?' Freda pushed a plate of scones across the table but Rose was not hungry.

Rose told the story Maudie had given her but Freda knew little. 'That was why Erik didn't like Luke,' Freda explained. 'He knew that Luke had been cheating.'

Rose changed the subject and drank her tea, then stood up. 'The donkey will be getting impatient, I'd better go,' she said. It was the wrong time to ask where Erik was and whether he was married, although she was sure she would have heard about a wedding at Wattle Tree.

As they walked through the garden to where Dougal waited beside the rail, Freda said rather awkwardly, 'How is Mr Barrington?'

Rose blushed and that made her feel even more embarrassed. 'He's recovering very well. I … found him badly injured and have been nursing him. I gather that Ada has told you all about it.'

'You can't have secrets where children are about, Rose,' Freda said lightly.

'There's no secret, Freda. None at all.'

Jim Carlyle lived on the block he had 'stolen' from the Carrs, or so they still believed. Rose had never called there but today she turned in at the gate and walked down the track with Dougal. Jim was coming towards her with a pony and trap. 'Rose! What brings you here?' Grinning from ear to ear, he jumped down to talk to her. Dougal and the pony eyed each other warily.

There was no time for small talk; better to come straight to the point. 'Jim, a woman called Maudie came to see me yesterday. Do you know her?' Rose looked up at him, wanting the truth.

'Er ... well, yes. Luke knew her before you came here, Rose, but he didn't see her once you were here. I don't think.' Jim took off his broad-brimmed hat and wiped his brow. 'Don't let it worry you, girl. It's a long time ago.' He looked very uncomfortable.

So far, so good. The next one might be harder. 'Did Luke really die in the forest? You only told me when it was all over, remember? Is it possible that he went off somewhere else?' Rose's lip trembled but she went on doggedly. 'I have a right to know.' Dougal was trying to give the pony a nip and Rose walked him up the track a little way.

Jim threw his reins over the horse's neck and followed her. 'Now, Rose, this can't be right. Did that woman suggest it? Luke had his faults, but he was ... fond of you. He was full of plans for the future. But unluckily, he died.' He stopped and there was silence for a while.

'Then – why wasn't I there at the funeral? Noojee is only a few hours up the track.' Rose moved nearer to Jim and looked straight at him. 'Can you swear to me that Luke is dead?'

Jim sighed and there was silence for a while; Rose could hear the thumping of her heart. 'No-o, I can't, Rose. You're putting a doubt in my mind.' Rose held her breath as he paused. 'You see, I'd ate something that disagreed with me that week. I was sick as a dog. So they went out and I stayed in the hut. Didn't see the accident or the funeral – I was too crook. I was shocked, of course, when Tom told me, but I've got no proof. All I saw was the cross, same as you.' His horse was wandering off and Jim went to bring it back. 'The first time I dragged myself out of the hut was the day we came to tell you about it.'

She remembered how pale and miserable Jim had looked that day. 'So I might still be a wife, not a widow. A deserted wife.' Rose started to move away with the donkey, sick with disappointment. She had thought that Jim would be able to give her the truth.

'Rose … I can't say. Really don't know what was in Luke's mind. Tom might know – he'd have had to get Tom to tell the tale. I suppose it might have been like that. Tom's a close one.' Jim looked shaken by the idea. 'Yes, it might have been … Luke was always looking for a change, something different.'

'That's why I thought … it might be true.'

'I could make some enquiries, if you like.' Jim swung back into his trap. 'Gotta go now, I have an appointment. But shall I tell you my news? We're going to be married next month – you'll be invited to the wedding.' Jim shook the reins and the horse moved off. 'Try not to worry too much, girl,' he said over his shoulder.

TWENTY

O*H, NO! I cannot believe it.* Erik stood in the mellow dusk, his hand outstretched and ready to open the gate. *I didn't want to believe it.*

Across her garden, prettier than he remembered it, he could see the veranda of Rose's house. This was the moment he had planned for. He was going to talk to Rose, to see whether she could marry him with a whole heart after all she had been through. He would take it gently, of course, but the time should be right. He'd brought flowers. They looked silly now.

Rose was there, but she was with a man. Barrington. He felt it like a physical blow.

One or two people had mentioned Barrington in connection with Rose, but like a fool he hadn't believed that there was a connection. But here she was on the veranda with her arms round the man. They were laughing together. *He must be twice her age*, Erik thought bitterly. *I've got it all wrong; I should have moved in as soon as Luke had gone, or soon after. It's too late now*. They were so easy together, they must be intimate.

So this was what Rose was doing, while he waited for her to recover from Luke's death. Well, she would have been lonely and that villain had taken advantage of her isolation.

Erik walked back up the track to Wattle Tree, his head down and his hopes in ruins, cursing himself for a fool. Barrington he knew slightly as a rather affected speaker who may or may not have been a lord. Rose probably liked him because he was

English – perhaps the title impressed her, although he couldn't imagine it. But then, he hadn't really known Rose, after all. This proved it.

How did you replan your entire life? It had been foolish, he knew now, to build all his plans and hopes on a woman without telling her, or even seeing her very often. It had been arrogant to suppose that she would be there waiting for him when he decided that it was the right time to speak.

Barrington was a fraud, Erik was almost certain, probably an actor with that deep resonant voice. He passed himself off as a lord to take advantage of people who were impressed by a title or by an air of authority. He was probably a felon from van Diemen's Land. Many boatloads of such people had sailed for Victoria some time ago when there was a shortage of food on the island. Victoria was proud of the fact that its people were free settlers, but there were plenty of convicts trickling in from elsewhere. Of course, not all were hardened criminals, but you had to watch out for people like Barrington.

The evening was now free. In fact, it was empty. Erik's farm work was done for the day, his mother had gone to play cards with the Watsons at the store and he'd expected to be home late. The rest of his life stretched ahead … empty.

Aimlessly he walked past the house he shared with Freda near the school, up the narrow track to his own house. It was finished at last, the result of three years of planning and hard work. It was meant for Rose.

Even in his desolate mood, the house soothed Erik as he sat down in the last of the daylight and looked round. The moon was rising, silvering the beautiful woodwork. Most of the settlers lined their houses with pressed tin from Britain or plastered the walls. Erik had been to Sweden to visit his grandparents and he loved the clean uncluttered look of the wooden houses there. His house had wood-lined walls and windows that looked out over the mountains, with no fussy curtains to hide the view. There were blinds he could roll down to keep out the heat and the cold. What if he had shown it to Rose at the start, asked her opinion? The thought was hard to bear; it was too late to have good ideas. But then, she'd been so single-minded about Luke for so long.

The house had several bedrooms, to allow for children. Freda had liked that, she wanted grandchildren. He'd had to admit to his mother that Miss Sinclair was not to be his bride, but he had not been able to bring himself to mention Rose. So poor Mother was in the dark as to Erik's intentions; she wouldn't be disappointed. A man had to have some private thoughts and plans. It would have been humiliating if anyone else had known.

Erik's dog Dan had followed him up the track and now he sat on the veranda of his new house with only the dog for company. 'Well, Dan, this is a pretty pickle,' he said and the collie licked his hand. 'What shall we do?'

The dog looked up at him and Erik was sure he could read Dan's mind. *Well, let's go droving*, the dog seemed to say. *Give it another go*. The faithful collie eyes looked into his and the bushy tail thumped on the boards. *What about the Brandy Creek run*, the dog seemed to say, his brown eyes never wavering.

'You've been eavesdropping again,' Erik said accusingly and then realized that he could be labelled as mad if anyone heard him. 'Well, Duncan did ask us …' The last time he'd seen Duncan, he'd been asked to collect some young cattle from Brandy Creek and run them up to Wattle Tree.

'Any time that suits you, there's no hurry,' Duncan had told him. Brandy Creek was only a few days down the track, nothing like the Melbourne trip.

The moon rose higher, slanting across the carefully planted garden. *Let's hope some woman enjoys the place one day*. 'Oh, Lord,' he said, head in hands. How could she take up with Barrington? Then he looked up and the dog was still waiting with a worried expression. 'Right, we'll go to Brandy Creek.' He patted the dog and stood up. Life must go on.

*

The Brandy Creek trip was just the change of scene that Erik needed. At the Cobb & Co. lodging house, Erik stabled his horses. The place was quiet, waiting for the next mail coach. It was run by a pleasant family and Erik noticed as she gave him soup that the daughter was quite pretty.

'You're from Wattle Tree, I think.' She smiled as she took his empty plate. 'I remember you coming through years ago. My name's Jenny.'

'My goodness, how you've grown. You were a little girl then.' Erik grinned. But he'd been much younger, too. 'I'm Erik.' The girl smiled and went back to her work. Later in the evening, her father Fred offered Erik a glass of beer and Jenny came to sit with them. He enjoyed the quiet chat but he wondered why Jenny was so interested in him. Whenever he looked her way, her dark eyes were turned on him.

The next morning, Erik enjoyed a good breakfast before saddling up. Jenny said to him quietly as he paid the bill, 'I hope you'll come through again soon, Erik.'

He looked down at the girl. Her teeth were white and her eyes sparkled with health. Jenny was neatly dressed and altogether an attractive young woman, fresh and efficient in spite of the fact that the Melbourne coach had stopped there in the middle of the night. 'I might do that – I enjoyed last night,' he said as he made for the door. What on earth would a young lass like this see in him? Perhaps she said that to all the drovers, in the interests of the business.

The small mob of heifers was in a safe paddock and they were docile, having been regularly handled. He and Dan grazed them eastwards, moving slowly along the three-chain road. They met a few carts and Erik spoke to the drivers as they passed. 'Any good land left up your way?' one man asked hopefully.

'Plenty, if you don't mind the hills.' People were needed, solid respectable settlers, not itinerant miners. The mail coach passed them without incident and by early evening they reached Shady Creek.

Erik sat on his horse and watched as the cattle drank eagerly from the creek; they were thirsty after a hot day. The dog Dan was always on the watch, rounding up any that even looked like straying from the group. The evening was deepening to purple, the mountains misty in the distance and the spicy scent of the bush wafted over him in a breath of cooler air.

Nearby was the drover's paddock where the cattle bedded down, safe behind fences, tired after the walk and not likely to give trouble. Erik slept in his bedding roll under the stars. They were off at first light the next day and Erik and Dan had the cattle delivered to his neighbour Sawley just before sunset.

Dan loved the whole trip; his tail was held high as he circled the cattle, watchful of any that showed signs of lagging behind. He went ahead to block off side roads or gateways. He didn't argue and he was the perfect companion. 'How much for the dog?' one traveller asked as he watched them, but Erik and Dan both laughed at him.

'Come in for a drink,' Ben Sawley urged him when the cattle were safely established in the paddock at their destination. So Erik and Dan went to sit on the Sawleys' veranda and drink a glass of homemade wine, looking out over the donkey paddock. 'It's a grand place, this,' Mrs Sawley said in her homely north of England accent. 'Would you live anywhere else, lad?'

'Never. I thought of leaving, but no … I'll stay here. You wouldn't find a better spot.' Erik breathed out slowly. Well, that was one decision made. He would stay, even if the new house was sold. In fact if he sold it he could buy more land. And perhaps he should spend some time with Jenny at Brandy Creek, although it seemed impossible to think of any woman except Rose. Life must go on.

Erik rode home, looking forward to a meal and bed. It was just after dark when he stabled the horses and went into the house. There was no light. That was strange; Freda always lit the lamps early.

The house was quiet except for the ticking of the clock. 'Mother! Freda?' Perhaps she was visiting a neighbour. Erik walked into the sitting room and found his mother lying on the floor.

Heart thumping, Erik knelt beside the still figure. At his touch she stirred and opened her eyes. 'You're home,' she said, and closed them again. 'Light the lamp, will you?'

At least she was lucid. With hands that shook a little from shock, Erik lit the lamp. 'Can you get up now, Mother?' He helped her and with a struggle, got her into a chair. 'What happened? How long have you been there?'

'It was after school ... I came in here and everything went black. I woke up on the floor and decided to stay there ... I felt so tired. I kept thinking I would get up in a minute or two. I didn't mean to alarm you, Erik.'

Erik brought her a glass of water and Freda said she was feeling almost normal. 'I'm taking you to the doctor in Moe tomorrow,' Erik said firmly. When she protested he said, 'I have to see the agent and get my pay – you may as well come along.' He would also see Mr Sinclair, to ask about drawing up a legal title for the new house. They agreed that Mrs Watson from the store could be asked to look after the school for the day.

When Freda came out of the doctor's surgery the next day she was agitated. Erik was waiting with the buggy, but when he saw her face her jumped down, tied up the horse to a rail and took her to a tearoom. 'I've got to rest,' she moaned. 'My heart's the problem. No more school until next term, he said.' She drank her tea and then admitted, 'I do feel like a rest. But what about the school?'

'We'll write to the Board, ask for another teacher. That's easy.' Erik felt guilty; he'd allowed Freda to do too much on the farm as well as running the school. 'There should be two teachers by now, the way Wattle Tree is growing.'

Leaving Freda in the tea shop with a second cup of tea, Erik went to see Mr Sinclair, who greeted him warmly. He asked politely after Harriet and was told she was very happy in Sale. They discussed the documents needed for the new house and then Erik said casually, 'Would you mind if I had a look at Burke's Peerage, sir? I want to check on our neighbour Lord Barrington.'

Sinclair laughed as he took down the heavy volume and began to turn the pages. 'No-o, there are plenty of earls, but he's not there.' He peered up at Erik through his spectacles. 'I believe he's a bit of a rogue, you know.'

'May I look?' Erik picked up the book just to be sure; he wanted Rose to know the truth. The man could be a lord without being an earl. His heart sank when he found an entry: 'The Viscount Barrington.' Jasper was there, large as life, and he was, as Erik had suspected, about fifty. 'He's not an earl, he's a viscount,' Erik told the lawyer. 'His lordship.' Well, if he was of blue blood he should behave better. A true gentleman would not have ruined Rose's reputation by living in her house.

The lawyer shook his head. 'No proof. There may be such a person, but is the man we know the real viscount? He may be an actor.'

With a sigh, Erik turned back to the problem of his mother. He borrowed paper and pen from Duncan Black and Freda wrote a letter to the education authorities before they went home, to catch the evening mail from Moe which would save a day. He would have to help with the school himself for a few days until the teacher arrived; Freda would tell him what to do. He was determined that she should not set foot in the school.

The letter from the Education Board arrived a week later and it was disappointing. Another teacher had been planned because of the expansion at Wattle Tree, but not until the next term. There was no teacher available at the moment. For the remaining six weeks of term, the Board recommended as an emergency measure that a retired teacher should be found to fill the gap, or an honest and sober citizen with some education who could supervise the important subjects, writing and arithmetic.

A few days later, they had drawn a blank. Erik had ridden round the neighbours, but it seemed there were no teachers in Wattle Tree and Haunted Creek.

'I know it might be difficult for you, Erik, but I think we'll have to ask Rose, if she can spare the time,' Freda said quietly. 'She was very good with the sewing class and is quite well educated; she reads a great deal.'

Erik looked at his mother sharply but she only smiled. 'You used to be friends but I've noticed you avoid her now and perhaps I can guess why.'

'Jumping to conclusions again, Ma.' He was not going to admit to anything. But there was no choice; Freda would hardly get well if she were worrying about the school. 'I'll ask Rose. I'll go there tonight,' Erik promised. 'I suppose I should admit that I – I'm disappointed she took up with Barrington.'

Erik felt a shudder pass through him when he opened Rose's gate. Taking a deep breath, he marched up the path. Rose was outside on her own, writing a letter. She looked up and smiled and Erik's heart turned over. This would not do. He tried to think of young Jenny, and failed.

'Where's Barrington?' he demanded, and then listened to the echo of his own harsh words. 'I'm sorry, Rose. I'll start again. Good evening.'

Rose stood up gracefully; she moves smoothly always, he remembered, and carries herself well in spite of the heavy work. 'Erik! It's good to see you. Did you want Jasper? I'm afraid he's gone home. He's quite recovered.'

She had pretended to take his question at face value. How could a woman who had lived with a man, shared her life and her bed with him for weeks and months – without marriage, just like a common harlot, to be biblical about it – be so calm? She should be hiding her head in shame.

'Barrington can wait,' Erik said. He wanted to punch Barrington.

Rose was waiting politely, head on one side. Erik's fists were clenched; he wanted to hit out. Had he always been so aggressive? He didn't think so. He swallowed the rage with an effort, put aside the thought of Barrington as a lover. 'We, Freda and I, need to ask a favour of you.'

Rose sat on the bench and patted the place beside her. She was wearing a soft green dress and she looked more beautiful than he remembered. 'Sit down, Erik, it's a long time since we met. Yes, I can help out at the school for a while, if Freda thinks I'm suitable. I was hoping you'd find a proper teacher.'

Erik relaxed a little. 'It's just for the rest of this term. I suppose you heard about it from Ada.' Everyone knew Freda was ill, because news at a school spreads through the place like the measles.

'I hope you'll stay here today, Erik, don't go off,' Freda said the next morning. 'Rose will need help. It's a lot for her to take on.'

Rose went first to see Freda and was given the school register and a list of the classes and subjects for the day. Her eyes widened when she heard that the teacher had been looking after thirty children by herself. 'That's the problem,' Erik said grimly. 'If you can't manage them all, I suppose I can take a few of them for geography. And you can let some of the girls sew, leave them to it.'

'If they were all the same age it would be easy. But they're all ages from five to fourteen,' Freda pointed out.

Erik was still furious with Rose for being so naïve as to take up with Barrington, but he managed to hide it. To his surprise she went calmly through the day. First of all she called the children together and explained that she would be there in Mrs Jensen's place until the end of term. 'We all want Mrs Jensen to get well again, don't we?' Vigorous nods. 'You can all help. If you work hard and try your best, Mrs Jensen won't have to worry about you. Now, do you want to help?'

'Yes, Mrs Teesdale,' the children chorused. Quietly Rose gave them all tasks and divided them into the usual age groups. After that the school was so quiet that Erik looked in at mid morning. He found the fourteen-year-olds giving the five-year-olds a reading lesson.

'A good way to learn is to teach,' Rose said, smiling at him. 'It's so good to be back here, Erik. I wish I had trained as a teacher.'

TWENTY ONE

A FEW DAYS later, Rose was alarmed to find she was to be left in sole charge of the school. 'Mother's going to Melbourne for a few weeks, to stay with her sister.' Erik was looming in the doorway. 'So you'd better see her about any problems with the school before she goes.' He seemed to be talking to a point above her head; how different from the friendly Erik she had once known. What was the matter with the man?

Then the message sank in. Freda going away? She would have no one to advise her. A thread of panic ran up Rose's spine. She was not a trained teacher; she had hardly any experience. To be running the school with the teacher sick next door was one thing, but to be on her own.... Rose lifted her chin. If Erik was distant there was no point in voicing her fears. 'Thank you. I'll see her at the lunch break.'

As so often these days, Rose looked out of the classroom window on to the scorched earth outside, where the boys were trying to play cricket in a cloud of dust. It was the end of November and already the green colours of spring had gone. Wattle Tree was dry as a bone, waiting for rain. A hot wind was sucking the last drop of moisture from the land.

Rose ate her lunch quickly and as she crossed the school yard she could smell smoke. For days the bush had been burning miles away in the hills, the scent carried on the breeze. She knocked rather timidly at Freda's door, then walked in. The teacher was sewing and glanced up with a smile; she was on the mend, but still looked tired.

Rose stood by the window. 'I'm worried about the risk of fire. Freda, what would you do if a bush fire came near the school?'

'I do hope it won't come to that. Erik says he's seen distant fires in dry years, but never one that threatened the township.' Freda put down her sewing. 'I suppose if there was warning, parents would keep their children at home to look after them. But ... well, Erik and I have talked about it. You know our big farm dam? I'd take all the children there and hope that we could be safe in the water. The banks are quite steep, so the fire should pass over the top. It does depend, of course, on how fierce the fire is – and also which way it comes. But I would never try to fight it, or save the buildings. The children ... we have to look after them, that's all.'

'I worry about the piles of dry bark and dead branches everywhere that litter the ground, Freda. The school yard is clear, Erik keeps the whole place bare in summer. But it's a worry. The only fires we saw in Yorkshire were on the moors, in the dry peat.'

Freda pointed to a chair. 'Please sit down, Rose. I do apologize for leaving you alone with the school, but the doctor insists that I should go away for a while. You can call on Erik for help, of course, and one or two of the mothers could support you. I'm quite sure you are up to the job and it will be good experience,' she finished brightly.

If she disagreed it would only worry the sick woman, so Rose smiled faintly. 'I'll do my best.' Erik would be too busy keeping out of her way to be of any help.

Ten minutes left and the bell should be rung for the end of lunch. Rose moved uneasily and Freda looked at her. 'What else, Rose? You've looked worried lately.'

Smoothing her dark blue school dress, Rose hesitated. 'I was told that Luke might not be dead, he might have faked his death, to make a start somewhere else.' She paused; it was still very painful to think of. 'You remember Jim Carlyle came with Tom to see me that day? Well, I asked Jim to tell me about Luke's death, but he says he saw nothing of the accident, or the burial. And Tom has gone away.'

Rather sadly, Freda said, 'I suppose you'd like to marry again and you need to know whether you're free.'

Rose felt hot. 'Marriage is the last thing on my mind. I just – well, I can accept his death, but if Luke really has gone off somewhere ... it's a terrible thing to do to your wife. I need to know, Freda.' This was about Luke and their life together and whether he had deliberately deserted her.

On her way to the door, Rose turned to say goodbye to Freda and the older woman said, 'I – I should tell you that a few people expect you to marry Mr Barrington, so I thought that was it.' The blue eyes were questioning.

Appalled, Rose felt herself turning brick red. So that was it. The gossips must have been busy. Maybe that story had affected Erik? 'Of course not! He's— He wants to marry someone else. He stayed with us because he was too sick to move, and now he's well again.' Anger was rising. 'I did what I could to help him and I was pleased that he recovered. I'd do it all over again if need be. If Lordy hadn't stayed in my cabin, he would be dead now.' Without waiting for an answer, she stalked out of the room.

Back in the classroom, Rose forced herself to simmer down. Calm and quiet was what the children needed. Once they were all busy with new tasks, she had a few minutes to herself. So they still thought she was going to marry Lordy! Only time would prove them wrong, and even time might not repair her reputation.

Lord Barrington was regarded as a rogue by all sober citizens and he kept the worst company. But she could hardly tell people that he had saved her from rape or even murder by the eucy men, as well as saving Ada from a snake, and that she loved him like a favourite uncle. It would probably be misunderstood.

Maeve knew the man well, of course. She'd said that Lordy had found a job for Sean, the young Irish lad whose life he had saved, on a farm near Moe. 'And him a Protestant, for all love, they're often against the Irish. Jasper has a heart of gold, so he has. He's taking Sean down to Moe this week.' Maeve was sending a man up the track to collect the produce, now that Rose was busy at the school, and the evening before she had come with him to see Rose.

The next day Erik drove his mother to Moe to catch the Melbourne coach and Rose was left alone with the school for the first time. She was kept very busy answering questions and smoothing out difficulties. The heat was intense and the sky was growing dark with smoke. It was not possible to see what was happening in the next valley; was the fire coming towards them? Mrs Watson at the store had told her that the smoke was coming from fires started by lightning strikes in the forest and that it was miles away.

As the air grew hotter and even drier, some parents came to collect their children with grim faces. Some of them took neighbours' children as well. When Rose asked them how near the fire was, they tried to reassure her. 'Can't tell,' said one sturdy settler. 'It's maybe not coming our way but we thought we'd better … we're off to Moe for a few days to see my ma. There's no stock on our farm just now.' He looked at Rose and then said, 'Don't worry, Mrs Teesdale, it's likely to die down by night. If the wind changes, and it surely will.' He clopped off on a big working horse with his little boy perched in front of him.

It seemed a good idea to close the school early and she decided to send the children home at two o'clock. For the last hour, Rose called all the pupils together and read them chapters of *Coral Island*. There were only seven children left by then. They all found it hard to concentrate and little Ada kept glancing nervously out of the window. Fire was on their minds.

Rose was uncertain what to do. Should she send the remaining children home? It was hard to tell whether there was real danger, or just a distant fire on a hot day. She tried to concentrate on the story. The wind was rising.

The reading was interrupted when Mr Sawley, the neighbouring farmer, came in without knocking, his face a mask of worry.

'Where's Erik? I would have thought he'd have you oooout of here by now.' Behind him through the open door Rose saw the sky was a livid red, not sunset but an eerie glow.

'He'll be on the way back from Moe,' Rose told him quietly. 'What do you think we should do? I was just about to send the children home … or if it's too dangerous, we could jump in Jensens' big watering hole.' Her lack of experience was putting the children in danger. Why had she not acted earlier and sent them all home? The pupils' eyes were large and round and they sat at their desks, absolutely still.

In the years at Haunted Creek, Rose had often seen fires in distant forests. At first they had scared her but she had got used to the smell of smoke on hot days. In spite of talking to Freda about it, she hadn't realized that the emergency was here, and now. 'Maybe we should go to the dam?'

Sawley tutted impatiently. 'That won't aaanswer, not this time. The fire's coming across the ridge. Wattle Tree's in line unless the wind changes, as faaar as I can tell. Every fire's different – you have to guess. Best get down the creek as faaast as you can, take the children with you. Go down as faaar as you can to the river. I think the fire will come across the high grooound, it shouldn't go into the valley.' He paused and then said, 'It's a looot for you to do on your own, but I've got to stay here and save what I can. If any folks come for their children I'll tell them where you've gone.'

Mr Sawley wasn't sure where the fire would strike, so how should she know? Rose felt afraid. If they went down the creek, what then? Directions were hard to tell in this part of the world and she couldn't imagine why Haunted Creek would be safer than Wattle Tree.

Rose thanked him and told the children calmly that they were going to walk along the creek. On the way they could call in at her hut. As they made their way down the track, the rising wind blew black ash over their heads, flakes of burnt bark and leaves. If any of that ash carried sparks they could be in trouble. Apart from the dark red sky, they could see no other evidence of the fire and Rose had no idea how far away it was. It was over the ridge – it could be minutes away.

At the hut, Rose gave each child a drink of water and then changed from her blue school dress into an old black one. She tied a rope round her waist. The pupils took the rope in one hand and this made it seem more like a game to them.

'Follow my leader,' Rose said cheerfully as she saddled up Dougal. The smallest child, little Lizzie, could ride and Ada was proud to lead the donkey.

After a minute's thought, Rose picked up the money she had saved and let the poultry and the goats out of their runs. A few eggs and vegetables went quickly into the donkey baskets and then they were off. It was more important to get the children to safety than to spend time packing up her possessions.

The strange procession picked its way down the track beside the creek as the sky grew darker and the wind rose again; it seemed to be following them down to the river. The mid-afternoon light was as dim as twilight. Rose kept glancing behind. They were all perspiring in the heat and as the fine black ash stuck to their faces and clothing, they were soon very dirty. 'My ma'll be angry,' one girl said, looking at her once white pinafore.

'Your mothers will all be pleased you are safe,' Rose said firmly. 'Let's go a little faster, if we can. We'll be able to wash our faces in the creek later on.'

They met no one on the track and the journey seemed to go on for hours. Birds flew over their heads, parrots and kookaburras, making for the river. Rose kept glancing at the creek, which was the usual shallow trickle of water after weeks of drought. Here and there were deeper pools and if the fire overtook them, they would need to jump in. 'Can any of you swim?" she asked hopefully.

'No, Mrs Teesdale,' the pupils said, looking fearfully at the water.

Lizzie who was riding the donkey piped up, 'My papa says you should go in the water if the fire comes, so we'll all get wet, Mrs Teesdale.'

'So we will,' said teacher calmly. 'It will be nice and cool after this heat.' Looking over her shoulder, she saw flames at the top of the ridge, leaping high into the air and playing in the tops of tall trees. It was the Noojee side of Wattle Tree, well alight. Would the little town be next? 'See how many different kinds of birds you can count.'

The wind increased to a roar. Tall trees were thrashing about and branches were breaking and falling, each one of them lethal if it hit you. Trying not to panic, Rose looked ahead down the track and realized they were not far from the All Nations hotel. 'Let's try running, shall we?' At least the building would give them some protection.

The children trotted obediently along, pushed by the hot wind behind them. It was darker than ever, but in the gloom Rose could see figures moving about. It would be good to be with other people, although it seemed to her that there was little any human being could do against the huge force of nature. Fires were natural here, the dark women had once told her, which was a good reason for not living anywhere permanently. You moved on and built a hut somewhere else.

Men with axes were chopping down trees and bushes round the hotel and others were spraying water over the roof and walls of the building with hoses. Maeve was supervising, dressed in black, and she swept Rose into her arms briefly before looking round the forlorn bunch of children. 'You poor dears, come in and we'll give you some lemonade.' She looked at Rose and added, 'You did well – Wattle Tree must have gone by now. Praise the saints, I think we'll be safe here ...' Then she looked up and saw the flames advancing. 'Have you seen Lordy? He went to Moe yesterday with Sean.'

The children trooped into the hotel and sat down obediently. Rose was glad to get them out of the danger under the trees. 'Please may we bring Dougal in, Mrs Malone?' Ada pleaded at the door, but Maeve shook her head.

'No donkeys in the bar, it's not allowed,' she said gently. 'There's a stable out there, he'll be safe,' she promised and Ada breathed a sigh of relief.

One of the men took the donkey, smiling through the grime on his face at the little girl. 'She'll be right, love,' he said and Ada muttered that Dougal was a boy, not a girl.

Rose could not see how they would be safe, any of them. The pub was a large wooden building and it would go up like a torch if sparks ignited it. The men with hoses and buckets were working on, sweating profusely. 'Got to save the pub,' they joked. 'Most important place in the district.'

Time went by. Boris the cook, bringing out drinks for the men, was very calm. 'Keep down low on the floor,' he growled at the children in his deep voice. It was now pitch black in the building as the smoke crept inside. Her heart thumping, Rose joined the children and found herself crouching next to Maeve.

'I'll never see Jasper again. He'll not live through this, he's had it this time. If only ... if only I'd told him I really do care for him,' she whispered to Rose.

'Jasper is a kind, brave man,' Rose said quietly. 'Did I tell you how he saved Ada from a snake?'

Rose had regrets of her own. *Oh, Erik, I wish we'd been friends and talked to each other*. She should have approached him, broken down that wall of reserve to find out why he had changed towards her. She should have realized how he felt when he heard about Lordy living at the hut. It all looked so simple now, when it was too late. Rose shook her head as she realized that her mourning dresses had been too effective.

The heat increased and the children whimpered. Rose found herself thinking about long ago – how long it seemed since she had seen snow! In its way, snow was as lethal as fire. People could lose their way on the moors above Kirkby in the snow, when it covered familiar landmarks. Sometimes a man had died up there. Was it better to die of cold or heat? Like everybody else, Rose was trying not to cough. It was likely that the smoke would kill them soon.

TWENTY TWO

ERIK DROVE AS fast as he could on the rutted road and his horse seemed to sense the urgency. The air was thick with smoke and ash and the wind was blowing leaves and small branches across the track. He turned to his passenger. 'I have to get back to the farm but you could have stayed in Moe. Are you sure you want to go on? The fire seems to be heading up Wattle Tree way.'

Lord Barrington's face was grimy but he looked quite cheerful. 'We can jump in a water hole if we need to, dear boy,' he said briskly. 'And I may be of some small use to you, or to one of the neighbours. Haven't fought a fire for years, but I still know what to do.' He paused and then added, 'I always like to get out of the town again, y'know. Go there as seldom as I can.'

'Well, I'm afraid we seem to be in for it this time.'

After this there was silence for a while, apart from the incessant moaning of the wind. Thank goodness, Freda was safely on the Melbourne coach, one less person to worry about. Erik's mind was busy with plans to meet various possible emergencies at home and in any case, he had no wish to talk to Barrington. But it seemed that his lordship wanted to get something off his chest.

'I had thought of coming to see you,' Lordy began. 'Would you mind very much if we had a talk, while you are driving? I believe it is time I set the record straight.'

Erik sighed. 'Very well, let's get it over with. I've a lot on my mind at the moment.' He wiped the sweat out of his eyes.

'It won't take long.' Lordy dived into a pocket and handed over a bottle of water.

'Thanks,' Erik muttered. It was just what he needed but he found it hard to tolerate the man. He drank some water and felt slightly less irritable.

'It seems that Mrs Teesdale's reputation is suffering as a result of my actions,' Lordy said quietly, looking straight ahead. 'I was badly injured, y'see, damned careless of me really, and she found me near her garden. I was barely alive.'

'So I believe,' Erik said coldly, peering at the glow from the nearest ridge. 'This is hardly the time to go over the past. I'm worrying about the fire.' He was probably going to announce their marriage.

'With great respect, Mr Jensen, this is important to me and I suspect it may be of some interest to you, also. If I could have removed from Rose's house I would have done so, but I was very weak and in need of care. So she gave me her new cabin for my own use, and tended my wound until it healed. There was no impropriety at all, I assure you.' The man was cool, you had to admit it. Lying in his teeth and also cool in the face of a huge fire.

The horse clopped on for a few minutes. Then Erik shook his head. 'I saw you together,' he said, all the bitterness welling up inside him. 'There was no mistake; you needn't lie to save her reputation. I suppose I shouldn't blame you – Rose is an attractive woman. But I'd rather see her with someone her own age.'

Lord Barrington went on with a touch of hauteur. 'I give you my word as a gentleman – and I am accustomed to being believed.' The old villain's eyes were flashing and his head was up. 'You may have seen Rose bandaging my wound, and mistaken it for an embrace. I assure you it was nothing of the kind.'

Erik felt his face growing even hotter. 'So you saw me at the gate, that evening … Then why did she suddenly stop wearing black? She went out of mourning when you arrived. It seemed obvious to everyone that she's found a new man.'

Lordy hesitated. 'As a matter of fact, Rose had another reason. I shouldn't tell you this … but I happened – unintentionally, of course, I was working in the house – to overhear part of a conversation she had with a lady from Moe who appeared one day.' They both ducked to avoid a flying branch and the horse danced nervously. 'This is a betrayal of confidence, but justified, I think. The woman said she was Luke's mistress, which shocked Rose to the core. And then she suggested that the hapless youth might not be dead, but might have absconded. Left her in the lurch.' He turned to look at Erik. 'It was bound to affect her deeply … she had always honoured his memory. Several of us knew that he had, um, indulged in an active social life, but evidently Rose did not.'

'I knew,' Erik muttered. 'The swine never treated her well.'

'Just so. The next day, I noticed that Rose had changed to a lighter dress. I have tried to make enquiries as to Luke's fate – without telling Rose, of course – but his employer has departed for distant places and apparently he was the only witness. There was no formal burial, no parson, they couldn't wait. The weather was hot, you understand.'

The wind was fiercer than ever as they neared Wattle Tree. To go on seemed risky, but what else could they do? 'We'd better stop here, give the horse a drink.' Erik pulled up by a water hole and as the horse drank he said, 'Thank you, Lord Barrington.' In spite of the fire, he felt lighter than for months. 'Poor Rose! If she'd asked me, I could have told her that Luke did die at Noojee.'

'That would be preferable,' Lordy said quietly. 'It would be impertinent of me to comment on your affairs, but … I happen to know that Rose thinks very highly of you.'

Erik led the horse back to the track and they jumped into the vehicle. 'And I of her,' he admitted. 'But we've got to survive today first, all of us. Let's see what we can do.' He squared his shoulders, now full of energy. If the wind would only drop they could have a chance. 'I only hope Rose and the children are safe.'

At a time like this, you realized what was really important. It was possible that none of them would survive, Rose thought with a strange feeling of calm. She held Ada's hand in hers and hoped that these children would live to grow up.

The All Nations was filled with smoke and with the noise of things hitting the roof, flying debris from the fire. Down on the floor they could just breathe. Should they have come here, or would the creek have been safer? The temperature rose even more and sweat ran down their faces.

'Let's sing,' Rose suggested to the children, who were wide-eyed with fear. 'Twinkle, twinkle, little star …' One by one, the children joined in, even Lizzie who sang out of tune. 'Up above the world so high …' The little voices sometimes rose above the roar of the wind. Over and over they went through their sewing room songs, clinging on to something familiar.

'Girl dear—' Maeve began, as the door burst open and one of the men rushed in. Behind him they could see the inferno; Rose shut her eyes. The end must be close now. One of the children began to cry and Rose stretched out and held her close. The rest went steadily on: 'Up above the world so high …'

The man gasped and coughed and Maeve gave him a drink of water. 'Wind's changed. Fire's within a few yards, but it's being blown back, away from us. Let's hope wind holds.' He staggered outside again.

'Saints be praised, we might have a chance!' Maeve turned to Rose with a sob of relief. It would take a miracle to save them but it might just happen. Rose allowed herself a deep sigh. 'Twinkle, twinkle …' the song went on.

There was movement in and out, as men took it in turns to come in for a drink. They said they were putting out spot fires all round the building, started by flying embers.

After a while the air cleared a little, as outside the wind blew the smoke away. Boris lit the lamps and made pots of tea and Rose looked round the room. Twenty or thirty grimy people with relief on their faces were slumped on the benches. The immediate danger was over.

It was a few days before Rose could go back up the track beside the creek. As soon as people could move about, fathers came on horseback to collect their children, very thankful to find them safe and well. Mr Sawley had told them where Rose and the class had gone. 'You'll have a sad time,' one man told Rose, but said no more. She waited until all the children except Ada had gone and then saddled up Dougal for the journey home.

Maeve was still a tragic figure, going about her work without a spark of her normal self. 'If you hear anything about Jasper, let me know,' she begged everybody that went out. 'If he'd been alive he would have been back here by now,' she said mournfully.

Rose made her way slowly back through an alien world. The sun filtered through bare branches. Trees were black skeletons, the ground was covered in ash and no birds sang. Only the creek was the same, making its placid way down to the river, a small fringe of green on the banks. 'It was a big fire, Mama,' Ada said, looking round from her perch on the donkey's back. 'Where did all the birdies go?'

'I think they flew away, Ada. I hope they'll come back one day.'

When they came to her home clearing, Rose could hardly recognize the place. The hut and the cabin were gone. There was nothing left except smouldering ruins. Ada sat wide-eyed and Rose had to fight back tears. She had hated the hut at first but it had been her home and the few things she'd possessed were there. Her memories were mainly happy ones.

There was movement on a stump and Rose looked down to find a huge spider staring at her, one of That Spider's family. 'Hello, you're alive!' Who thought she would ever be pleased to see a huntsman spider?

'We'll find somewhere else to live,' Rose told Ada gently. There was a little money but not enough for a house. What was she to do, a lone woman with nowhere to go? The child was shocked, and no wonder. Ada needed reassurance.

Who among her neighbours had survived? It was eerily quiet. Perhaps she and Ada were the only ones left. Feeling the shock and the strain of the last week overwhelming her, Rose stood in the ruins for some minutes. Her mind was a blank.

The child tugged at her hand and for Ada's sake Rose shook herself out of the trance. Something had to be done. From here they would go up the track with the donkey to Wattle Tree, to see whether anyone was there. But first, painful though it was, Rose decided to sift through the ashes where the cabin had once been. There might be some relic left, some twisted keepsake from the past. She moved aside a tangle of tree branches and started in horror. There was somebody here ... a man was standing in the ruins. Possibly a thief.

A second look and Rose saw a figure bowed down with grief, holding the charred remains of her blue dress, the one she'd worn at school on the day of the fire. Somebody here was mourning for her, thinking she had died in the fire. Somebody cared; she was not alone after all. Quietly, she went up to Erik and put her arms round him. 'I'm here,' she said gently. He didn't react at first.

Erik looked years older than when she'd last seen him, with singed hair and ragged clothes. His eyes lit up and his whole face changed when he realized that although the hut was gone, Rose and Ada were alive. He was speechless, but he took them both in his arms and hugged them tightly. Rose felt the old surge of love. Erik was alive; that was all that mattered. 'You're here, too, thank goodness.'

'I was sure you were dead. That was the dress you were wearing ...' They clung to each other.

'All the trees are dead, Mr Jensen,' Ada said wistfully.

Erik squatted down to be level with the child. 'Not dead, Ada. A lot of Australian trees wake up again after a fire, they put out green branches. And the tiny seeds in the earth will soon sprout and grow more … a fire gets them going.' He looked up at Rose. 'It's true, fire makes some plants germinate. This land of yours will regenerate quite quickly, you know.'

'I hope so.' Ada wandered off to look at the ruin of the garden. Rose and Erik held each other, with no words.

Eventually Erik said, 'I think you know how much I love you. We should have been together long ago. Only this week did I realize how wrong I've been, leaving you to fend for yourself.'

Now was the time to overcome his shyness, to break down the barriers while emotions were still raw. Gently pulling away from him, Rose considered what to say. 'Erik, I was never involved with Jasper Barrington.' She took a deep breath. 'It was unconventional to look after him in my home, but necessary. He's a decent man, he would have died if I hadn't cared for him.'

Erik was listening. 'I thought you were … committed. I know how loyal you are.' He hesitated. 'I've just found out the truth.' He kissed her gently. 'My darling Rose, I'll never leave you again. We'll rebuild our lives together.' He looked down at her, more his old self. 'The school has gone, Freda's house too, but my new house – it's empty but still standing. The fire went round my new block of land – a lot of it was ploughed and I think that saved it. We've been lucky … the fire swept down to the creek but it missed Sawleys and the shop, and the donkeys survived. And do you know, your goats came up the hill – they're at my place.' He took a deep breath. 'We have the land, we can start again. Can't we, Ada?'

The child had come back and inserted herself between them. 'Mr Jensen, do you want to marry Mama? She's not going to marry Lordy, he's going to marry someone else. Can I come to your wedding?'

'I'm going to marry your mama as soon as I can, if she'll have me. But for now … how would you like to camp out in an empty house, Ada?' Erik was bubbling with joy. 'We can all camp until we get some furniture.'

Ada smiled, a wise smile for so young a child. 'And the birdies and possums will soon come back.'

That night they sat on the veranda of Erik's new house. His land was an oasis in a sea of blackened stumps. Erik had bought some bread, cheese and apples from the store for them to eat. 'There's been no loss of life, as far as I know. You've accounted for all the children … everybody had time to get out. My horses and dogs are here, the sheep are scattered, but I hope to get them back eventually. It could have been a lot worse. I thought it was a lot worse, when I found your dress,' he whispered.

They were quiet for a while, exhausted. Ada went to sleep and the first stars came out. Erik stirred eventually and took Rose in his arms as the moon came up and turned his blond hair to silver. 'Please marry me, Rose. We must never be apart again. Ada has it all planned – we mustn't disappoint her! But is it possible? Do you love me?' He held her at arm's length and looked into her eyes. He was not taking her for granted, even now.

'I've loved you from the start, Erik,' Rose confessed. It had been hidden, locked away for so long. She shivered. 'Erik, I'd forgotten … I might not be able to marry, after all. Luke may still be alive. He could have, well, gone off to start a new life.'

Erik reached over and held her hand. 'He didn't, Rose. He's dead. It was bound to upset you so I didn't tell you. But I know what happened.'

'How on earth could you know?' Was he trying to smooth it over for her? Rose couldn't understand him.

'Not long after Luke died, I wanted some dowelling and so I rode over to see the Noojee carpenter. And old Fred was very subdued. He makes the coffins for the district, you see … he says you get used to the job. But one particular death had upset him so much, he couldn't forget about it. A poor lad that was killed by a falling tree.' Erik paused and Rose looked into the distance. 'It was Luke all right, he even remembered the name. And he says he'll never forget the sight of the body.'

There was silence for a while and then Rose sighed. 'Thank you.'

'I should add that Fred told me all this without any questions on my part … but it proves that Luke didn't just abandon you. He met with an accident – may he rest in peace.'

Goodbye, Luke, forgive me for thinking badly of you. Rose sat quietly hand in hand with Erik, looking at the night sky. 'Twinkle, twinkle …' still echoed in her head.

'Just one thing,' Rose said hesitantly after a while. 'Do you happen to have seen Lord Barrington?'

'You're worried about him? He and I sheltered together from the fire – we got into my biggest dam,' Erik said, looking at Rose. 'I gave him a ride from Moe and the man was keen to mend your reputation. In a delicate way, he let me know why he was at your house … and why it happened that you had your arms round his waist, one night when I came to see you. Just bandaging, that was all.' He smiled at the memory. 'I must say he was very cool when the fire came right over our heads. Kept on talking about fishing, except when we ducked under the water.'

'Goodness me, that sounds dangerous. You saw me bandage him? No wonder you thought the worst.' Rose sighed. 'But Maeve Malone is grieving. She thinks he's dead.'

Erik laughed. 'Oh, yes. He's waiting a bit longer to soften her up, make her worry a bit. And he thinks that when he does turn up, then she'll give in and marry him. I always knew he was a rogue … a charming rascal.'

The night was warm and scents were rising from the shrubs beside the house. Hand in hand, they wandered through the garden down to a little lake, fringed by weeping willows. 'Water for the garden,' Erik explained. 'But I wanted it to look beautiful as well. I always imagined that you would share it with me, one day.'

They stood looking at the moon on the water and Rose said, 'Let's bathe.'

It seemed quite natural to take off their clothes and go into the water. Erik swam a few strokes and then came back to Rose. The water was cool on her skin and she felt that the past was being washed away, along with the dirt and ash of the fire. Moonlight danced on the surface, reflections broken by their movement. *I will always remember this moment.*

Laughing, they floated together and then Erik took her hand and they came out of the enchanted pool. Water streamed from their bodies and Rose watched their moonlit shadows on the grass as they moved together and merged. There was no need for guilt, no need to draw back.

CULTURE IN ACTION

Hip-Hop

Jim Mack

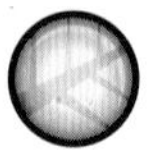

www.raintreepublishers.co.uk
Visit our website to find out more information about Raintree books.

To order:
Phone +44 (0) 1865 888066
Fax +44 (0) 1865 314091
Visit www.raintreepublishers.co.uk

Raintree is an imprint of Capstone Global Library Limited, a company incorporated in England and Wales having its registered office at 7 Pilgrim Street, London, EC4V 6LB – Registered company number: 6695582

First published in hardback in 2010

Edited by Louise Galpine, Abby Colich, and Laura J. Hensley
Designed by Kimberly Miracle and Betsy Wernert
Original illustrations © Capstone Global Library Ltd.
Illustrated by kja-artists.com
Picture research by Hannah Taylor and Mica Brancic
Production by Alison Parsons
Originated by Dot Gradations Ltd.
Printed in China by CTPS

ISBN 978 1 406211 97 9
14 13 12 11 10
10 9 8 7 6 5 4 3 2 1

Acknowledgements

We would like to thank the following for permission to reproduce photographs: Corbis pp. **6** (Thinkstock), **8** (Brenda Ann Kenneally), **19 right** (Neal Preston), **22** (James Leynse), **25** (Reuters/Ethan Miller), **26** (epa/Joelle Diderich); Getty Images pp. **4** (Stone/Bruno De Hogues), **5** (Ty Milford), **7** (Antonio Luiz Hamdan), **10** (WireImage/Jemal Countess), **14** (Jason Blaney), **17** (FilmMagic/Lyle A. Waisman), **18 bottom** (Rick Diamond), **19 left** (Peter Kramer), **20 bottom** (WireImage/Kevin Mazur), **21 top** (WireImage/Arnold Turner), **21 bottom** (WireImage/Bob Levey), **24** (Vince Bucci); Photolibrary p. **12** (Tony Hopewell); Redferns pp. **11** (Janette Beckman), **13** (Ebet Roberts); Rex Features pp. **18 top** (Leon Schadeberg), **20 top** (Geoff Robinson), **27** (Voisin/Phanie). Shutterstock p. **16** (© charobnica).

Icon and banner images supplied by Shutterstock: © Alexander Lukin, © ornitopter, © Colourlife, and © David S. Rose.

Cover photograph of a DJ playing music reproduced with permission of Corbis/Blend Images/Andersen Ross.

We would like to thank Nancy Harris and Jackie Murphy for their invaluable help in the preparation of this book.

Contents

Some words are printed in bold, **like this**. You can find out what they mean by looking in the glossary on page 30.

Planet hip-hop

In a club, an **MC raps** into a microphone while a **DJ mixes** records. The work of **graffiti** artists decorates a wall outside, and teenagers are **break-dancing** on the pavement. Hip-hop is not just a musical style. It is a **culture** (way of life) that started on the streets of New York City, USA, in the 1970s. It quickly spread throughout the United States and the rest of the world.

Hip-hop is rooted in the **rhythms** (regular beats) of African and Caribbean music. It mixes rhythmic, repetitive song with rhymed storytelling. Hip-hop musicians combine styles of music such as rock, jazz, soul, rhythm and blues (R&B), and more.

Music through the decades

The **lyrics** (words) of rock and folk music in the 1960s often centred on problems in the changing world. Music in the 1970s was generally less serious. This included the lighthearted dance music of disco. Hip-hop exploded in the mid-1980s. It had a completely different sound from anything that had come before it.

Drums are an important part of traditional African music.